Praise for *A Hero of France*

A *New York Times* Bestseller

"Emotionally gripping and hugely satisfying . . . Furst rolls all this out with his usual steady-as-she-goes pacing and a prose style that nicely mixes the elegant and the matter-of-fact. And it's not giving anything away to say that in the end many readers will want to stand up and sing 'La Marseillaise' through their tears."
—*The Washington Post*

"Furst's descriptions of occupied Paris are certainly sinister . . . but his is a Paris where the people never seem to give up hope, where their love for France and for their beloved city inspires them to take defiant risks." —*The New York Times*

"Tense, evocative, and greatly satisfying . . . Mr. Furst's great gift for re-creating the sights, smells and spirit of World War II European milieus is again on fine display." —*The Wall Street Journal*

"Considered one of the premier writers of historical spy fiction, Furst delivers a vivid portrait of a French Resistance fighter in World War II Paris and of a city still alive and very much itself— even as the Nazi grip tightens." —*O: The Oprah Magazine*

"[*A Hero of France*'s] power resides in how Furst uses the wartime scarcity of everything—food, clothing, hours of the day, kindness—to evoke immediacy. . . . So much of Furst's strengths, past and future, rests in . . . the knowledge of human nature, the belief in liberty, and the understanding that women can be men's equals in courage as well as pleasure." —*NPR*

"A masterpiece . . . The suspense builds as readers turn the pages."
—*San Francisco Book Review*

BY ALAN FURST

Night Soldiers
Dark Star
The Polish Officer
The World at Night
Red Gold
Kingdom of Shadows
Blood of Victory
Dark Voyage
The Foreign Correspondent
The Spies of Warsaw
Spies of the Balkans
Mission to Paris
Midnight in Europe
A Hero of France

A HERO OF FRANCE

A NOVEL

A
HERO
OF
FRANCE

ALAN
FURST

RANDOM HOUSE NEW YORK

2017 Random House Trade Paperback Edition

Copyright © 2016 by Alan Furst
Maps copyright © 2016 by David Lindroth, Inc.

Published in the United States by Random House, an imprint and division
of Penguin Random House LLC, New York.

RANDOM HOUSE and the HOUSE colophon are registered trademarks of Penguin Random House LLC.

Originally published in hardcover in the United States by Random House, an imprint and division of
Penguin Random House LLC, in 2016.

LIBRARY OF CONGRESS CATALOGING-IN-PUBLICATION DATA
Names: Furst, Alan, author.
Title: A hero of France : a novel / Alan Furst.
Description: New York : Random House, [2016]
Identifiers: LCCN 2016004998| ISBN 9780812986464 (paperback) | ISBN 9780812996500 (ebook)
Subjects: LCSH: France—History—German occupation, 1940–1945—Fiction. | World War, 1939–1945—
Underground movements—France—Fiction. | BISAC: FICTION / Thrillers. | FICTION /War & Military. | FICTION /
Espionage. | GSAFD : War stories.
Classification: LCC PS3556.U76 H47 2016 | DDC 813/.54—dc23
LC record available at http://lccn.loc.gov/2016004998

Printed in the United States of America on acid-free paper

randomhousebooks.com

987654321

Book design by Carole Lowenstein

In the spring of 1941, as British bombing raids over Germany intensified, some of the returning aircraft, badly damaged and losing altitude, managed to escape German territory, their pilots and crews parachuting into the Occupied Zone of France. Here they were hidden, until they made contact with small groups of French men and women who had organized escape lines that led out of the country and, eventually, back to England.

This was the beginning of what came to be known as the French Resistance.

Paris, 1941

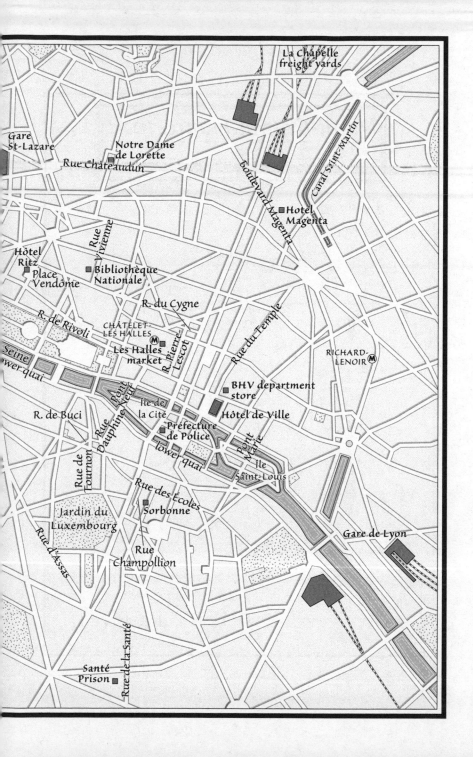

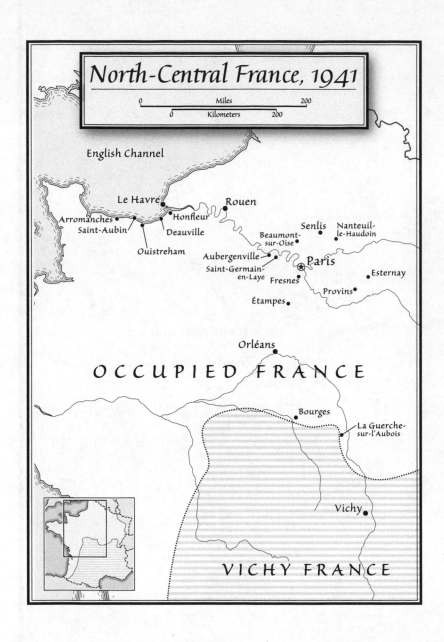

North-Central France, 1941

Miles
0   200
0   200
Kilometers

English Channel

Le Havre
Rouen
Arromanches
Honfleur
Saint-Aubin
Deauville
Senlis   Nanteuil-
le-Haudoin
Beaumont-
sur-Oise
Ouistreham
Aubergenville
Saint-Germain-
en-Laye
Paris
Fresnes
Esternay
Provins
Étampes

Orléans

OCCUPIED   FRANCE

Bourges
La Guerche-
sur-l'Aubois

Vichy

VICHY   FRANCE

YOU
MUST NOT
MEET THEIR
EYES …

OCCUPIED PARIS, THE TENTH DAY OF MARCH, 1941.

At eight-twenty in the evening, the man known to his Resistance cell as Mathieu waited in a doorway where he could watch the entry of the Métro station on the Boulevard Richard-Lenoir. He tried to look beyond the entry, at the tree-lined boulevard, but there wasn't much to be seen, only shapes in the night—the streetlamps had been painted blue and the windows of apartment buildings draped or shuttered in the blackout ordered by the German Occupation Authority. A sad thing, he thought, a dark and silent city. Silent because the Germans had forbidden the use of cars, buses, and taxis. But in that silence, nightingales could be heard singing in the parks, and in that darkness the streets were lit by silvery moonlight when the clouds parted.

A night earlier, at the same Métro, Mathieu had noticed a gray bicycle, bound to the trunk of a chestnut tree by a stout chain. Now he saw that it was still there. Bicycles had never been more valuable, and soon enough this one would be stolen if its owner did not retrieve it. Where was he? What had happened to him? In a cell at some police Préfecture? Possibly. But if the Paris police arrested you, friends or family would be notified and someone would have come for the bicycle. Maybe its owner was floating in the Seine—a bad fate but not the worst fate, the worst fate was to be taken by the Gestapo. And if that were so he might never be heard of again: *Nacht und Nebel,* night and fog, Hitler's very own invention; people disappeared and nobody would ever find out what had become of them. They went out to do an errand and never returned. A sharp lesson for family and friends, punished forever by their imaginations.

Now the ground trembled beneath Mathieu's feet and he could hear a rumble from down below as the train pulled into the station. Moments later, the passengers appeared, climbing up the stairway to the boulevard. They were still wearing winter clothes because it was cold in the city, apartments and offices barely heated for want of coal. As the crowd emerged, one woman caught his eye, she was lovely to look at; the face of a fallen angel, and dressed in the latest Paris fashion: she wore ski pants—warmer than a skirt—a ski jacket, and boots. She was lucky to have the boots; some passengers wore clogs, wood-soled shoes, as there was no leather to be had for repair. To Mathieu, the passengers looked tired and worn—they might well have looked like that at the end of a working day before the war but for Mathieu the weariness was different, deeper. Lately one heard the expression *Je suis las,* it meant *I am tired of the way I have to live my life,* and this was what Mathieu saw in their faces, in the way they walked. But then, he would think that, he cared for the people of Paris, as though he were a guardian. The woman in the ski jacket returned his look; a glance, nothing flirtatious, rueful perhaps, *in other times than these . . .*

Ah, at last, here was Lisette, seventeen years old, a *lycée* student. She appeared not to notice him but, as she walked past the doorway, she said, her voice low and confidential, "They have crossed the border. They're in Spain."

12 March. In Senlis, thirty miles north of Paris, RAF sergeant Arthur Gillen was hiding in the cellar of a barbershop.

At six-thirty in the evening, Mathieu found him sitting on a blanket—as much of a bed as he had—and whittling a block of wood with a clasp knife. Looking up at Mathieu he said, "Are you the man taking me to Paris?" Mathieu spoke good English but Gillen, with a heavy Manchester accent, was hard to understand.

"Yes, that's me," Mathieu said and offered Gillen a cigarette.

The RAF man was very grateful. Mathieu, lighting it for him, said, "We have a few minutes to make our train, Arthur, so we better be going."

The barber, shaving a customer, gestured to Mathieu as they left the shop. It was a chilly twilight in northern France, with a lead-colored sky and a mean little wind, so the two walked quickly, heads down, as they made their way to the railway station. Gillen was young, surely not yet twenty, and looked to Mathieu like a worker—likely a worker in the Manchester fabric mills. He was small and thin with something of the factory gnome about him, he just needed a stub of cigarette stuck to his lip and a worker's cap. He wore a soiled gray overcoat and was, Mathieu saw, walking with a limp.

"Are you hurt, Arthur?" Mathieu said.

"Not much. Sprained an ankle when my parachute came down, but I'll be fine. I just want to go home."

"Well, we'll try and get you there."

With luck, he would get there and then, after a brief furlough, he'd go back to the war, and that was very much the point of Mathieu's work in the Resistance. It would have been nice to think that

Mathieu's efforts were inspired by humane instincts, but Europe was not so humane that year. Sgt. Gillen was trained and experienced in a demanding job, radioman on a Wellington bomber, and was in fact a *weapon*. And Britain needed any weapon—especially pilots but aircrew were almost as valuable—it could get its hands on because it was losing the war.

When the railway station came into view, Mathieu said, "No more talking, Arthur, we don't want anybody to hear you speaking English." The station platform passport control was, as usual, perfunctory—local police glanced at the passengers' identity documents and waved them on toward the waiting train. There were fewer trains now—French coal was used to make German homes cozy and snug—and they were all overcrowded; the compartments filled, the aisles packed with cold, tired travelers shifting from one foot to the other; with the train crawling at this pace they would never get home.

Then, twenty miles from Paris, the locomotive was shunted to a different track, one that swerved away from the passenger line. A businessman next to Mathieu said, "What the hell are they doing now?"

A man standing nearby said, "There's no depot here, this is a track used by freight trains, leads to a water tower and a coaling station."

A few sighs of despair and a muttered curse or two could be heard in the aisle—*now what?*

Very slowly, the Senlis local passed lines of freight cars on two tracks to its left. On the right-hand side, a weedy field bordered by partly thawed mounds of soot-blackened snow. At last, with a hiss of steam from the locomotive, they stopped by a water tower. "They must need water," the businessman said. "Couldn't they get it in Senlis?"

When a conductor appeared from the next car everybody turned toward him, waiting for what they sensed would not be good news. "Mesdames and messieurs, all passengers must leave the train."

As Mathieu and Gillen got out, they saw a nightmare: in the white glare of floodlights, a surprise control; gendarmes—French military police in khaki uniforms—were everywhere, there were two of them by the steps that led to the ground, herding the passengers toward a concrete slab beneath the water tower, where four tables manned by gendarme officers awaited them, the control guarded by gendarmes carrying submachine guns. As the passengers formed a ragged line, getting their documents ready for inspection, the businessman said, "They are looking for somebody, a fugitive."

Mathieu pressed the inside of Gillen's arm, holding him back, trying to get as far away from the tables as possible. Gillen would be asked questions, there was no way he could answer them. For fifteen minutes, the lines moved slowly; stopping, taking a step or two, and stopping again. Then, something went wrong at the tables. A well-dressed older woman, harassed beyond patience, was screaming at the officers. A moment later, two of the gendarmes took her by the elbows, arresting her, which drew growls of muted protest from the passengers. She refused to move and, when they lifted her off the ground, she kicked her feet—one of her shoes flew away—and shrieked. From the crowd of passengers, a gasp.

"Now," Mathieu said and, with Gillen following, dropped to the ground and, expecting a police whistle or a bullet in the back, rolled beneath the coach, crawled over the rails, and, with Gillen beside him, crouched behind the high wheel of the local train. Then they climbed over a coupling to reach the next track, where a locomotive was taking on coal. By the cab of the engine, two railwaymen, one in an engineer's cap, were talking and having a cigarette. When Mathieu approached them, the engineer said, "What's going on over there?"

"Surprise control. We have to get away from here or we're dead."

The engineer paused for a close look at the two, then said, "On the run? Is it you they're looking for?"

"No, but my friend can't be questioned."

"What'd you do? Hold up a bank?"

"Defied the Boche."

"Hmm, they could do with a little defiance. Well, you can ride down to Paris with us but we can't stop on the way, we're going to the La Chapelle freightyards." The engineer led them to one of the freight cars and rolled the door back. "We'll let you out in Paris. In an hour, maybe, we have to go slow, we had to paint the locomotive's windows blue because of the blackout, so we can't see much. And don't disturb the freight in here, it's going to Germany on another train. Oh yes, and good for you, whatever the hell it is that you're doing."

Sitting with his back against a pile of wooden crates, Mathieu, who had been a tank captain in 1940, smelled Cosmoline, the grease used to protect weapons when they left the armory. Mathieu shook his head. "Look at this, Sergeant, a shipment of arms made in French factories, headed for the Wehrmacht."

Gillen made the sound of spitting. "Maybe some of my mates will take care of them once they're on German railway tracks, could be some ammunition there too, it makes a great show when you hit an arms train."

For a time they were silent—the only sound in the darkened freight car the rhythmic clatter of the train's wheels—then Mathieu said, "How did you get to Senlis?"

"I landed near a village and found the local priest, that's what we're taught to do if we bail out over France. Fine old man, Père Anselme, looked like a prophet in the movies, you know, white hair, face like a statue. I'd been in the woods for two days, I was wet through and banged up, shaking like a lost dog. He fed me, gave me some brandy, got in contact with the right people, and took me to the barbershop."

"You were shot down over France?"

"Well, hit in Germany, came down in France. We were on a night bombing run, after the railyards at Essen, and dropped incendiaries and regular bombs, there were fires below us when we banked in a turn and headed back toward the RAF airfield at Croydon. A good amount of flak that night but I've seen worse." He paused, then went on. "And then, as we headed west, the portside engine caught fire, probably hit by ack-ack, and failed, and when the pilot tried to restart it he couldn't. The Wellington can fly on one engine but we faced a headwind over France and, with loss of power, we began to lose altitude. Lower and lower we went and then *something,* not one of their eighty-eight cannon, maybe it was quad-mounted fifty-calibre machine guns, which are very fast and put out a lot of rounds. Whatever it was raked us, nose to tail, we saw tracer bullets pass through the cabin.

"In the Wellington, the radio operator and the navigator sit in a raised position above and behind the pilot, and that saved our lives. The pilot . . . the pilot had his head back over the seat with his eyes open, and there was blood on the cabin wall. There's only one pilot in that bomber and when he was killed there was nobody at the controls and the plane's nose dropped down and we began to dive. By now there was smoke in the cabin and on the intercom we could hear the tail gunner shouting, 'Get out! Get out!' We never saw him again, and when we called the bombardier there was only static. The navigator and I jumped from the midship door and I saw his parachute open, but we drifted away from each other and came down in the woods. That's when I hurt my ankle, I landed on a tree root. As loud as I dared, I called out the navigator's name but nobody answered. I was still in the air when the Wellington came down, there was an explosion west of me and I saw the flash reflected off the clouds. You know the rest, I walked through the woods all night, because I knew the police were going to show up as soon as they could get there."

A minute passed, then Mathieu said, "I'm sorry about your comrades, Arthur. The worst part of war is when you lose friends."

Gillen nodded but said nothing—what was there to say?

. . .

It was after ten when the train stopped and the door of the freight car was slid aside. What awaited them was darkness—no streetlamps or lit apartment windows, a sky overcast with dense clouds, so no starlight or moonlight. Mathieu could make out objects only a few feet away from him—after that, whatever was out there was swallowed up by the night. The La Chapelle freightyards were three blocks wide and some thirty feet below street level, with a dozen tracks appearing from one tunnel, then, a few blocks later, crisscrossing past switching equipment and disappearing into another tunnel that led to the Gare Saint-Lazare.

When Mathieu and Gillen jumped to the ground, the engineer was waiting for them. "That's your way out of here," the engineer said, pointing. "Just about directly across from where we are now, there's a steel ladder set into the wall that leads to the street above— it's about thirty feet high. Now is the time to get away—there are German inspectors who show up here in the morning. Be quiet about it, you'll have to watch out for the railway police, who patrol the yards all night long." As the locomotive moved off, Mathieu watched as its light eventually disappeared.

They set out in the direction the engineer had indicated. When they had to circle around parked freight cars, Mathieu made sure they returned to the path he was trying to follow, counting tracks to give himself some idea of where he was. Then Gillen grabbed his arm and whispered "Stop" and cupped his hand around his ear. What he now heard were footsteps, and an idle conversation. *Railway police.* As the voices came nearer, Mathieu and Gillen slid under a freight car. The approaching footsteps stopped and one of the policemen said, "What the hell was that?"

"I don't hear anything," said the other.

Mathieu held his breath, the voices were close to them.

After a minute, the first policeman called out, "Come over here, whoever you are. *Now.*"

Silence. "Maybe a rat," the policeman said.

"Could be."

The two policemen began to walk, coming closer and closer until Mathieu could see their boots as they passed the railcar. Then they stopped again, waiting for their prey to break cover. Finally one of them said, "Whatever was here is gone." When their footsteps were no longer audible, Mathieu and Gillen made for the wall. After a try in the wrong direction, they found the ladder. As Mathieu looked up, it seemed much higher than thirty feet—three stories of a building.

On the narrow ladder they would have to climb one above the other, so Mathieu led the way but he was only a few feet off the ground when he heard Gillen below him—breathing hard and unable to stop a muffled sound of pain every time he put pressure on his injured ankle. Mathieu stopped and said, "Can you make it, Arthur?"

"I will."

"I am going to help you, we'll use a double-grip—you hold my wrist, I'll hold yours—and when you push off on your bad ankle, I'll pull you up." The method slowed them down but they took one rung at a time together and managed to climb two-thirds of the way to the top. Then, from the foot of the ladder, the policeman's voice. "What the hell do you think you're doing? *Get back down here!*"

Mathieu whispered, "Keep going, Arthur."

From down below. "We're railway police, I'm going to shoot you if you don't stop."

They kept going.

"Look, be sensible, we just want to question you."

A few more rungs, Mathieu could see the curved handles at the top.

"Do it, Corporal."

The corporal tried shooting from below but the bullet pinged off a steel rung and whined away into the darkness. Mathieu felt the impact where his hand gripped a rung, instinctively pulled it off, fought for balance, then started to climb again. A second shot passed behind him.

"The angle's no good," the policeman said. "We have to back up a few feet."

His breathing hoarse with effort, Mathieu reached the curved handles atop the ladder and, with Gillen still hanging on, dropped flat at the edge of the street. "One more, Arthur, I'll pull from here." For a moment Mathieu felt that his shoulder joint was going to give out, then Gillen struggled over the last rung and fell next to him.

Down below, more shouting, more threats, as the two moved off down the street.

14 March. Taking the Métro, then walking through the darkness, Mathieu made for the neighborhood of crumbling tenements by the Les Halles market. On the Rue du Cygne, a giant doorman with gold epaulets on his uniform stood beside a discreet sign that said LE CYGNE, the swan, a nightclub named for its address. As Mathieu turned toward the entry, the doorman said, "You are early, monsieur, we don't open until ten-thirty."

"I'm here to see Monsieur de Lyon." The name was pronounced like the animal, not the city.

The doorman put two fingers to the visor of his cap and said, "Ah then, welcome to Le Cygne."

Descending the stairway to the cellar, Mathieu could hear a piano—a slow version of the cancan—and a woman's voice, rising over the music, that called out, "And *one,* kick . . . and *two,* kick . . . and *three,* kick . . . and *four,* oomph!"

The piano player, a cigarette held between his lips, said, "Again, madame?"

The woman calling out the numbers, apparently the dance director, clapped her hands twice and said, "Once more, ladies." She had a pale, refined face, the body of a ballet mistress, and wore a kerchief over her hair. Four young women, or maybe not so young, wearing only bra and panties, kicked in time to the music, then stuck their bottoms out on the "oomph!"

At a table on the far wall was, Mathieu supposed, the man he'd come to see, the owner of the nightclub. De Lyon stood as Mathieu reached the table and extended his hand. "I'm Max de Lyon, you must be Mathieu. Red wine? Champagne? A cognac for a cold night?"

"A cognac, please."

De Lyon, perhaps fifty, had a still face and hooded eyes— narrow and low-lidded with a faint downward slant—that were at once amused and threatening. The gaze in those eyes was conventionally known as *penetrating;* they read deep and they knew who you were. For the rest: a receding hairline, a compact build, and a double-breasted suit over a black shirt and a pearl-gray tie. He looked like a gangster, but Mathieu knew this was a costume. A gangster de Lyon might be, but not the sort who wore such clothes. He looked the way a German officer might expect him to look: the owner of a nightclub on the dark side of Paris. The effect was completed when he spoke: low, determined tones with just a hint of a Slavic accent.

De Lyon produced a packet of long cigarettes in brown wrapper leaf, offered one to Mathieu, then lit both with a brass lighter designed to work in the wind. "They're made in Turkey," he said. "And what I have to pay now, since the Occupation . . ." He shook his head. "It's *everything*. You can't imagine what it costs to buy an ostrich plume these days, but we must have them, for the dancing girls, just like the Folies Bergère."

"To please your new clientele?"

"Yes, German officers. At first, they came here to watch the typical nightclub crowd, you know, thugs of the better class, swindlers, Parisians getting rich off the black market, their fancy girlfriends, a spy or two, some local courtesans. But now we need dancing girls who look good with their clothes off—they used to wear G-strings, but not lately. So, as you see, we're having an audition tonight, which one do you like?"

"They all follow the routine," Mathieu said diplomatically. "Is one better than the others?"

"Oh yes. It will be the one on the far left with the big behind—
Germans are partial to big behinds."

Standing by the piano, the director said, "Alright, ladies, turn
your backs to me and jump, up in the air, as high as you can. Now,
one at a time, starting from the left, and . . . *jump!*" The dancers
did as they were told. When de Lyon's candidate jumped, her behind jumped with her, then bounced as it landed. The director
walked over, placed a firm hand across the dancer's lower derriere,
let it rest there, then said, "Very nice. What is your name, dear?"

"My name is Lulu, madame."

"A stage name?"

"Yes, madame, my real name is Marie."

"Very well, Marie, let's you and I visit the ladies' WC and take
your pants down."

"My, my," de Lyon said, raising his eyebrows.

The three remaining dancers stood together and talked, while
the man at the piano began to play something classical, which Mathieu recognized, after a few bars, as Chopin.

A waiter arrived with Mathieu's cognac and a red wine for
de Lyon, who said, "So Mathieu, my lawyer tells me you're a man
doing good work, I know you can't say too much, but . . ."

"My friends and I take downed RAF pilots out of France."

"That kind of thing costs a lot of money."

"It does. Before the war I had a job and an everyday life, but I
ran out of savings long ago. Now, people like your lawyer and a few
others help out, otherwise . . . I don't know."

"Don't go robbing banks, Mathieu, that's the old Bolshevik
style, very unhealthy."

"No, no, that takes professionals." He paused, then said, "But
we must do *something*."

"I agree," de Lyon said. "But what is it that makes you say
'must'?"

Mathieu hesitated, then said, "When we lost the war, the heart
went out of the people here. It was as though the city had died.

This *reached* me, and soon enough I began to *do* things, small things, but they made me feel better. And the more I watched these arrogant bastards strutting around the city, my city, the more I did."

From de Lyon, a sympathetic nod. "I understand, believe me I understand. This was my refuge, this Paris. I was born in a shtetl in the Ukraine, then, when my mother died, I was sent to live on my father's estate in Poland, among Polish nobility, the result of my father's youthful folly with a Jew. But these people didn't want me there so, at the age of fourteen, I ran away and came here, where I'd never been before, but I knew I was home. Now they've taken my refuge, so, yes, I will give you money." He drank some of his wine, then a little more. "Call it my way of fighting back. I hate them, of course, but I must have customers or I close, and the customers these days are German officers." He shrugged. "Everyone in this city will tell you the same story, though there are those who go much further, who collaborate. Which, someday, God willing, they will regret."

When Mathieu answered, he spoke slowly. "You are no collaborator, monsieur, I'm sure of that."

"No, I am not, but how can you be sure?"

"It's one of the things I do—make decisions about people, can they be trusted. I am good at it. And I'd better be, because I can be wrong only once." He had a sip of his cognac. "Very good cognac," he said. "I wonder if, someday, I could call on you for a favor?"

"More than money, you mean."

"Yes."

De Lyon smiled and said, "Are you recruiting me, sir?"

"I am."

De Lyon thought it over, then said, "My answer is 'maybe,' we'll see when the time comes. But, for now, the money. When they finish up here we'll go to my office, and I can let you have five thousand dollars."

"A generous gift, monsieur, American dollars get an extraordinary rate on the black market, because people in flight desperately need them. Also, at a certain level, they are the currency of choice for bribery."

De Lyon laughed. "How well I know," he said. "There was a time when I was an arms dealer, on a small scale, and I bribed everything that moved."

The director and the dancer came out of the ladies' WC; the dancer's face was flushed pink. The director signaled to de Lyon, who said to Mathieu, "You see? I was right, she'll have the job. Now we'll go up to my office and visit the safe. I wasn't planning to give you that much, but, once I met you . . . Anyhow, in the future, please call me Max."

Back in the night, Mathieu made for the Châtelet–Les Halles station, where he would take one of the last trains—the Métro shut down at eleven as the curfew began. Eyes searching the darkness, he had to move slowly, pausing at doorways where he could hide if necessary, hurrying to cross a narrow street, and listening intently for the telltale sounds of police patrols. The Parisian police often talked to each other as they rode their bicycles, their voices loud in the strange silence of the city. This was intentional, the theory went, the *flics* making sure you knew they were around so they didn't have to arrest you. As for the German patrols, the ring of their hobnailed boots on cobblestones carried a long way: useful for people like Mathieu, hated by the Parisians, captive in their blacked-out apartments.

The Parisian male of a certain class was finely made, slim and elegant, insouciant, and faintly amused. This was not Mathieu. To some, at first glance, he looked like an American. Perhaps he did, a former athlete with thick shoulders and big hands and, from an amateur boxing match when he was twenty and a student at the Sorbonne, a small, curved scar by his right eye. He leaned forward when he walked, as though in a hurry, and watched the world around him with a particular intensity. His eyes were a rich brown, his hair, always a little too long, a shade darker, his voice both strong and low pitched, and he laughed easily. He had always been strong; a leader, a protector. From the age of twelve, he was the one who had confronted the school-yard bullies when they pushed some kid too hard.

At the end of winter, he wore what he'd worn before the war: jacket, muffler and gloves. An old jacket but expensive, in a brown-and-gray Harris Tweed, collar up, over a heavy woolen muffler looped at the throat, then a charcoal-black, home-knit sweater. This had started out to be a turtleneck but here his aunt had tired of the project and left the neck low, a soft roll that didn't quite fold over. Which was fine with Mathieu, who didn't like turtleneck sweaters. Or hats. Against the cold, he wore black leather gloves lined with rabbit fur.

Mathieu had never married, he'd had some long and serious love affairs but the wedded life—shared home, children, in-laws—had never appealed to him. Still, it was always there if he changed his mind: women found him attractive, rough around the edges but with two notable qualities that won hearts; he was funny and he was kind. Mathieu would turn forty in the summer of 1941—he had always looked younger than his years but, after he'd begun to work in the Resistance, a patch of gray had appeared above his ear. The pressure of clandestine work had aged him and there, in the mirror, was the result.

When Mathieu left the nightclub, headed for the Métro, he passed beneath a propaganda poster: a portrait of Marshal Pétain, the leader of the Vichy government, with the printed legend RÉVO-LUTION NATIONALE. In June of 1940, the Germans held the upper third of France and, when Pétain signed the surrender, this area became the Occupied Zone, ruled by the Germans, while the remainder of France was governed by Vichy and led by Pétain.

Traitor, Mathieu thought, anger rising within him. A traitor with a snow-white mustache that some took as a symbol of his moral purity. Pétain was the one who, in the 1930s, claimed that France had been weakened by decadence—too many love affairs, too much wine, rich food, and liberal politics. And then, in June of 1940, when the French lost the war, well there you had the reason. Thus the phrase National Revolution; no more soft, corrupt people, no more indulgence, now France, and the French, would have to change.

Instinctively, Mathieu reached in his pocket for a pen, meaning to draw a Cross of Lorraine with two bars, the Gaullist symbol, and write VIVE DE GAULLE beneath it. He had begun his resistance in just this way, a "small thing" to be sure, still, it had helped him feel better in the summer of 1940 that followed the Occupation. But the pen stayed where it was. In the summer of 1940 he hadn't cared about being arrested but not now, not on a night when he was carrying a lot of money.

And that wasn't all he was carrying.

He turned into the Rue Pierre Lescot, not far from the Métro, but his luck didn't hold. Up ahead of him he heard the sound of shattering glass, followed by a gleeful, triumphant snicker, and out of the gloom came three teenaged boys in uniform. Uniforms of a sort, cheaply made jackets, trousers, and ties, which meant membership in one of the youth organizations created by Vichy operatives. Called the Garde Française or the Jeune Front—Young Guard, French versions of the Hitler Youth, they were packs of teenaged thugs who roamed the streets and set upon those they took to be enemies of the Vichy regime.

For Mathieu, it was too late to slip away. Inspired by the bully's edge—three against one—they decided they didn't like him and that they would do something about it. One of them, the smallest of the three—scrawny, hair shorn above the ears, and, from the set of his face, mean as a snake—showed Mathieu a tire iron, likely used to break the shop window. "See this?" he said. Mathieu stood where he was, stared, and was silent—if they thought he was going to grovel, they were wrong. When the Young Guard took a step toward him, Mathieu reached under the back of his jacket and drew, from his belt, an Italian automatic pistol, a Beretta, then held it loosely by the side of his leg.

For the Young Guard with the tire iron, a moment of reflection. There were those who gestured with a weapon, most would never use it. Was showing the gun an act of bravado?

Mathieu read his mind, and smiled. A tolerant smile—he understood them, could only hope they understood him.

The Young Guard glanced at his friends, would they think he was a coward? But then he came to a conclusion and stepped aside. If this went any further Mathieu would kill him and he knew it.

It was frigid inside the Métro car, and there wasn't much electricity, so the lights were dim. In the semi-darkness, the crowd was silent, a sea of white faces. The train stopped at Vaneau, then Sèvres-Babylone. Next came Mathieu's station, Mabillon, where he left the train and hurried along the platform as he looked at his watch. He might just make it indoors before the curfew began.

Leaving the entry, he took the Rue de Buci, a market street where produce was set out on stalls in front of the stores, a street that smelled like rotting vegetables. Just after eleven, he turned onto the Rue Dauphine—a few shadows, walking fast, late like Mathieu, headed the other way up the street. The Rue Dauphine was home to small shops—umbrellas, lamps, cookware—and battered old hotels with sensible room rates. He passed the Louisiane, the Tarane, the Hôtel du Petit Mouton—the little lamb, essentially a brothel, followed by his hotel, the Saint-Yves.

As Mathieu opened the door, there was an eager whine from the vestibule and Mariana, the hotel dog, her tail wagging at full speed, ran up to him and gave him a fast lick on the hand. *Where have you been? Why do you make me worry like this?* Mariana was a Belgian shepherd bitch of the Tervuren variety, with a thick brown and white ruff at her neck. Yes, it was there to keep wolves from biting her throat but it also felt good to touch, and Mathieu combed his fingers through the fine hair and said, "*Bonsoir, bonne Mariana.*" He was her most favored tenant and she had adopted him as her owner, sleeping across the threshold of his bedroom at night, and lord help anybody who tried to get past her; fear had been bred out of the Tervuren a long time ago. Mariana led him up five flights of stairs, occasionally looking back to make sure nothing had happened to him. When he opened the door to his rooms, she charged in and leapt onto the sofa, mouth open, tongue out, panting with pleasure. Once again, life was as it should be.

Mathieu had discovered the Hôtel Saint-Yves six months earlier. On the top floor, the previous tenant had turned three adjacent rooms into an apartment: a bedroom with a desk and sofa, a bathroom with a porcelain claw-foot tub, and a kitchen with stove, refrigerator, and a sturdy walnut table that looked like it had made more than one trip to the flea markets. Under false name and identity papers, Mathieu rented the apartment by the month and used it as a base of operations.

It was a familiar place, the rooms like those to be found in cheap but decent hotels anywhere in France: wallpaper with pink roses and green leaves on a tan background, thin brown carpet, a narrow bed with iron bars at head and foot, a green chenille bedspread, and a sagging mattress.

As Mariana watched, Mathieu used the claw of a hammer to prise up a floorboard and there he deposited de Lyon's five thousand dollars. It had company: Swiss francs, Spanish pesetas, occupation francs, and French francs minted before the Occupation. These had the former national motto, *Liberté, Égalité, Fraternité,* while the occupation francs had the new, Vichy motto, *Travail, Famille, Patrie,* thus liberty, equality, and brotherhood had become work, family, and fatherland. From the Vichy point of view, healthier ideals for the new France. Before he put the board back in place, Mathieu laid the Beretta on top of the money.

· · ·

He would need some of the money later in the week when he saw Ghislain, his second-in-command, to be used for repayment of railway fares, various bribes, and payments to *passeurs,* who escorted fugitives into the Unoccupied Zone south of the Loire. Business done for the night, Mathieu went over to his bedroom window and looked out into the darkness. The Rue Dauphine led directly to the Pont Neuf, and from his vantage point he could see the river. There was a three-quarter moon that evening and its light made the Seine visible, a ghostly gray, its surface showing the swell of the current that ran with the spring tide.

At twelve-thirty, two faint taps at the door.

Mathieu had been lying on the sofa, hands clasped beneath his head, so excited by anticipation that he couldn't read his book. By the time he got to his feet, Mariana was waiting at the door, ready to welcome the visitor—she'd recognized the person in the hallway as a friend.

"Come in, Joëlle," Mathieu said.

She opened the door, scratched Mariana on the chest, then embraced Mathieu. He kissed her lightly on the lips, his finger touching her lower back, just where the cleft of the bottom parted. There was wine on her breath. For scent she wore vanilla extract.

He held her at arm's length, his eyes moving up and down, then said, "And how are you?"

In answer, her face and hands moved a certain way, a variation on the Gallic shrug which meant *not too bad.* She lived in a room on the fourth floor of the Saint-Yves and worked in the records department of the Hôtel-Dieu hospital on the Île de la Cité. A month earlier, she and Mathieu had begun a love affair. Joëlle was in her thirties, with the creamy-brown skin of southern France. She was slim and lithe, had shining eyes, a warm, irresistible smile that could turn mischievous, and chocolate-colored hair that hung below her shoulders. "I have a request," she said.

"Which is . . . ?"

"Before we . . . do anything, I would like to wash myself."

"I'll heat you a pan of water," he said. "Don't attempt the bidet"—the powerful spurt of his bidet was ice-cold—"you'll hit your head on the ceiling."

"My God, I miss hot water."

Mathieu went into his kitchen, filled a pan with water and set it on the burner atop his kerosene stove. The tiny flame flickered blue but, if you waited, it would heat whatever you had. In the corner of the kitchen was a folded blanket that Mariana settled on when she wasn't wanted in the bedroom—dogs knew not to disturb intimacy but still, they watched. Now Mariana lay down on the blanket and sighed.

"How was work today?" Mathieu called from the kitchen.

"Pretty much like always. My friend Valérie has a new man, we asked her about him but she doesn't really know who he is—she said it was like making love to a stranger, now and then he disappears, and he lives in a hotel somewhere, that's where they meet."

Like us.

He had never told Joëlle of his secret life, trying to protect her, trying to make sure that if, God forbid, she were interrogated, she could say nothing that would suggest she was involved with what he did.

He tested the water with his finger, then went into the bedroom. "Very well, *ma petite*," he said, as though to a child, "time for your bath."

She slipped off her sweater, slacks, and much-darned wool stockings, and wriggled out of her long underwear. Mathieu took her hand and led her to the bathroom, then brought in the pan of tepid water, a bar of soap, and a washcloth. Gesturing with the washcloth he said, "May I, mademoiselle?"

"Oh, I see," she said. "Well, yes, you may, but as I am undressed, you must be too."

He took his clothes off and hung them on a hook on the door.

She met his eyes and smiled.

"And now, please raise your hands," he said.

She raised her hands above her head, he dipped the washcloth in the water, swiped it on the soap, and began to wash under her arms. This drew, from deep inside her, a grateful sound of mixed pleasure and relief.

He dried under her arms with a towel, knelt before her, washed her feet, and, gently, began to wash between her legs. She said "Oh!"—playing at being shocked. Mathieu moved the cloth up and down and, after a time, she exhaled a breath of air and said, "Dear me."

"Feels good?"

"Yes, very good. Don't stop."

"Now, now," he said, teasing her. "This is just to warm you up." Still on his knees, he washed her loins, then said, "Turn around and bend over, dear."

She turned around and bent gracefully from the waist, her hands pressed against the wall. Following the practice of Parisian women, she wore the same style two-piece bathing suit all summer, so that a splendidly white ass shone stark between the dark skin of her thighs and lower back. As he washed, she bent lower, moving a little toward his hand.

At last he stood and bit her lightly between shoulder and neck, then put his arm around her shoulders, walked her into the bedroom, and lay down beside her on the bed. "I can see that you enjoyed the bath as well," she said.

"I did. Something different is always inspiring."

"How would you like me?"

"On your knees, but not yet."

Taking his time, he kissed her mouth, then her small breasts, reading her response by the pressure of the hands that gripped his upper arms. After a time, she rested her palm on the top of his head. He understood the signal and did as she wished, worked his way down until his head was between her legs. In the past, this act had needed some time but not now. She shivered briefly and moved away from his mouth. When he looked up at her, she ruffled his hair with her fingers. "You are a tender soul," she said, adding the name—not Mathieu—that he used at the hotel.

Later, he turned off the nightstand lamp and, now that the bedroom was dark, he went to the window and opened the blackout drapes. She left the bed and joined him at the window, he put his arm around her, she rested her head below his shoulder, and together they looked out at the stars in the night sky above the city. A few minutes later, as the cold reached him, he said, "Time to get under the covers."

As she pulled the quilt up, he took an ashtray from his desk, lit two cigarettes, and joined her. She inhaled and blew smoke from her nostrils, saying, "Mmm."

"American cigarettes," he said. "Black-market cigarettes."

"Everybody I know rolls the horrid tobacco they sell now."

"I do too, but not tonight. And there's more to come."

"Yes? What is that?"

"I have a present for you."

He had never given her a present, and she turned on her side in order to see his face.

"The present is in the kitchen, you'll take it with you in the morning."

"I can't imagine," she said.

"Cheese, my love, a big wedge of some kind of Brie, I think, from a dairy farmer down in Provins."

"Thank you," she said. "Before the war I loved cheese, all kinds, but, since the Occupation . . ." The cheese ration dictated by the Occupation Authority was seven ounces a month.

"I know," he said. "That's the way things are, for the moment."

She put out her cigarette, laying the remnant carefully on the nightstand, then slid up against him. He finished his own cigarette and, when he turned on his side, she put her arm around his chest and pulled him closer. In a cold world, he thought, there is nothing so warm as a lover next to you in bed. He didn't think it for long. He'd done a lot that day, then made love, now fell asleep.

Suddenly he was awake, thinking, *What woke me?* He groped for his watch on the nightstand, saw that it was three-twenty, then heard the low drone in the distance that grew louder as he listened. Next to him, Joëlle was propped on her elbow. "Do you hear that?"

"Yes."

"They are getting closer."

Then the air-raid sirens began to wail.

The formations of British bombers, headed for Germany, flew over northern France, sometimes near Paris, sometimes not—the RAF tried to vary the flight paths of their aircraft. Paris was blacked out, as the Germans tried to deny navigation aid to their enemy, but they couldn't black out the moon, which glinted on the rivers and the steel of railroad tracks and led the RAF navigators as they flew toward the industrial cities of the Reich. Now the first searchlight came on, a white disk sweeping back and forth across the sky as the German anti-aircraft batteries hunted for a target. "They are just above us," Joëlle said. "They're not going to bomb Paris, are they?"

"Not intentionally," he said.

Mathieu slipped free of the covers and went to the window, Joëlle followed. It was foolish to stand in front of glass if there was any chance of an explosion, but they stood there anyway. The sound of the RAF formation grew very loud and they could hear the beating of heavy engines overhead. One of the searchlights crisscrossing the sky must have fastened on a bomber because the anti-aircraft batteries stationed on the outskirts of the city opened fire, the sound so loud that it made the floor vibrate. In the sky south of the Seine, little puffs of smoke appeared, harmless looking, but lethal.

A moment later, a rain of shrapnel began to fall, the steel shreds rattling down on the roofs and streets of the city. When dawn came, the kids of Paris would rush out of their apartments for the hunt, seeking the biggest pieces to add to their shrapnel collections.

As Mathieu and Joëlle watched the sky, there was a flare in the darkness above the river, then a trail of fire, like a shooting star, crossed the top of the window.

"Maybe the airmen got out," Joëlle said.

"Maybe."

"Did you see parachutes?"

"I didn't."

A few minutes later, the thunder of the bomber formations faded to a drone and drifted away to the east, the anti-aircraft cannon stopped firing and the searchlights went dark. Mathieu and Joëlle crawled back into bed but there would be no sleeping anytime soon. "I hope the airmen got out. They do, sometimes," Joëlle said.

"It's true."

"I know the Germans hunt them down, but some of them escape, and are hidden by people in the countryside until they can be taken across the border into Spain."

"Yes," Mathieu said. "I've heard the same thing."

"Hold me for a while," Joëlle said.

Mathieu wrapped his arms around her.

16 March, 1941.

The afternoon local made its way north from Paris toward the village of Beaumont-sur-Oise through a gray springtime mist, close enough to rain that droplets trickled down the windows of the third-class car. Mathieu, sitting on the window side of the wicker seat, stared out at what he could see of the fields passing by. Then the train slowed, barely making way, and the passenger on the aisle side of the seat said, "It always does that here." Mathieu turned to see a well-dressed man in his thirties, who had a cane propped by his leg.

"Any special reason?" Mathieu said.

"The track here was bombed by the Germans last May. It was repaired, but not very well, so the locomotive has to go carefully."

"You ride this train often?"

"I come up here once a month, to see family, then back to Paris the next day. It makes for a change," he said.

"Do you work in Paris?"

"I do. I'm an engineer with the Department of Public Works, in the Bureau of Roads and Bridges. I can't do as much walking inspection as I did before the war, but I manage." He patted his leg and said, "War wound, up at the Meuse River."

Mathieu nodded. "I was there too. My reserve unit was mobilized in April, just around the time they called up the forty-year-old class. And when the fighting started in May, I was a tank commander until we ran out of ammunition and were ordered to surrender."

"Damned sad, that whole business. Which tank?"

"Renault R-35. Two-man crew, the driver was up front, I stood in the turret, loading and firing the gun, such as it was."

"Yes, I know, thirty-seven millimeter, did nothing to the German armour."

"A bad tank, no radio, I had to direct the other tanks with hand signals. What a farce, our fuel trucks had wheels instead of treads, so they couldn't cross the terrain."

"Did the Germans let you out of prison camp?"

"I never went. The Wehrmacht captured so many French soldiers they put us in a soccer stadium, at Charleville-Mézières this was, and, when night came, I made a run for it, with two of my men. The stadium exits weren't lit, and there was only one guard and some barbed wire, so we distracted the guard, hit him a few times and tied him up, then used his bayonet to loosen the bottom strand of the wire and slid underneath. We spent a night in the woods, walked west when the sun rose, and eventually reached Paris. We thought we'd find an army unit and join up with them but, by then, what was left of the army had retreated to the south. They certainly weren't in Paris, the city was in chaos. Half the population was out on the roads, trying to get south, trying to get anywhere. What didn't we see! Ambulances from northern France, farm carts pulled by oxen, fire engines piled with furniture, hearses, one of them carrying a cage full of parrots, monks in robes, riding bicycles." Mathieu shook his head. "A farce, truly that's what it was."

"A terrible time," the engineer said. "You see why Pétain had to make a deal, that's what saved Paris."

"Yes, we can thank him for that, not much else."

The conversation was veering toward politics and they both sensed it was a subject better avoided. The engineer produced a one-page newspaper and started to read, Mathieu looked out the window and fell back into reverie. When the conductor announced the next stop, the engineer struggled to his feet and, leaning on his cane, took a business card from a leather case and handed it to Mathieu. "My card, monsieur," he said, then, with difficulty, walked toward the end of the car.

Mathieu put the card in his pocket. One never knew, but an inspector of roads and bridges might someday be useful.

A classic March day, the seventeenth; blustery and bright, with a stiff wind that blew the mist away to reveal a rich, sunny sky. In such weather, the old-clothes market in Clichy, up in the Eighteenth Arrondissement, was crowded with Parisians hunting for something, anything, they could wear. It was a tough neighborhood, Clichy, home to the Moulin Rouge nightclub and its cancan, as well as the Place Pigalle—a woman in every doorway with a leer and a suggestion for the men passing by. The old-clothes market took up one side of a street off the Boulevard Clichy, a row of carts piled high with what looked like mounds of tangled rags.

One of the vendors, who wore a knit cap and had three days' growth of white beard, watched as a woman approached his cart. What, he wondered, is *she* doing here? The woman wove her way past the shoppers, carefully, as Parisians in a crowd were determined to go wherever they wanted to go and if you were in the way they might help you, with shoulder or hip, not to be. But nobody pushed this woman. One wouldn't.

The woman, who used the nom de guerre Chantal, was, in the proper light, not yet fifty and had the look and bearing of the French upper bourgeoisie: chin up, back straight, complexion slightly roughened as though by time spent outdoors—it would have been no surprise to see her in waxed Barbour jacket, coming out of the woods with a shotgun in the crook of her elbow. Her hair was the color of bronze, worn parted to one side and swept across a noble forehead. She had prominent cheekbones, a determined gaze, a lean body, and spoke a musical, perfect French, spoke directly, with none of the breathless cooing—*Oh, monsieur!*—of the Parisian flirt. She had dressed for the Clichy market in an iron-gray belted overcoat, a maroon scarf wound into the opening at the top.

At last, Chantal reached the cart. "Good morning," she said. "I am told you sell cast-off French army uniforms."

"As you see," the vendor said, waving a hand toward his cart. "Some of them are almost new."

"Actually, I would like something worn and tattered, in a small size. I work for a costume department out at the Joinville studios. May I hunt around?"

You can't think I'm going to *serve* you, he thought. "It's all yours, madame," he said.

Patiently, she worked her way through the mound of clothing, which gave off the sour smell of old sweat, with an undertone of something burned. It made her sad to handle these uniforms and to think of the men who had worn them. Chantal came from a military family and had lost her father, two uncles, and a nephew in the

1914 war, while her estranged husband had disappeared in 1940, was probably in a POW camp in Germany. She hoped he was, she'd always liked him, though he'd been a terrible husband—couldn't keep his hands off the maids, which had distressed her, thus she couldn't keep the maids, which distressed her even more.

She found a soldier's tunic at the bottom of the pile and tugged at its sleeve until it came loose. Yes, perfect as a disguise, muddy and ripped at the shoulder, but without bullet holes or bloodstains. Now, for the trousers and the shirt. Boots would have to be bought, for a staggering price, on the black market, but Mathieu would take care of this himself. As she held the tunic up for inspection, the vendor said, "You told me you wanted something in sorry shape, well, you've got it there."

"Perhaps you'll give me a good price," Chantal said.

"Can't go much lower on any of it, I'm afraid. Plenty cheap as it is." After a moment he added, "Madame."

"Very well. I'll want the shirt and trousers."

The vendor shrugged. "You can have anything in the cart, if you like, and, for a little more, I'll throw in the cart."

Chantal laughed; surely a well-modulated laugh, but uninhibited and joyful. Now the vendor thought, *She's not so bad.* "Let me help you, madame," he said. "I know my way around in that cart."

"How very kind of you," Chantal said.

Chantal took the uniform—a bundle tied with a string—back to her apartment in the Rue d'Assas, on the far side of the Jardin du Luxembourg, not far from the border of Montparnasse. There she hung it up on two hangers by a partly opened window—if she couldn't wash it, she could at least air it out. Then she fixed herself a plate of lentils and onions and, with the last of her bread ration for the week, had lunch.

Next, to the central police station, the Préfecture, on the Île de la Cité. At the door, Chantal steeled herself, this was where one had to go for travel documents and the place breathed a century of sor-rows. *We regret, monsieur, that we cannot . . . But look here, the date stamp shows that your eligibility has expired . . . You need, madame, a letter from the Portuguese consulate.* And on and on and on. The vast room had gray walls, hard wooden benches, a worn-through linoleum floor, a crowd of angry, frightened peti-tioners, and clerks, who hung cardboard squares printed with num-bers on a wire stretched above the reception desk so you would know when it was your turn. 38 was being seen now, you had 144. Behind the reception desk was a counter where the clerks would direct you to an office, or send you away. It was a *high* counter. Chantal, who had brought along a battered old Colette novel, sat on a bench, and waited.

It took more than an hour but, eventually, she was admitted to the office of *Inspecteur Principal*—Captain, Marcellin. He rose and greeted her; she'd been here often and he was, in his way, wel-coming. He was an old cop, with strands of hair across his head, pouches beneath his eyes, and the face of a melancholy hound. He had, some years earlier, fallen on the street while in pursuit of a thief and had injured his knee, and was therefore relegated to work in this hell. At least he had a private office.

Inspecteur Marcellin wasn't much to look at but his eyes, the eyes of an old soul, fascinated her. Sometimes at night, in a mo-ment of private pleasure, she thought of Marcellin. He wore a pa-jama bottom, she reached inside the fly, held him, then drew out what she wanted. There was more, but it was that image which caught her imagination, and she found herself repeating it, she liked it so well. Why? What was it with this man? He was married and had six children, had never flirted with her, and she was sure the fantasy would never come true but neither did it go away. Chan-tal had a rough friend who lived a daring life and had once said of a would-be suitor, "He's handsome enough, but no news from down below." Well, with Marcellin, there *was* news from down below.

"It is good to see you, madame," he said. "How has life been treating you?"

"Well enough, considering how things are. And you, Inspecteur?"

"I don't know . . . I carry on, as best I can. But it's a hard job, pretending. All of these people"—he nodded toward the waiting room—"come here seeking permits: to stay in France, to reside in Paris, to work, to leave Paris, and they believe the state will help them but I know it will not. Of course I can't *say* anything, I have to play my part, the neutral civil servant." For a moment, anger flashed in his eyes, then it disappeared.

"Difficult, I think, very difficult."

"It is, because I am on their side. These fugitives . . . it was hard enough in the thirties but, since the Occupation . . . Jews, Spaniards who fought for the Republic, Poles, German intellectuals, Russians, Serbs, they all find their way to Paris with hope in their hearts, all of them, men, women, children, all of them in flight, most of them doomed. And then, when I read the newspaper, there's a name I recognize, yet another suicide."

"I know," she said gently. "My friends and I do what we can."

From Marcellin, a nod of appreciation. "Yes, but we all have to be careful, I hope you understand. The exit visa, which brings you here today, is subject to review, first by my superiors, some of whom are good friends to Vichy, and then by an office at German headquarters, the Kommandantur at the Hotel Majestic. I assume that one day I will be found out, and then . . ." He shrugged.

"We try, Inspecteur, not to ask too often."

"That's true, but don't stop asking. The *flics* here have to do the Germans' dirty work, so helping you is my way of telling them to . . ." As if in illustration, he turned his swivel chair to face a typewriter on a small table. To one side of the machine, a row of assorted rubber stamps, ink pads in red and black, and a franking device that, when squeezed, impressed an official seal on a document. Next the card, labeled PERMIS DE SORTIE—permission to leave, which he slid into the typewriter, then worked the roller bar until he had the dotted line he needed.

Chantal stared at the table, *The tools of life and death,* she thought.

The inspector said, "The name?"

Chantal had memorized the details because, according to what the members of the cell jokingly called the Code Mathieu, it was better not to write things down. Memorize, then destroy the notes. "Jean Dubois." She spelled the last name slowly, then said, "He is, or was, a corporal in the French army."

As Marcellin, using two fingers, typed the name, he said, "He'll need demobilization papers, you know."

"He will have them," Chantal said. "Those come from a Vichy office in Paris."

"And his age?"

"Nineteen."

"Height?"

"Five feet three inches tall."

"Eye color?"

"Brown."

"And I suppose he is of French nationality."

"He is."

"Address?"

"That would be twenty-two, Rue Marcadet, in the Eighteenth."

Marcellin worked away, then said, "And now, the photograph."

Obtaining this had not been easy, requiring Père Anselme to bring Sgt. Gillen to the Samaritaine department store in Paris, where a Photomaton booth, much used for photographs that would be attached to official documents, was available to the public. In such photographs, the right ear had to be visible.

The inspector rolled the card out of the typewriter. Using a brush and a small jar of paste, he fixed the photograph in the box provided on the card, then slipped the card into the franking device so that half the impression was on the photo, the other half on the card, making it impossible to exchange the photo for another. This technique annoyed the forgers, as it demanded extra work.

Marcellin held the card up for inspection, then chose a stamp and applied it to the card, followed by two more—*thock, thock, thock*. Next he signed, with a steel-nibbed pen dipped in a bottle of ink, the bottom of the card. As he handed the card to Chantal he said, "Now it is official, Corporal Dubois may leave Paris. The *permis* only says he can leave, to stay somewhere he will need a separate approval. And if he wishes to cross into the Unoccupied Zone, he will need an *Ausweis*."

"Yes, I know," Chantal said. "That has to come from the Kommandantur."

"I trust you are able to obtain the permission—perhaps I have a fellow knave over there."

"I would wish, but we must handle it . . . another way." She smiled, *You know I can't reveal that kind of information.*

Marcellin returned the smile and said, "You are discreet, madame . . ."

"Yes, in all things, I am discreet." She wanted to press her hand to her mouth—how had she let that slip out? *Merde!*

Perhaps the far edge of one of Marcellin's eyebrows lifted slightly. The tiny gesture thrilled her. *No, you mustn't!* she told herself. In answer, her mind produced the favored image from her nighttime fantasy. She'd better, she thought, change the subject. "Tell me, Inspecteur," she said, "how long must we be oppressed by these people?"

Marcellin leaned back in his chair. "If you read history, the answer to that question is troubling. The Ottoman Turks held their empire for three hundred years, and there are plenty of other examples. It would seem that once a nation gets its fangs into another, it's very hard to make it let go. Conquest, you know, for some it is a kind of drug." He paused, then said, "But I mustn't ramble on." He stood and offered his hand. She held it briefly: a cool, dry hand, the skin smooth and hard. *A lovely hand.*

"Then I'll say *à bientôt*." I'll see you soon. "But not *too* soon," Chantal said.

"Whenever you might need me, I'll be here," he said.

A woman on the station platform at Beaumont-sur-Oise, waiting for the afternoon train back to Paris, watched as a young man, aided by an older woman, prepared to board the third-class car.

Oh, this is sad to see, she thought. Yet it wasn't all sad; the good side of human nature was there as well. Here was a wounded French soldier, walking with a crutch, a bandage around his throat, helped by his poor mother, who held his arm as they climbed the steps into the car. Standing just behind the pair, the woman said, "There, there, take your time, the world will wait for a wounded soldier." The mother turned and smiled. Chantal wore a dowdy little hat, a church hat, while an old, black leather handbag rode her forearm, a symbol of staunch membership in the lower bourgeoisie.

When the train reached Paris, the woman said, "May I help you, madame?"

"I think we can manage."

"Poor boy, I hope he will mend soon."

"Thank you, madame, he is young, he'll come through it."

At the Gare de Lyon, the pair had to change for a local that went to Orléans, and there, on the platform, was a *contrôle,* a young policeman and an older detective. "Your papers, please," the detective said.

"Yes, of course. I have them right here," the mother said, snapping open the metal clasp of her purse and bringing out two *permis de sortie* authorizations and two identity cards.

The detective had a glance at the cards, looking up from each photograph to see that the faces were the same. The detective's eyes now settled on Sgt. Gillen. "Have you your demobilization certificate, my boy?"

The mother said, "Here it is." She brought out the document and handed it to the detective.

"Seems to be in order," the detective said. Then, to the sergeant, "Are you feeling any better?"

"Oh yes," the mother said. "He is healing nicely."

The detective's eyes changed. "Can he not speak?" he said.

"A wound in the throat," the mother said. "The doctors say his speech will return. In time, they say it will."

The detective looked them over. Chantal could practically see his mind working and her heart started to beat hard. Then people in the line behind them, afraid of missing their trains, shifted their feet, someone cleared his throat, others mumbled—*What shall we do?* In its way, the crowd was confronting authority. The detective had just about decided to pursue the matter, then he saw the faces of the people in line, pleading faces—most would have to wait hours for another train if they missed their connections. Yes, he could have made the pair stand aside while he checked the other passengers, but the idea wasn't appealing: the wounded soldier with a crutch, the caring mother. *Oh the hell with it,* he thought. He handed the documents back to Chantal and said, "Very well, you may go ahead."

The pair moved slowly along the platform, Chantal holding Sgt. Gillen's arm in a grip like a vise. She feared tricks: the detective calling out, in English, "Good luck, soldier" or "Say, you've forgotten your hat," so, no matter what happened, her English fugitive was not going to turn around.

The Paris/Orléans local left twenty minutes late. Chantal and Sgt. Gillen took seats in a compartment in the second-class car—third class was jammed, not a seat to be found, passengers standing in the aisles, so Chantal paid the conductor the difference when he came to punch their tickets. The Mathieu cell preferred third class, where German travelers never ventured, they all rode first class.

Chugging along at a leisurely pace, saving coal, the local rattled down the track beneath a sky of wind-blown clouds.

Chantal relaxed, relieved to be in the countryside, *to be back in France,* she thought, for Paris was its own nation. At the Étréchy stop, she looked across the track to see passengers returning to Paris with their treasures. You were lucky, if you lived in the city, to have family or other connections in the country, as they could buy food from the *paysans:* ham, sausages, cheese, and more. One couple stood guard over a lumpy burlap sack that likely contained potatoes, and almost all the Paris-bound passengers had bundles and large suitcases.

In the compartment, Chantal and Sgt. Gillen had joined an older man and two young girls, perhaps fourteen and twelve, who looked like sisters, which left one empty seat. Just as the train pulled away, a face appeared in the glass panel above the door to the compartment, a tubby gent with a little mustache entered, tipped his hat, said good afternoon, slid a good-sized suitcase into the luggage rack above the seat, and sat himself down with a contented sigh. And he was, evidently, in the mood to talk. "Headed for Orléans?" he said to Sgt. Gillen, who was in the opposite seat.

"That's right," Chantal said, polite but brusque, and not inclined toward conversation.

"Going there myself. I'm a traveler in dry goods." He pointed to his suitcase on the luggage rack.

There was no response—the passengers knew a pest when they saw one. The salesman appeared not to notice—if nobody wanted to speak with him he would continue the conversation without them. "Yes, it used to be a good business, but now it's hard to come by any decent fabric. Still, one must do one's best, eh?"

Silence. Sgt. Gillen looked out the window. The salesman was undeterred. "I see that you were in the military. I didn't serve myself, bad back, from hauling a sample case about. But I admire those who did, like yourself."

Chantal had to intervene. "It is difficult for my son to speak, monsieur."

"Too bad! Nothing like a good war story to make the time go by. Where are you folks from?"

Chantal's first instinct was to ignore him, but that was, she realized, a mistake—making it seem that she did not wish to speak to a social inferior. She knew this type of personality—it could not tolerate such a slight and would want some form of revenge. "We are from Paris," she said.

"A delightful city," he said. "Yes, Paris . . . I myself am from Lyons but I often visit Paris . . . what brings you to leave such a delightful city?"

Nosy! "There is an excellent doctor in Orléans, I am taking my son for a consultation."

That seemed to mollify him. He said, "Mm," in answer, then stood, reached up to his suitcase, unlocked it with a tiny key, probed inside, and brought forth an orange. This was a remarkable sight, no one in the compartment had seen an orange since before the war, and the two sisters were wide-eyed as they gazed at it. Producing a multi-blade knife, he took out his breast-pocket handkerchief, folded neatly into three points, shook it loose, and spread it on his lap. When he began to peel the orange, the powerful scent filled the air. "I'm on the trains every week," he said. "All the conductors know me." He loosened a section of the orange and, using the point as a fork, popped it into his mouth. He chewed for a moment, then said, "They tell me stories, the conductors, about what goes on . . ." He shook his head. "If you knew . . . well, all sorts of people traveling about lately. All sorts, it's hard to believe." He speared another segment of the orange, saying, "Some of them, I'm told, wanted by the authorities." For the salesman, that last word had some considerable weight. "Even English soldiers on the run! Imagine!" He paused to eat the segment and wiped his lips with his fingers. "Quite a substantial reward, if you snare one," he mused. "Thousands of francs."

Chantal felt Sgt. Gillen stiffen by her side.

"There may even be one . . . on this train," the salesman said. "Could be . . . could be. Right, soldier boy?"

Sgt. Gillen stared out the window.

"Seems like he doesn't hear me." The salesman returned to his orange. In the compartment it seemed very quiet. As he ate, the salesman now stared at Sgt. Gillen, the stare lasted a long time. He finished the orange and put the peels into the ashtray on the arm of the seat. "Well, time to . . ." He rose, pushed the compartment door open, looked left and right, then walked away down the corridor. After a few minutes, the older sister whispered to the younger, then stood, and left the compartment, going in the same direction the salesman had taken. Chantal knew that this led away from the WC at the end of the car, so where had the salesman gone? To do what? She told herself to be calm, but she wasn't. She began to feel threatened and reproached herself for having an overactive imagination but the feeling didn't go away. As the train crawled along a sweeping curve, a long moan from the whistle. *Nearing the next station,* it meant. The older sister now returned, sat next to the younger, and the two began an urgent, whispered exchange.

In the corridor, the conductor called out, "Étampes. Next station Étampes."

Chantal stood and retrieved a small suitcase from the luggage rack while Sgt. Gillen, following her example, rose and propped the crutch beneath his arm. *"Bonsoir, tout le monde,"* Chantal said— goodby everybody, pushed the door open and held it for Sgt. Gillen. As the train rolled to a stop on the platform, the waiting passengers, edging in front of each other, gathered where they knew the steps would be. Chantal preceded Sgt. Gillen and gave him a hand as he descended to the ground, then she looked up and down the platform, found the station house, and headed in that direction, which meant they had to pass by the car they'd been traveling in. Glancing up, she saw the salesman, staring down at her from the window, his face puckered with rage as he raised a small, white fist and shook it at her.

"Fooking bastard," Sgt. Gillen said.

Chantal shushed him.

As they neared the station house, the two sisters went past them, almost running, the older sister holding the hand of the younger, who was biting her lip as tears rolled down her cheeks. Chantal watched them as they went past the door of the station house and disappeared around the corner.

"What's gone wrong?" the sergeant said.

"The salesman frightened them."

"He never spoke a word to them."

"But they knew what he was. And they were afraid of him because they're on the run. The older girl followed him on the train, probably saw him talking to the conductor. In a certain way, talking."

"On the run? Where are their parents?"

Chantal shook her head, slowly, a gesture of sorrow. "I don't know," she said. "I don't know."

Chantal let the next local pass, then took the one after so, by the time she and Sgt. Gillen reached Orléans, it was almost ten in the evening. They were met on the platform by a tall, lanky man with unruly white hair. He kissed Chantal on the cheek and shook hands with Sgt. Gillen. "I was beginning to worry," he said. "You were due earlier."

"We ran into trouble," she said, "and had to change trains."

"You can tell me in the car," he said.

Dr. Lambert, Chantal explained, was allowed to have a car because he was a veterinary surgeon. He led them across the street to a dented, old Renault, its original red color faded to a pastel, that looked like it had been down too many dirt roads. After a few tries, the car started up and, with piston rods clattering and black smoke streaming from the tailpipe, they set off for the doctor's house.

Chantal had been in Orléans years earlier and remembered that she had liked it; an ancient city, still beautiful despite a history of wars—its residents had helped to fight off Attila the Hun in the year 408, and the city had been taken from the English in 1428, during the Hundred Years War, the army led by Joan of Arc. As the doctor drove slowly on a stone bridge over the river Loire, Chantal recalled one of the better moments of her last visit: a meal in a side-street restaurant, morsels of young venison with *griottes*—dark, sour little cherries—in a peppery sauce, a local specialty. Had she been with her husband that night? Likely she had been, they were still together then.

"What happened to make you change trains?" the doctor asked.

Chantal described the salesman, and the young sisters.

The doctor listened carefully, his expression growing darker as Chantal spoke. When she was done, he said, "Poor France, denunciation has become a national disease. You didn't happen to get a name, did you?"

"I didn't."

"Too bad."

"What would you have done with a name?"

"I would have written it down."

As for the two sisters, he said there were fugitive children running loose all over Europe. "Maybe, one night, the parents didn't come home. Perhaps the parents had told them what to do in case that happened—go to your aunt's house in Orléans. Or, at worst, the girls were scared of being put in some *institution*, so they took whatever money they had and got on a train."

A few minutes later, they reached the doctor's residence on the Rue Saint-Marceau, a three-story brick building with a walled garden—thus there were two entries, requisite for a safe house. Inside, Dr. Lambert led them to the kitchen and introduced the pair to his wife, sister, mother, and two RAF airmen, Flt. Lt. Hinton and Sgt. Wicks, also trying to make their way to Spain.

The doctor had made sure that dinner was saved for Chantal and the sergeant, a bowl of soup: potatoes, carrots, and onions, flavored by a few bits of chicken. Chantal was famished, and found the soup delicious. As for Sgt. Gillen, he finished his meal quickly and, more than happy to see fellow airmen, and happier yet to speak to people from his own country, asked the two what unit they'd been with.

"We were with the three-oh-eight squadron, Fourth Bomber Command, flying Wellingtons out of Biggin Hill," Hinton said. He had thin, wispy hair, a mild face, and looked to be in his middle thirties.

"I was also in Wellingtons, the four-one-three, out of Croydon Field."

"What did you do?" Hinton asked.

"Radioman." Gillen said it with pride.

"I was the pilot," Hinton said, "and Wicksy here was our bombardier."

Wicks had wavy hair combed back from his forehead and, clenched in his teeth, a pipe with no tobacco. In the cardigan sweater and corduroy trousers that a courier had found for him, he looked like a schoolteacher, just about to work in his garden on a Saturday morning. *Yet*, Chantal thought, *a bombardier, setting cities on fire.*

"What happened to your throat?" Wicks asked.

"Not a bloody thing, the dressing is just an excuse not to talk because I can't speak bloody French."

"Nigel here speaks it pretty damn well," Wicks said, "but the couriers won't let him say a word."

"School French, y'know, not French French," Hinton said.

Hinton continued, "We saw plenty of tracer and we were damned lucky it didn't hit us, but the evasion used up our air time and somewhere over northern France I realized we weren't going to have the fuel to make it across the Channel, so I found us a field and landed. Tore the wheels off, no more than that. We all got out, then we saw flashlights and heard people shouting in German and made a run for the woods on either side of the field. The four who went left were caught, Wicksy and I weren't. So, after two days of wandering about, wet and cold, we knocked on a farmhouse door."

"We had an engine go bad," the sergeant said. "Lost altitude, then we were hit by machine-gun fire. Two of us parachuted out but I never found my mate and . . ."

There was an old telephone on the kitchen wall—a wooden box with a receiver hung in a cradle on one side—and now it rang, two hoarse stutters, then rang again. As the doctor put the receiver to his ear, he held up a hand for silence. "Yes?" he said. Then, "I see, oh dear, poor Didi, I'm afraid you'd better." He hung up and said to his wife, "That was Ronel, his poodle swallowed a bone, and he and his wife are bringing her over."

"Dreadful people," Madame Lambert said to Chantal. "Loyal to Vichy, more than loyal, and they don't shut up about it."

The doctor met Chantal's eyes, pointed upward and said, "*Now,* please, Chantal."

The doctor's wife and sister hurried to clear the table, because the Lambert family surely didn't have supper after ten. Meanwhile, the doctor herded Chantal and the airmen up the stairs, then used a key to open a door on the landing at the top of the staircase. Inside, an attic. There were two blankets on the floor and Wicks said, "Here's where we sleep." The doctor took two blankets from a pile in the corner and handed them to Chantal. "You cannot talk while these people are in the house. Not a word," he said. "I'll be back to tell you when it's safe."

The attic smelled of mildew and it was cold, the air damp and still, like the air in a room that hasn't been heated for years. Chantal sat down, wrapped the blanket around herself and leaned against the wall. It was an old blanket that had, she soon realized, spent its earlier life on a horse. Next to her, Sgt. Gillen stared up at the beams, then his eyes closed and he went to sleep. *It would help to know the time,* she thought, but it was too dark to see the numbers on her watch. When a light rain started up, pattering on the roof above her head, the sound was hypnotic and soon had her asleep. Some time later, she woke to find the doctor squatting at her feet. "So, how is Didi?" she said.

"Very groggy at the moment, from the anesthetic, but she'll survive."

"Glad to hear it."

"What time is your train tomorrow?"

"Midday."

"The Ronels paid me with eggs, so there will be breakfast in the morning. And, as it's after midnight, you may as well go back to sleep."

"I will . . . I am tired all the time, now."

"All of us, Chantal. It's the work."

Chantal and the sergeant reached the town of Bourges late in the afternoon, then took a two-car train to the tiny village of La Guerche-sur-l'Aubois, just to the north of the Unoccupied Zone, where, at the end of the village's main street, Chantal found the small house she'd used before. She had told Sgt. Gillen what to expect, but he was still surprised. In the parlor of the house, ten people were waiting to be taken across the demarcation line into Vichy France.

From time to time, a *passeur*—a guide who led fugitives across borders—would appear and for a small fee, fifty francs, lead two or three people along a twisting route which left them in the Vichy Unoccupied Zone. Sometimes the local border guards would raid the house but they always made sure to let the *passeurs* know they were coming. Most of them were related to the *passeurs* and they weren't going to arrest family.

When it was their turn, Chantal and the sergeant followed the guide through an oak forest, across a rushing stream spanned by a tree trunk, then around a farmyard where the dogs barked at them but didn't attack, and, at last, to the edge of a cow pasture. "Watch your step here," the guide said. "Mind the cow flops. You're in Vichy now, so I'll go back for the next customer."

Now Chantal and the sergeant walked a half mile to a cow barn, where the next courier would pick up the sergeant and take him into Spain. As they waited, Chantal said, "You will be on local trains down to the border. Crossing the mountain pass will require hard walking—I expect the smugglers will see your crutch and put you on a mule."

They watched from the open door as a young man, dark and serious, made his way up a hill to the barn. Chantal said, "That is your courier, Ramón, a Spaniard who fought against Franco, then fled to France. I will go down there and talk to him, for I must be off if I'm to make the Paris train." From Chantal, a tender smile. "Good luck, and safe journey."

"Thank you, Chantal," the sergeant said, "for all you've done . . . you risked your life for me."

"For you, and for France, and I could go on, but your courier is almost here and it's growing dark, so I will say goodby."

Paris. 29 March. That afternoon the city wore its habitual colors— gray skies, gray stone—*triste* if you were melancholy, soft and inspiring when life went your way. Mathieu was meeting with Ghislain—the resistance name of his second-in-command—in an office at the Bibliothèque Nationale, the national library, that was made available to Ghislain for confidential meetings, its usual occupant arranging to be elsewhere for an hour. The office looked down on a courtyard and was apparently used by a senior librarian—there were books, some of great age, stacked on a long table with slips of paper inside their front covers, while the scent of old dust, old books, and the sweetish smell of library paste perfumed the air.

Mathieu and Ghislain had been friends long before the war, so their real names and circumstances were no secret, which was also true of Chantal and many others in their cell, trusted friends, acquaintances, and business associates, who had chosen to resist the Occupation. But, when they were engaged in clandestine work, in

cafés, railway stations, even in private meetings, they used their resistance names: this was standard practice because it was safer—
private meetings were sometimes not so private as you thought.

They had met initially when Mathieu attended Ghislain's lectures at the Sorbonne, the latter a prominent ethnographer who,
following Margaret Mead and Bronisław Malinowski to Melanesia, had published a book called *The Kahwa People of the Trobri-
and Islands,* and this much-praised publication had earned him a
senior professorship at the Sorbonne. Mathieu had taken to the
professor, fascinated by a view of culture directly opposed to the
typical colonial assumptions—these were complex societies and
their members were not "natives." Mathieu would approach the
lectern when the professor was done speaking and ask questions
and, in time, he was invited to visit Ghislain's office and the professor became a kind of father figure to the young student.

Ghislain was now in his sixties, with white hair, and eyeglasses
in thin silver frames—the sort of eyeglasses that a priest might
wear—his face set in a speculative, patient half smile, and, always,
he paused before he spoke. Pear-shaped, and wearing loosely fitting
gray suits, he seemed to be at peace with the world around him. A
few months after the fall of France, Ghislain had become a coun-
selor to the resistance cell, and second-in-command to Mathieu,
who found his critical, penetrative mind to be of great value.

Both men lit cigarettes and, as they chatted about the news of
the day, Mathieu counted out half of the five thousand dollars that
Max de Lyon had given him. "This is much needed, right now,"
Ghislain said. "It's been three weeks since Bertrand was arrested,
his wife was told she could expect help but it hasn't come yet and
she's getting anxious. So I'll have the lawyer convert the dollars into
francs and bring some money over to her. Today. Then I'll pay the
expenses of a few couriers, and keep the rest for the future."

"How is Bertrand doing?"

"Being in the Santé prison for two years will be difficult, but
he'll survive it. The lawyer will visit him every week, which will let

the prison administration know that he has friends, and we paid to make sure he wasn't sent on to a German camp."

"And the English airman?"

"In fact a Scot. He is in a POW camp in Germany—there won't be enough to eat but they'll take decent care of him. There's a kind of gentlemen's agreement between the English and the Germans: the English treat their military prisoners well, which the Germans appreciate, so they don't misbehave in *their* POW camps. Of course, if the war should begin to go badly for the Reich, that may change—Germans can be vengeful if they aren't winning."

"How is the wife taking it?"

"Not well. She has always thought of Bertrand as naïve and dreamy and she believes that we used those qualities to recruit him. She expected him to take over her father's business, but he became a dramatist . . . to spite her, she suspects."

"Might she go to some office and tell them stories?"

"Not as long as we pay her. Also, I think she knows there might be consequences."

"We don't do such things, Ghislain."

"Not yet, we don't." Ghislain sat back. "That's always the question with underground work—how rough do you play the game? I knew a man a few years ago, a Russian, he'd been to some training school for the secret services and he told me that his instructor had played a sort of game with one of the students.

"He asked him, suppose your country had been suddenly occupied, you never expected any such thing but it has happened. Then, one afternoon, your phone rings, it's a man you've seen now and again, not quite a friend, who says he's in your city for the day and needs a favor. It seems he has a heavy package, he can't carry it around from office to office, can he leave it with you? It's hard to say no, so you say yes.

"An hour later, a man shows up at your door with a package— your friend couldn't come, so this man agreed to deliver the package, he'll be back later to pick it up. You wait, and then, quite a bit later than you'd imagined, someone else shows up and takes the package. Now you sense you've been drawn into someone's secret operation.

"A week goes by, and here's your friend again, on the telephone. 'Thank you for helping us,' he says. *Us?* Which confirms what you feared—you've given them a hold over you. Now he needs one last favor, and makes it clear you don't have a choice, do it, or they'll give your name to the police. 'I understand,' your friend says, 'that you know X, and that the two of you have lunch now and then.' *How do they know that?* 'Why not make a lunch appointment with him? For next Monday, say, at one o'clock, at such-and-such a restaurant.' It's only a lunch, so again you agree.

"Then, the morning before the lunch, your friend calls and says, 'You are meeting X at one. At one-twenty, excuse yourself and go to the WC.' You follow orders, and the assassins arrive a few minutes later. You, and all the other customers, run like hell. From now on, you belong to them, whoever they are.

"Or, take a different view. You refuse to accept the package and, that afternoon, your friend is arrested, and shot. Well, you just avoided a serious problem. But you didn't. Because the occupier is now expelled from your country and, a week later, somebody shows up and says he's from some justice committee and you stand accused of causing the death of a patriot."

It was quiet in the office, then Mathieu said, "Ghislain, are you suggesting that, sometime in the future, we will operate that way?"

"Tomorrow, no. But if the British lose this war, and there's some chance they might, we may become desperate, and desperation leads to the actions described by the Soviet instructor."

"If the Americans enter the war, the British won't lose."

"That's true. That's why we listen to the BBC French service, that's why we talk endlessly with friends, we want to know, when will the Americans save us? As they did in the 1914 war. And what we fear is that they won't arrive, they'll stay behind their ocean—there's a good deal of powerful sentiment in the USA against intervention."

"Let Hitler win?"

"They don't say that, they say that Stalin is the real enemy."

"And your Russian friend, what became of him?"

"Shot in the 'thirty-six purge, so I was told."

When Mathieu left the library, he went for a walk on the Rue Vivienne, which ran from the Palais Royal up to the Bourse, a fancy street that featured the Galerie Vivienne, an enclosed passage with fancy shops beneath a glass dome. Walking along, his mind far away, Mathieu came down from the clouds and saw that he had just passed the Restaurant Maurice, an old favorite from before-the-war times. Mathieu was always hungry but today he felt it more than usual, and decided to have lunch at the Maurice and eat whatever rutabaga or sweet potato *plat* they'd cooked up for that day. At the maître d' station he was asked, "Table for one?" As Mathieu opened his mouth to say yes, the maître d' added, "Or does monsieur wish to dine in the upstairs room?"

He didn't wink, a good maître d' doesn't have to wink, his voice and eyebrows do the job for him. Mathieu had plenty of money in his pocket, not resistance money, his own, and said, "The upstairs room, please." Which meant he would be served real food, black-market food, at black-market prices. As he followed the maître d' up the stairs, he smelled *frites,* thin-sliced potatoes deep-fried in beef fat, and thought, *I would kill for a steak frites.* The steak seared and running blood, the *frites* in a sizzling mound by its side. Dark gold. Crisp. And, if he were in luck, plenty of rich, brown sauce with peppercorns.

He *was* in luck. He tried to eat slowly, to savor the taste, ordered a second glass of red wine, but he was done before he knew it, swirling the last of the *frites* through what remained of the sauce on his plate. As he waited for his dishes to be cleared, he noticed a couple seated a few tables away, who had arrived just after he did. They were well dressed, in their forties, the woman, with an animated face and expressive hands, was amused by something her companion said and . . .

My God it's Klara!

Yes, he was sure, it was his Sorbonne girlfriend from years ago, rabid communist, rabid lover. Klara Zeller came from an old Alsatian family, and looked Jewish but, technically, she wasn't. In 1870, when the Prussians won a war with the French, they had absorbed the disputed province of Alsace-Lorraine. There had been a fair-sized Jewish population in Alsace but then many of them decided to emigrate across the new border to France, others changed religion, becoming Lutheran, hoping to be spared the tender affections of the Prussian government. Klara's grandfather, who owned a department store—a profitable business that wouldn't travel—had done that very thing, and the records were there to prove it, should the Germans inquire.

Eighteen years old, Mathieu had been, and feverish, overheated, in a permanent state of arousal, and it was the same for Klara. She had aged: there were scowl lines between her eyes, some descent beneath her chin, and her abundant hair, once curly and wild, which she'd pulled back and tied with an Indian-print scarf, was now carefully cut below the ear and set. No more the cracked leather coat, now an ankle-length black wool coat trimmed with fur.

And who had she married? A rather plain fellow, powdered and neatly barbered, a man of substance. Who squinted briefly at the *addition,* then produced a wallet from an inside pocket, drew out a few large-denomination bills, and handed them to the waiter. When the waiter reached for change, the man-of-substance stopped him with an imperious wave of the hand. Then he stood, pulled Klara's chair back for her, and took her elbow as they left the upstairs room. Mathieu wondered if Klara had noticed him, and decided she had not. Anyhow, what did he want with her? This answer he knew—memories of the affair had manifested themselves beneath the tablecloth. *Oh well.*

But, as Mathieu was served a green salad, she reappeared, went back to her former table and, from a chair, retrieved a pair of suede gloves, then hurried over to Mathieu's table, kissed him lightly on the forehead and handed him a five-franc note—a telephone number written on it with a waiter's pencil.

They had first made love twenty-two years earlier. Klara's aunt and uncle had asked her to water their houseplants and, after making sure she had a key, they left for Cap Ferrat and she and Mathieu were in the maid's room by late afternoon. It was the first day of August, hot and humid in Paris, and quiet, with the Parisians off for vacation, so when Klara opened the window there was only the sound of birds singing in the trees that bordered the street below. Klara unrolled the mattress on the narrow bed and covered it with a sheet she found in the linen chest.

Facing each other, they began to undress—Klara had worn pink panties for the occasion and, after a moment of hesitation, pulled them down. After that, they just stood there and stared at each other, getting a long, hungry look at what they'd wanted to see for three months. Finally, Mathieu took her hand and led her to the bed. Klara was a virgin, cried out when he entered her, then spent the night with a towel between her legs.

Mathieu was not a virgin, had been twice with prostitutes in cheap hotels, where he'd been shown how it worked—his early sexual education little more than a pamphlet with instruction on the order of "The daddy uses his penis to plant the seed in the mommy," and the prostitutes had led him well beyond that.

It had been a lengthy courtship; the first time he put a hand on Klara's breast she took it off, the next time she let it stay. They danced at a summer pavilion and as they circled slowly her thigh accidentally pressed against him. When he called her a naughty girl, she submitted to a playful spanking. He rubbed oil on her back at the beach and she returned the favor, moving her hand slowly, babbling about God-knew-what as she caressed him, the soft pressure of her fingers like nothing he'd ever known—she was *good* at this, it was far more natural than artful. What else might she touch so sweetly? When, as he kissed her good night at the door, her parents snoring away in their bedroom, she guided his hand where it had never been before, he didn't know exactly what to do so held it still until she said, breathing hard, "I think you had better go now."

After the night of the towel, they became serious lovers. Each time she undressed, he liked to look at her before he touched her: the lush body of an eighteen-year-old, silky skin a shade of ivory and, when she opened her legs for him, the color known as *rose de dessous*—the pink of underneath.

Meanwhile, Klara read *Ten Days That Shook the World,* John Reed's story of the Russian Revolution, and attended communist rallies as civil war raged in the USSR. She handed out leaflets in the street, she marched, calling out *"Front de Gauche!"*—Left Front, as she thrust her fist in the air. Mathieu was often at her side, but could not abide the *meetings,* and did not join the party. By autumn they were experienced lovers, and he'd discovered how much he treasured the moment when she gasped and quivered, and later realized that this was what he desired of women more than anything else. The affair lasted five months—she met someone she liked more than she liked Mathieu, someone far more passionate about politics than he was, also better looking. That was hard on him, he moped for a couple of weeks, but there was this girl he'd met and . . .

Mathieu telephoned the day after the meeting in the upstairs room. Klara was obviously not alone; when he said, "Klara, can we meet sometime?" she said, "It's Michelle." Then she paused and said, "Oh Michelle, an afternoon tea, that would be wonderful. At Monique Vallon's apartment? I haven't seen her for ages!"

"And where does Monique live?" Mathieu asked.

"Wait a minute, yes, twenty-two Rue Champollion, is that right?"

Mathieu repeated the address and wrote it down.

"Wonderful, then I'll be there, Thursday at four."

"So will I," Mathieu said.

"*À bientôt,* Michelle. Until Thursday."

Thursday, four in the afternoon. The Rue Champollion was in the Fifth Arrondissement, the student district, battered old buildings near the Sorbonne. Number 22 had a cheap restaurant at street level—*Klara lives here?* Nostalgia for student days maybe, but hard to believe that the Klara he'd seen at the Restaurant Maurice would be comfortable in this *quartier.* When Mathieu rang the bell at the exterior door, the concierge let him in and said, "Madame is expecting you, she's on the third floor."

Klara heard him coming up the stairs and when he arrived on the third floor she was waiting at the open door. Polite greetings and Parisian-style kisses were exchanged, then, once more, they stood gazing at each other, twenty-two years had gone by but there is nothing quite like your first lover. She wore a silver-gray knit sweater dress with a belt, a long, lavender scarf tied loosely at the throat, and Chanel perfume. She said, "Won't you come in?"—the formality relieved by a certain sparkle in her eyes. As he followed her into a large, airy room, he saw that she was rather more ample than she had been but to him that was no bad thing. On a coffee table in front of a sofa there was a bottle of wine and two crystal glasses.

"This isn't where you live, is it, Klara?"

"Oh no, it's a spare room I rent from a friend—it belongs to the adjoining apartment but it has its own door. It's somewhere I can come when I want to be alone."

Mathieu's professional interest asserted itself; to any resistance cell, spare rooms, often unused maid's quarters, were like gold in the crowded city. *You could hide three fugitives in here,* Mathieu thought.

She lowered herself to the sofa, legs together and swung to one side, and patted the cushion next to her. "Let's have a glass of wine, dear, and talk about old times."

They talked, they flirted, her phone rang but she didn't answer it. She asked him what he thought about the Occupation and he said this was no time to think about such things. She angled her face, moved toward him, and closed her eyes. It was a long, busy kiss, she put a hand to the side of his face while he stroked her back, and, when the kiss ended, they looked at each other with fond smiles. Now that she was seated, the hem of her dress lay just above the knee and he moved it up a little further, and then more, to a point where the clips of her garter belt were fastened, which left a few appetizing inches of bare skin for his fingertips.

"Slowly, dear," she said. "We have the entire afternoon to ourselves." She reached down and tugged her dress back where it belonged. "Would you care for a little more wine? I think I'll have some." She took the bottle from the coffee table and refilled their glasses.

Perhaps, he thought, *a pang of guilt.* After all, she was a married woman, about to stray with an old boyfriend. "Klara," he said, "the man who was with you at the restaurant, is he your husband?"

"He is. A decent man, difficult at times, but we get on well together."

"But you do what you like."

"Yes, I always have, it seems to be my nature." After a moment she said, "I try to live from pleasure to pleasure but that's not so easy now. If only the horrid Boche would go away."

"We all wish for that, Klara."

"Is wishing enough, do you think?"

"What else is there?"

"Well, some people resist, you know. They write leaflets or deface the German posters or . . . other actions that oppose the Occupation."

"Yes, of course I've heard about it," he said. "The Resistance."

"I have a few friends who are prepared, when the time comes, to do just that," she said, determination in her voice. "Are you ever tempted? I remember you as a man who didn't like to be pushed around, what happened to him?"

Merde, she was *recruiting* him—this room was the equivalent of his apartment at the Saint-Yves, a safe house. "Klara, I'm curious, are your political opinions the same as when we were together? Are you still faithful to the party?"

"Yes, I've never changed."

"But, the way things stand right now, with the Hitler-Stalin alliance, the party opposes resistance, no?"

"For now, that's true, but it won't be forever. Hitler will invade Russia, and then we'll be able to work against the Nazis. Will you join us?"

Mathieu sighed. "Klara, this is all a little deep for me, I'm just trying to live day by day."

"Still, you should think it over. We would work together, you and I, with my friends."

Regret in his voice, he said, "I don't think I would be very good at conspiracy." The meeting at the Restaurant Maurice had been no accident, he realized. Klara and her husband, if he was her husband and not a fellow operative, had followed him, because Soviet spymasters, aware of their long-ago love affair, had determined to take advantage of it. Clandestine networks run from Moscow were nothing new in Paris—there had been a series of highly publicized trials during the thirties as the police uncovered espionage operations.

"One learns conspiracy, in the same way that one learns a foreign language," she said, her tone now challenging and hard. "And in time you'll *have* to learn it, because the day is coming when we'll all have to take sides—the old regime or the new, that will be the choice."

"Yes, I suppose it will be, but, for now . . ."

"I would ask you, please, to keep our rendezvous a secret. My friends don't like to be talked about." Her eyes met his to confirm the threat.

"From me, not a word," he said, looking at his watch.

"Do you have to be somewhere?"

He nodded, rose from the couch, leaned down and brushed her cheek with his lips. "Another time, perhaps, we'll see each other."

"Yes, I hope so," she said, clearly disappointed. By an old love affair that would not have an encore? Or by a failed recruitment? Maybe both, he thought, but he was wrong and he knew it.

It was after six when he left Klara's apartment, headed for the Saint-Germain Métro station. As he worked his way along the crowded boulevard, it occurred to him that this part of the evening, five to seven, *l'heure bleue,* had been much loved by Parisians, the time for love affairs, the time for discreet hotel rooms, but the people on the boulevard, Mathieu suspected, were going home to hide away until they had to go to work in the morning.

Up ahead of him, Mathieu saw a German officer stride past a Parisian man—a small, unremarkable fellow, then the officer spun around and shouted, "You! Halt!"

"Me?"

"Yes, you."

"What did . . . ?"

The German's French was terrible, but the man understood what he ordered: "Stand at the edge of the sidewalk and face the traffic." The man did as he was told but nothing happened right away, the German let him stand there for a few moments. From people hurrying by, sidelong glances, but nobody dared to stop. Finally, the officer drew his leg back and gave the man such a hard kick in the backside that he stumbled and went sprawling facedown in the street. The officer walked away.

Mathieu hurried over to the man and, with hands beneath his armpits, helped him to his feet. The man, brushing himself off, said, "That sonofabitch could really kick."

Mathieu said, "What happened? Did you say something to him?"

"No, not a word. But I stared at him, looked him in the eyes, and that made him mad."

"Are you hurt?"

The man rubbed his bottom and said, "I'll be sore in the morning."

There was an older woman who had stopped after she'd seen the incident. "May they burn in hell," she said, voice trembling with anger. Some people gathered near her muttered in agreement.

It was one-thirty in the morning, rain beating down on the pavement outside the Le Cygne nightclub. Mathieu had received a hand-delivered note at the Hôtel Saint-Yves: Max de Lyon, the owner of the nightclub, had asked him to come and meet a friend—Mathieu could stay in a room above the club until the curfew ended. So, in time for the meeting, he descended the stairway to the basement.

From the foot of the stairs, Mathieu looked out over the scene. *What a zoo!* Le Cygne was packed: Parisian underworld types, black-market royalty, German officers of high rank—some wearing monocles, some with sabre scars—and their showy girlfriends in glittering gowns, the whole crowd as drunk and merry as could be. Amid a haze of cigarette smoke, in darkness cut by theatrical spotlights, the floor show: to the accompaniment of a trio, saxophone, piano, and drums, a line of twelve naked dancers did the cancan, bumping, grinding, and kicking their legs high in the air. And there among them, Mathieu saw, the young woman he'd watched as she auditioned for a dancer's job.

Seated at his usual table, in suit, black shirt and pearl-gray tie, de Lyon waved him over, and Mathieu sat next to a man who'd stopped by to see the nightclub owner. "This is Stavros," de Lyon said, nodding to a swarthy bear of a man with oiled hair who wore a baggy silk suit.

"Pleased to meet you," Stavros said, then turned to de Lyon and continued a conversation—with a glance at Mathieu, the outsider who'd joined them—saying, "So we think that Albert will, um, take care of it."

"Quietly?" de Lyon said.

"With him? Always, you know Albert, and, uh, this kind of job is something he does well."

"And money?"

"Don't think about it—Albert is grateful, you know, for getting him out of . . . trouble. I will tell him it's, the number we said, and he'll nod, in that way of his."

De Lyon said, "Then we'll go ahead, Stavros, and you'll let me know when it's going to take place."

Stavros stood and said, "I'll be going back to my table," then offered a hand to Mathieu—he had a grip like a steel vise—and said, "Glad to meet a friend of Max's."

When he was gone, de Lyon said, "Good old Stavros, he is from Macedonia and, at age fourteen, was already fighting Bulgarian bandits. After that, being a gangster was easy." De Lyon smiled. "Valuable, a man like Stavros, not much he won't do . . . actually, nothing he won't do."

A German officer, not so steady on his feet, approached the table. De Lyon stood, Mathieu followed his lead. "Colonel von Hartz, allow me to introduce my friend Henri." The colonel clicked his heels and, with a brief bow of the head, spoke through a fume of alcohol. "Honored to meet you, monsieur." Then he drew a chair closer to de Lyon, sat down, and said, in an undertone, "Monsieur Max, I am enchanted by one of your dancers . . . the one at the end of the line, on the left." He meant, Mathieu realized, the dancer from the audition.

"Oh yes, you mean Lulu, pretty girl."

"Pretty, and more, her . . . she has a comely shape, such a comely shape, she has."

"She does, doesn't she. A gift of nature."

"Would it be possible, that is . . . could one have . . . an introduction?"

"I don't see why not," de Lyon said.

"Ach, I would be so pleased to meet Lulu!" He smiled a great, beaming smile.

"I will speak to her in the dressing room," de Lyon said. "But . . . well, you ought to know, she is not entirely in good health, so, *protection* is always important, we men must be careful."

The colonel's smile disappeared and he said, "I see. So . . ."

"Shall I introduce you to Lulu?"

"Perhaps later, Monsieur Max. Later on . . . Thank you." The colonel said good night and staggered away.

De Lyon sighed, then said, "I try to protect them—the ones who want to be protected, some of them are eager to sleep with the conquerors." He paused, then said, "Did you see the medals on him?"

"Yes, quite a few."

"Battlefield decorations, Mathieu, from the invasion of France."

Mathieu just shook his head.

"Enough of that," de Lyon said. "So tell me, Mathieu, how goes the war?"

"We're working hard," Mathieu said. He rapped his knuckles on the table and added, "Touch wood, all is going well."

De Lyon looked at his watch and said, "In a few minutes we'll go to my office to see an old friend of mine—maybe 'friend' is not quite the word—who has asked to meet you. He is called S. Kolb, generally believed to be a spy, thought to work for the British but nobody is really sure. He appears suddenly, here and there in Europe, does whatever he does, then vanishes."

"And he is from . . . ?"

"His nationality? I don't have any idea—he speaks many languages, none of them as a native. I have heard him described as a citizen of the shadows."

Mathieu was amused and said, "A sinister description, I would say."

"But maybe, in this case, accurate. You will be doing me a favor, when you talk to him. He has helped me, now and again, in ways no one else could."

"Can he be trusted?"

De Lyon hesitated, then said, "Yes, I believe so."

De Lyon had a small, cramped office above the basement nightclub: a typewriter, two telephones, papers everywhere, and a small lamp that left most of the room in darkness. Mathieu could hear the trio, working away down below, and occasional shouts in German followed by raucous laughter.

Ten minutes later, S. Kolb knocked at the door and entered the office. He was bald, with a fringe of dark hair, wore eyeglasses, and had a sparse mustache—a short, inconsequential man in a tired suit. When de Lyon introduced him to Mathieu, they shook hands briefly and, for just an instant, Kolb looked directly into his face, then lowered his eyes. Mathieu felt something like a chill.

As Kolb sat down, de Lyon said, "I'll leave you two to talk," and left the office.

"So, here is the brave Mathieu. An honor to meet you, monsieur."

"Thank you for the compliment, Monsieur Kolb."

"I know some people in London who speak highly of you, you should be proud."

"And, if I may ask, which people are these?"

"People who read the debriefing reports of the airmen your efforts have saved."

Mathieu waited.

"These airmen are urgently needed, as I'm sure you know, if Britain is not to lose this war. The people in London are grateful, and sent me over to France to see if we might be able to help you. Of course I had to find you, but now here we are." He smiled.

"Was it difficult . . . to find me?"

"A proper question, Mathieu. I can only say that finding people is one of our jobs, we are practiced at it, and it was done in such a way that you were protected. The last thing in the world we would wish is to damage you in some way, we want to *help* you, Mathieu, if you'll allow us to do that."

"And how would you help me?"

"To begin with, money. Connections to the civil administration, even to the German Kommandantur. I'm sure you have similar arrangements, but ours are quite dependable and they may reach higher than yours. And then, we would provide a radio, for coded wireless transmission to London, as well as a contact, here in Paris, someone you could seek out if you require assistance. We hope that you never find yourself in difficulties but, in this kind of work . . . the weather can change quickly, if you know what I mean."

"And, in return?"

"We ask no more than you continue to do your best."

"Monsieur Kolb, please understand that I appreciate your offer, but I would like some time to think it over. Is there some way I can reach you?"

Kolb reached into his pocket and produced a small slip of paper. He handed it to Mathieu and said, "Here is an address in the Occupied Zone, simply telegraph the message on the paper."

Mathieu studied the paper, a few words written by a typewriter with a faded ribbon: *Agence de Voyage Havas 8 Boulevard Bineau Neuilly-sur-Seine confirm reservation Hôtel Pont Royal signed LeBeau.*

Mathieu said, "I thank you for your offer, Monsieur Kolb."

"Please consider it carefully—we hope you will make the right choice." Kolb stood, and moved toward the door.

"You are going out during curfew?"

Kolb looked playfully grim. "Yes, always *something*, but I will manage. I have a paper I can show if need be—nobody will inconvenience me."

And with that he was gone.

11 April. Under a sky of fleeting cirrus cloud, the courier Daniel rode his bicycle through the streets of Rouen. He was to meet an English RAF officer and escort him back to a safe house in Paris. Rouen was in sorry shape, half of it had burned down during the fighting in 1940, when Wehrmacht units refused to let firefighters extinguish the blaze. For the rest, a classic Norman town—the narrow streets lined with timber-and-plaster buildings—where the English had bought Joan of Arc from a French enemy and burned her at the stake. Worst of all, for Daniel, Rouen was an important port on the upper Seine, part of the German coastal defenses, and there were patrols everywhere—he'd already been stopped by the military police and that had scared him. They had taken a long look at his identity card. And a long look at him.

Daniel was a Jew. He had, before the war, taught mechanical engineering at a technical school in Montpellier, but that ended. He did not look Jewish, in his twenties he was short, with the sinewy build of a runner in track competitions, dark hair, and five o'clock shadow a few hours after he shaved. He had heard that the Germans were now executing couriers and if they discovered a Jewish courier, they would, he knew, kill him.

Marshal Pétain and the Vichy administration, eager to please Hitler and crawling with deference, had attacked French Jews soon after the armistice—the Statut des Juifs became law on 3 October, 1940, when Jews were prohibited from public service and the military, and barred from positions that could sway public opinion: journalism, radio, film, theatre, and teaching. So Daniel had returned to his family in Nanterre. Watching his parents struggle, after the Germans had stolen his father's shoe factory, had only fueled his desire for revenge.

Daniel had heard about British fugitives on the run and determined to take part in the Resistance, asking this friend and that until he reached someone in Mathieu's cell. Mathieu had taken his time, making a decision about Daniel. He knew Daniel wanted to kill Germans because they had ruined his life and, he sensed, in time Daniel would do just that. But Mathieu did not have the heart to exclude him—he had already been excluded by the Vichyite fascists, now their French opponents?—and though he accused himself of weakness Mathieu did at last accept the young teacher. He could, he thought, control him; Ghislain hadn't been so sure.

The English officer, Daniel had been told, was fifty years old, a technician flying on a photoreconnaissance mission over the German submarine base at Saint-Nazaire. In other times, he would never have been allowed to do such a risky thing—he was a camera technician, in possession of all sorts of secret information—but Britain was so desperate that old and sensible rules were violated every day. When the pilot spotted a group of fighter planes to his west he fled east and, after losing himself in heavy cloud, managed to land in a field, not far from Rouen. The pilot went off in search of a farmhouse but when, after a few hours, he did not return, the technician made his way to a hotel in Rouen. Now it was Daniel's job to get him out and, eventually, back to England.

It was dusk when Daniel found the Rue du Grand Pont in the old section of Rouen, near the quay that bordered the river Seine. On a street with burned-out buildings, the Hôtel Rouen still stood, its stucco façade stained black with soot. Daniel shifted his weight on the pedals, about to dismount and walk the bicycle the rest of the way to the hotel. But there were two men walking toward him on the Rue du Grand Pont and one of them noticed him, the one wearing a very expensive double-breasted suit and a grand hat with the front of the brim turned down. Daniel sensed he was an authority of some sort, stayed on his bicycle, and averted his eyes. But too late.

The man in the suit called out some words Daniel didn't quite hear and raised his hand, palm out: halt. Daniel thought about speeding up but he knew that would bring police cars and they would chase him down, so he came to a stop. Now he could see the man's face: coarse skin, gross features—Daniel had never seen such a smug expression, heightened by a cruel smile. Next to him stood a flabby, pasty-faced young man wearing a pin, a Francisque—the old battle-axe of Gaul and Vichy's chosen symbol—in his lapel. The man in the suit beckoned Daniel to him and took from his pocket an oval-shaped metal disk showing an eagle atop a swastika—the Gestapo badge. Daniel must have reacted to the badge because the man's smile broadened, then he said a few words in German and the man by his side, a translator, said, "Show me your papers."

Daniel rested his bicycle against a lamppost, then stood before the two men as the Gestapo officer snapped his fingers and held out his hand. Daniel gave him his identity card, the officer studied it, running his finger over the surface, then said, through his interpreter, "You are from near Paris, what are you doing in Rouen?"

"I have a girlfriend here, I've come up to see her."

"On a bicycle?"

"Yes, the weather is good." As in, *Why not?*

"Don't be insolent, you little prick. Not with *me*." Even though he did not speak French, the Gestapo officer could hear a faint note of defiance in Daniel's speech.

"I am sorry, sir, I meant no disrespect." *What's the matter with you?* Daniel couldn't help it, as much as he tried to be diffident there was a certain shading of tone that leaked from his emotions into his words.

The Gestapo officer glared at him and said, producing a pad and a pencil, "Tell me your girlfriend's name. And, if you don't tell the truth, I will know."

Daniel told him a name, the officer wrote it down.

"And she lives where?"

Daniel gave him an address.

The officer asked the interpreter a question, then, when it was answered, said, "There is no such street in Rouen."

"It's the only address I have for her."

"You French are all the same; lying scum, you lie and lie and lie. Well, let's go back to my office and have a long talk." With that, he grabbed a fistful of the back of Daniel's jacket, turned him around and began walking him down the street. As they walked, the interpreter by the officer's side, the officer began to whistle a tune, a jolly tune, a march.

It was the jolly tune that did it. The rage festering inside Daniel now burst free and he spun around and, with the base of his open hand, struck the officer at the midpoint of his nose. Daniel felt it break; the officer's hat fell off, he took a step backward and yelped with pain as blood coursed down his face. Daniel jumped toward him and punched the officer in the temple—a far more vulnerable spot than the chin or the jaw.

Stunned, the officer fought for balance, then fell hard on the seat of his pants. From there, he drew an automatic pistol from a shoulder holster, armed it by working the slide, and pointed it at Daniel. Who grabbed the interpreter by the collar and the belt and moved behind his back, using him as a shield. This tactic so frustrated the officer that he fired twice, hitting the interpreter in the heart. The force of the shot threw them both backward, Daniel heard a moan, then felt the man die. Keeping the interpreter in front of him, no less a shield for being dead, Daniel dragged him a few feet toward a building, then let him collapse and ran for the doorway.

It was a burned-out building with a board nailed across the space where there had been a door, but Daniel used his shoulder to force the board, ran into the building and up a stairway. The interior of the building was in total darkness and the smell was overwhelming: burned plaster, burned electric wiring and its rubber coating, burned paint and furniture stuffing, charred wood rotting after months of rain, and the lingering odor of death. The weakened steps began to flex as Daniel ran upward, then, almost at the next floor, the wood gave way and left Daniel dangling from a step above him. Someone down below fired a shot, close enough, Daniel heard the ripping-silk noise of a passing round.

Gritting his teeth, Daniel hauled himself to the top of the staircase, then, guided by his hand on a wall, worked his way down a corridor to a place where the second flight should have been. But it was no more. Retracing his steps, his guiding hand found a door hanging on one hinge. Inside, lit by the night sky shining through a window with no glass, the remnants of someone's life: a blackened sofa, shards of broken crockery underfoot, burst cans of food. He was now on the other side of the building and below him was the cobblestone quay that bordered the river. From the hallway beyond the broken door, flashlight beams began to probe the darkness and Daniel decided to jump the ten feet to the quay, dive into the river and swim for his life. He braced a foot on the window frame and leaped out.

His ankles gave as he landed, he went down on all fours, then crawled to the edge of the river and rolled into the water—cold as ice, with a strong current flowing north toward the sea. Daniel let it take him, sweeping his hands in small circles, kicking so that his feet did not break the water. Even though his shoes were growing heavy he did not kick them off—he would need them later, if he survived. There was all sorts of debris floating around him—a partly submerged tire, a drowned rat, the end of a wooden packing crate—while patches of oil on the surface shone iridescent in the moonlight.

When he heard the high-low wail of sirens, from police cars driving slowly along the quay, he let himself sink. Even so, his pursuers had a good idea where he was, swept the river with their searchlights, and began to fire randomly into the water. Some of the bullets ricocheted off the surface and whined away into the darkness, others penetrated the water. Then Daniel felt a band of fire burn across his lower leg. He came up for air, reached down to his leg and found a groove where the bullet had creased his calf. When a beam of light came toward him, he again went under, kicking and paddling as fast as he could. It seemed to take forever— perhaps two minutes—but when he again broke the surface, the quay was behind him.

He began to tire, his body had done whatever it could, now he needed help or he would drown. Just ahead of him, he could see the end of the packing crate, trailing strands of wire from its edge, and, using whatever strength he had left, he caught up to it, got both hands on the strips of wood reinforcing its frame, and, slowly, the current towed him north. After a time, he had no idea how long, he felt sleep trying to claim him—the temperature of the water was sucking the life from his body. He had to get out, and made for the shore, a strip of gravel at the edge of a wood. He spent a long time on his knees, then understood that the cold air blowing on his wet skin would soon enough do what the water had tried to do. *Walk. You must walk,* he told himself, and struggled to his feet. The pain returned to his leg, and he limped, but he managed to walk. Occasionally he had to stop and rest but the walking had brought his blood back to life and the breeze had dried his clothes. An hour later, he saw a small fire ahead of him and then the outline of a bridge. By the time he neared the fire he was staggering with fatigue.

"What brings you out, this time of night?" A rough voice, a low growl. Coming from a wizened little fellow wearing an overcoat held together by a length of rope. A tramp, Daniel realized. A moment later, a few more appeared from, apparently, an encampment under the bridge.

One of them said, "Go overboard did you, son?" Then, "Fall off your barge?"

"I'm running away," Daniel said. "From the police."

Somebody laughed and said, "We all know about that. What'd you do?"

"I'm wanted by the Germans."

"Oh? For what?"

"For fighting against them, I . . ." He started to wobble but one of the tramps grabbed him before he could fall and said, "We better get him warmed up or he'll die on us."

Holding him upright, the tramp walked him over to the fire and lowered him to the ground, then fed a few dry sticks to the flames. As the warmth flowed over him, Daniel closed his eyes, fought to stay awake, then lost consciousness.

Later, when he came to, he was being carried in a blanket along a path through the wood and saw that someone had tied a rag around the wound in his leg. Still dazed, he mumbled, "Where are we going?"

"Ah, you're awake . . . that's good, son . . . only a little while now and you'll be safe . . . we're taking you to the convent, up on the next hill."

"The convent?"

"Carmelite sisters, bless them, they help anyone who asks, and they will take good care of you. As for the Boche, well . . . don't worry about the Boche . . . they don't bother the nuns."

WEAPONS OF WAR

"Success in the game is the great incentive to subdue fear. Once you've shot down two or three the effect is terrific and you'll go on till you're killed. It's love of the sport rather than sense of duty that makes you go on without minding how much you are shot up."

—*British fighter pilot, 1940, as quoted by Lord Moran in* Anatomy of Courage

12 APRIL, 1941. ON A SOFT AFTERNOON IN THE ENGLISH countryside—the fields newly green, the sky clear but for a few wispy clouds—a dozen young men were passing their time by not doing much of anything; they sprawled on lawn chairs or lay on the grass, smoked cigarettes, made idle conversation, a few slept, others stared up at the sky. They all shared a certain mood, a mix of boredom and tension: boredom because they had spent the last eight months in just this way, tension because any one of them might be dead by nightfall.

The field where they waited was called Northolt Aerodrome, some fourteen miles from London. The young men were fighter pilots, Polish fighter pilots of the 303 squadron, also known as the Kosciuszko pilots, famous for their courage in combat—which was just this side of crazy, some said—had fought brilliantly in the Battle of Britain and still continued to fight, attacking Luftwaffe formations that bombed targets in the British Isles. Hawker Hurricane aircraft were parked on a macadam runway, while a few feet behind the men, up the slope of a hillside, was a Quonset hut with two desks, a few battered couches, a map that covered one wall, and a telephone.

A few minutes after five, it rang.

Its ring, two short jingles—they never heard more because it was always answered immediately—had become a crucial sound in the lives of the airmen, who came crashing back to earth from wherever reverie had taken them and leapt to their feet. This telephone line was a direct connection to the air defense system: from coast watchers to radars to young women who kept track of the bomber flights as they headed toward England.

The pilots, in leather caps, goggles, and Mae West life jackets, ran for their planes and were taking off moments later. The thunder of their ascent was deafening—the battle for the skies of Europe was fought with the most powerful engines to be had: BMW and Daimler-Benz for the Luftwaffe, Rolls-Royce for the RAF.

Sgt. Jan Kalisz was second in line as the Hurricanes climbed for altitude—the goal of any flying predator was always the same: high above the prey. Leveling off at thirty-five thousand feet, Kalisz fired a few rounds from his 20-mm cannon to make sure they were working. Five minutes later, the flight commander came on the radio: Messerschmitt 109s at eleven o'clock, Dornier bombers in tight formation a thousand feet below. Kalisz had been ordered to attack the bombers while others in the squadron would take on the German fighter planes assigned to protect them.

Kalisz had been a pilot in the Polish air force and then, when the Poles surrendered to the Nazis in 1939, had flown a trainer airplane to France. When France fell, he'd flown his Dewoitine fighter to England. He was twenty-seven years old and had nine confirmed kills to his credit, which earned him the title of *Pilot Ace*, one of two in the Kosciuszko Squadron, but he looked nothing like the handsome pilots on the war-bond posters. In fact he looked like a factory worker—the wise-guy welder who smiles for the girls when the photographer comes around—with an honest face and clipped, straw-colored hair, the type always ready to take part in a practical joke.

Now, to work. As he dove at the bombers, targeting one at the rear of the formation, he heard a warning shout on his headphones and a 109 flashed past his cockpit. No chance to fire so he again closed on the Dorniers below him, stayed in the dive, engine scream-ing, until he was three hundred feet away. Then he fired a short burst and pieces flew off the bomber while its portside engine trailed a thin stream of smoke. *Almost.* He pulled out of his dive and banked the Hurricane into a tight turn, meaning to attack again and finish off the bomber.

But now orange tracer rounds flew past his cockpit, coming from a 109 flying directly at him. As the 109's gunports twinkled, Kalisz felt the impact of machine-gun rounds hitting the fuselage of his Hurricane and fired his own cannon, the rounds passing above the oncoming fighter. They would hit each other in seconds but the German pilot flinched first and, just as he sideslipped away, showed Kalisz a fist with a raised middle finger.

Meanwhile, chaos. Aircraft everywhere, tracer streams glowing bright in the dusk, a Hurricane spinning nose down as it fell from the sky, two fighters speeding through the clouds—a Pole chasing a German, both planes on fire, while in the far distance a parachute was floating slowly toward the ground.

From down below, Kalisz now heard the steady rumble of ex-ploding bombs and, a few seconds later, the Dornier formation changed direction, turning away, their mission completed. Kalisz followed them and was about to start a new attack when he saw what he thought was the same 109, climbing away from him. Al-most in range, he had a try with his cannon but the 109 kept flying. Kalisz had missed his shot.

Or had he? The 109 banked right and began to lose altitude—a tactic of evasion? Or a damaged aircraft? As Kalisz pushed his engine to full throttle, the pilot in the 109 changed his course and flew south, heading for his airbase on the coast of France. But Kalisz wasn't going to let him get away, saw that he was gaining on the 109 and again he fired, and was this time rewarded with a fiery flash from the fuselage just behind the cockpit. *That did it.* As the 109 descended toward the sea, Kalisz realized the pilot was dead or wounded, so all Kalisz had to do was make sure that the plane hit the water. *Tenth kill,* he thought.

Then the French coast came into view. Kalisz, having once experienced the fierce anti-aircraft fire that awaited him there, banked into a tight turn and headed home to Northolt. The chase had taken him over the wide part of the Channel and he was alone in the sky. His mind wandered; soon he would be back at Northolt, he wanted a cigarette and a large vodka, and another. Such pleasant thoughts absorbed him, but then his engine missed, and missed again, and a glance at the fuel gauge revealed that he was almost out of gas, the needle quivering near EMPTY.

"Kurwa!" Fuck. That dead Nazi had taken his revenge. Firing his machine guns as the two planes flew toward collision, he'd punctured the Hurricane's fuel tank, so Kalisz wasn't going back to Northolt. Then his engine cut out and did not come back to life, its roar replaced by the sigh of the wind, the plane's propeller turning slowly with the momentum of the aircraft. Kalisz made sure of his parachute harness, slid the canopy back and stood on the seat. To the west, below tumbled masses of black cloud, the top half of the setting sun glowed dark orange above the sea on the horizon.

14 April. Mathieu waited in a café across the street from the Père-Lachaise cemetery, the wind blew gusts of rain against the window and by the cemetery gates the old women who sold bouquets of anemones, waiting in vain for a customer, chatted beneath their

black umbrellas. Dusk at three-thirty in such April weather, the branches of the old trees at Père-Lachaise still bare, the deserted street shining black in the rain. The café was almost empty, the barman working at a crossword puzzle, his newspaper spread out before him.

Mathieu was here to meet a young woman recruited, and highly recommended, by Chantal and the two of them had chosen the nom de guerre Annemarie for her. Ghislain had done the research: Annemarie came from the high aristocracy, an ancient family bearing titles bestowed for battles won in the Middle Ages, such titles accompanied by grants of gamelands, vineyards, and villages in Burgundy. The family then prospered further with the French Empire and now lived on income from investments, principally in the French colonies of Indochina—rubber, and Senegal—phosphates and sugarcane.

Through the raindrops running down the window, Mathieu could see the blurred form of the young woman, their newest courier. She looked around as she entered, spotted Mathieu and nodded at him. She was wearing a mocha-colored raincoat tied with a belt at the waist and carried a silk umbrella, lime green, with a carved ivory handle. She shook water off the umbrella and slid it into the urn kept by the door.

As she walked to his table she seemed self-confident and determined, perhaps in her midtwenties, with the look and bearing of an aristocrat. She had a fair complexion, closer to pale, a tip-tilted nose, her hair ash-blonde with white fuzz at the temples. At the base of her throat she wore a tiny gold cross on a gold chain, and, on the fourth finger of her right hand, a signet ring. Not a wedding ring—according to the concierge that Ghislain had questioned she was escorted to occasional social events by young men of good family but never spent the night away from home, and attended mass twice a week.

Mathieu stood, they greeted each other, then she sat across from him, met his eyes with a straightforward gaze and rubbed her hands, delicate skin chilled and reddened by the wind. "Would you care for a brandy, mademoiselle?"

"Indeed I would . . . what a *day*," she said. "My dog really did not want to go outside this morning."

Mathieu called out to the barman and ordered brandy and coffee for each of them, then said, "Terrible day, Parisian spring at its worst, but at least you have a fine umbrella."

"Pretty, isn't it," Annemarie said. "My grandmother brought it home from Shanghai."

"Shanghai?"

"Yes, that generation imported tea from China. Anyhow that's the story we tell. For me, I suspect they were in the opium trade, but you can't *say* such things."

The barman returned with the brandy and coffee and Mathieu had a sip of each: the former was bitter to the taste and burned all the way down, the latter was *National Coffee*—ground chestnuts and chickpeas and a hint of the real thing.

Staring out the window at the cemetery gates, Annemarie said, "We always came here on the Jour des Morts, after All Saints' Day in November. We brought along soap and stiff brushes and scrubbed the family mausoleum—a little stone house with urns and an iron bench. It's on one of the main avenues, a few feet from where Corot is buried. We used to see a young man, an art student, we suspected—thick glasses, a beret—who every year set a bouquet of anemones on Corot's grave."

"Do you like Corot?"

"I do indeed, particularly the roads, lanes, really, that he painted."

"We have that in common," Mathieu said.

"I suppose the portraits are favored, the one we have is a portrait, a woman holding a book, but I would like to have a road, someday."

"Is it still at your house?"

"Heavens, no! When the Germans were approaching Paris we

moved the art to a vault in Switzerland, along with some of the jewelry. We did what we could—we have a Bentley hidden in a village, parked in a barn."

"Did your family lose anybody in the invasion?"

"Thankfully we did not—we're a naval family, when the wars come, so I have an uncle with the fleet in North Africa. Chantal is from a *military* family, they lost all sorts of people in the 1914 war."

"Tell me, Annemarie, why do you want to take part in the Resistance? You will be in danger."

"Yes, I know. But I am from an *old* family, we have fought for France since the Middle Ages. And I am a *Frenchwoman,* so honor plays a part in my decision. Really, one must do *something.*"

"So you shall. We will provide you with false documents—you should get photographs from the Photomaton at the Samaritaine department store, with your right ear visible."

Annemarie nodded, then took a polite sip of her coffee, placed the cup carefully back on the saucer and said, "Well, it has been good to meet you, Mathieu, but I must be on my way," stood, and shook hands.

Mathieu watched her as she retrieved her umbrella and stepped out into the downpour. Seen through the rainswept window, Annemarie walked vigorously, shoulders back, head high. Mathieu took another sip of his brandy, the gloomy day had worn him down, and, for a moment, he realized just how lonely he was, then drove the thought away: not good to be thinking too much about oneself, a doctrine firmly impressed on him by his mother as he was growing up. With a sigh in his heart, he paid the bill and left the café for his next meeting.

He was late getting back to the Saint-Yves, where Mariana, the hotel's Belgian shepherd, was waiting for him in the hotel vestibule. At such moments he would lean down to comb his fingers through her ruff and she would greet him with two fast licks on the cheek. But, that night, she did it twice.

. . .

The following morning, the giant doorman from the Le Cygne nightclub came to the Saint-Yves with a message for Mathieu. He delivered the message in a bass rumble of a voice with a strong Russian accent. "Monsieur de Lyon ask me to say that Monsieur K has a friend he wants you to meet. Eight-thirty tonight, at nightclub. It's alright? You will come to the meeting?"

"Tonight at eight-thirty," Mathieu said and the doorman, casting a wary eye at the watchful Mariana, said, "Good dog," and left the apartment.

"Monsieur K" was S. Kolb, and the "friend" was, Mathieu guessed, the contact mentioned in the deal that Kolb had offered him. Mathieu had said he would think it over, which evidently meant *yes* to S. Kolb, and whatever secret service directed him. *No time for dithering, do what we tell you.* Thus spoke power. And how much more of this, Mathieu wondered, would there be?

Mathieu was prompt, the nightclub empty but for a couple of waiters—one reading a newspaper, one sleeping in a chair—and an old man in an apron, pushing a mop around the floor. Later on, the cellar would be all darkness and candlelight but now, illuminated by ceiling lights, the seductive gloss was gone, the Art Deco chic no more. As Mathieu stood there, de Lyon came down the stairs that led to his office, said, "He's waiting for you," and pointed upward with his thumb. His tone and the expression on his face suggested that Mathieu might not be pleased with what he found in the office.

Mathieu's reaction to what he found was: *Rich English bastard from Mayfair.* Or some other posh neighborhood in London. Based on his former life, and nights at the cinema, Mathieu recognized the breed. Kolb's "friend" stood when Mathieu entered the office, he was wearing an ordinary tan raincoat and an ordinary gray hat and, like the French businessman he meant to imitate, carried a buckled briefcase under one arm. His face lit with welcome as he said, in decent French, "Ah, here is the famous Mathieu!" From his pocket he produced a dim, out-of-focus photograph taken through a shop window that made Mathieu, hurrying down a street, look sinister and hunted. "A fair likeness, I'd say, don't you think?" To Mathieu he seemed like an arrogant, supercilious jackass trying not to seem arrogant and supercilious by being cheerful. His handshake was firm as he said, "I'm to be called Edouard, please do sit down."

When Mathieu was settled, Edouard said, "Care for a cigarette?" Rather self-consciously he took a tin case from his pocket and held it out: rolled cigarettes, as smoked by almost everyone in Paris, but these were produced by a cigarette-rolling apparatus. When Mathieu had taken one, Edouard lit it with a wooden match. Mathieu inhaled—the usual occupation tobacco. He was sure that all of Edouard's clothing had French labels.

"My associate S. Kolb says you are a dependable sort of fellow, and that we can do business with you."

"Does he? Perhaps I am, but we'll see about business."

This answer was not what Edouard expected. "Now look here," he said, "we might have let our arrangement mature in a more natural way, but at the moment we have an urgent problem and we need your help."

"And the urgent problem is . . . ?"

"We understand that you are a specialist in exfiltrating fugitive airmen from France and back to Britain, is that true?"

"Specialist? Well, we've done our best, worked hard . . ."

"Yes, we know, very good. Our problem is a fighter pilot, a Polish fighter pilot in what's called the Kosciuszko Squadron. An *ace* pilot, the sort of man we need back in Britain, where he will be put forth as a hero—war-bond tour, visits to arms factories, that sort of thing, good for the public morale, which could stand a boost, just now."

"You don't need him to fly planes?"

"Oh he'll do that alright, but first a bit of propaganda."

Mathieu hesitated, sensing he should go carefully with this

man, then said, "If your pilot is in France, can you tell me how he got here?"

"He had a punctured fuel tank and ran out of gas chasing an Me-109 over the Channel and parachuted into the sea."

"And then?"

"The French mackerel fleet from Saint-Malo was just about to head for port when somebody saw a splash and went and fished him out."

Mathieu raised his eyebrows. "So far as I know, all the fishing fleets are patrolled by German E-boats."

"They are, but fishing trawlers spread out as they work and it was almost night, so the rescue wasn't seen."

"Still, brave souls, taking a chance like that."

"No doubt. Anyhow, at dawn the pilot was in the back of a truck, hidden under a load of mackerel, and headed for the Les Halles market. From there, he was taken to the American Hospital in Neuilly."

"Was he injured badly?"

"Not a bit, the American Hospital has been hiding fugitives since the first day of the Occupation."

"I had no idea," Mathieu said.

"Music to my ears. It's a well-kept secret, you see."

"Does he speak any French?"

"Not a word. Almost all Poles at a certain social level speak French, but this man comes of a working-class family." With that, he unbuckled his briefcase, brought out a well-stuffed manila envelope, and laid it on the table in front of Mathieu. Who let it sit there.

"Twenty thousand dollars," Edouard said. "You may want to count it now, or wait until later."

Mathieu slid the envelope back toward Edouard.

Shocked and puzzled by this reaction, Edouard said, "What are you doing? Is it not enough? I was led to believe that money was a part of our bargain . . . surely you need money."

"Yes, we need money, but not *this* money."

"Oh? Can you tell me why?"

"This money would help us, but it's meant to establish your influence over our resistance operations, is that not so?"

"You have my *word,* Mathieu, the people in your cell will always see *you* as their leader, *you* are their chief, *you* give the orders. There may be times when we require some action taken, but nobody will ever know that. Now be a sensible fellow and take what we're offering. Please."

"No."

"You won't help?"

"We will help, we will get your pilot down to Spain, because we are an escape line, it is what we do for the Resistance."

Now Edouard was angry and a pink flush spread across the skin over his cheekbones. "Let me tell you something important, *Mathieu*"—he emphasized the name, *whoever you think you are*—"with our help you may survive—may. The average life of these escape lines is about six months. If I count from December, you have a month left, then you and your people will be arrested, at best sent to prison in France, at worst taken to Germany, where you will be put in a prison camp—Dachau, Buchenwald—or executed. You know, *le petit mur.*" The little wall, in argot meaning the wall where one stood to be shot. "Can you see them? Your friends who trusted you? Your . . ." Warned by something in Mathieu's eyes, he stopped there.

"We know the danger, Edouard, and we are very careful."

Edouard was furious, his voice cold as he said, "Very well," snatched up the envelope and shoved it back into his briefcase. "Have it your own way." There was more, a threat perhaps, but Edouard left it unsaid. He stood, thrust his briefcase under his arm, said, "I wish you good day," and left the office.

Mathieu sat there, staring at the wall, the nasty little twit had tried to scare him. No, *had* scared him. Hearing two light taps on the door he said, "Yes?"

De Lyon entered the office, said nothing, but took a bottle of cognac and two glasses out of a cabinet. When he sat down, he looked Mathieu over carefully, poured two drinks and handed one to Mathieu, saying, "So? How did it go?"

"Badly." He drank off his cognac.

De Lyon poured him some more and said, "Well, it had to happen. Now it has. What did you do?"

"He went home with his money, is what I did."

"He'll be back, or there will be another one. The sun, at one time, really did *not* set on the British Empire, they know how to deal with the natives."

"*Quel connard.*" Damn fool.

De Lyon shrugged. "The British intelligence had good networks in France, professional networks, but they were badly damaged during the invasion. Enter Edouard, sitting around in his club in 1939, then Hitler goes into Poland and it's war; so Edouard must join up, must find a job suitable to his station, a job he can brag about. He talks to friends, but nothing happens right away, then somebody learns he speaks French, perhaps was raised in France by British parents, and now Edouard has his job, a secret job, so he can tell his friends, 'Sorry, old man, I really can't say what I'm doing.' Wink."

"I never expected somebody like that, not after meeting Kolb."

"I doubt very much that S. Kolb is an employee of the British service, he works for S. Kolb. And he would never involve himself with anyone like this Edouard creature. His job was to find you, and to see if you might accept their offer. After that, he went on to something else."

Mathieu described the meeting. When he mentioned the photograph, de Lyon was amused. "He was supposedly making sure that you were the real Mathieu, but, to their way of thinking, a little intimidation never hurts—'We've been watching you,' that sort of thing."

"But Max, we've been working with the British service for

months, we depend on them, once we're in Spain, to take the airmen the rest of the way back to Britain. And they've been nothing but helpful, *grateful*."

"Maybe a new section at work, a new strategy."

"What do the people behind Edouard want from us, specifically?"

"My best guess? Possibly espionage, spying. Clandestine underground groups do one of three things: resistance—including propaganda and escape networks, espionage, or operations, meaning sabotage, assassination, all that. But you won't find out what they want until you agree to work for them."

Mathieu was silent, unsettled by the day's events. He reached for a cigarette and lit it.

De Lyon could see how he felt and said, "Don't take it badly, my friend. You own a business, which has prospered, now somebody wants to buy it. Way of the world."

17 April. A tender scene: a young student from a nearby *lycée* walking her bicycle home while, by her side, her adoring papa spoke earnestly to his cherished daughter. The seventeen-year-old student was Lisette, the postmistress for Mathieu's resistance cell, who, after school at three-thirty, rode her bicycle through the streets of Paris and delivered messages, sometimes written, usually spoken.

The papa was Mathieu who, the night before, had received another visit from S. Kolb: the secret service was frantic, had now decided to send a Lysander—a speedy monoplane with fixed landing wheels—to pick up the Polish pilot. All Mathieu had to do was fetch him from the American Hospital and take him by train to a village north of Paris, and they had specified that Mathieu himself was to be the courier.

Mathieu agreed, but, he told Kolb, two men of military age, traveling together, drew far too much interest at document controls—they had tried this twice in the early days of the cell and had nearly gotten caught both times. What worked was mother and son, uncle and nephew, or a married couple. "Do what you have to do," Kolb had said. "Take someone along as camouflage, but be at that village in two days. Here are the details." He handed over a few typewritten lines on a scrap of paper, then said, "What's causing the flutter in the service is that the politicians have become involved." The look from Kolb which accompanied this news was meaningful.

Parting from Mathieu at a Métro station, Lisette pedaled along on the damp spring afternoon, weaving her way through crowds of bicyclists, ringing her bell when somebody got in her way, avoiding the *gazogènes*—taxis with wood- or charcoal-fired engines that had now appeared on the streets of the city.

Reaching the Seventh Arrondissement, she found the tiny *impasse*, cul-de-sac, where Annemarie, the new operative, lived, locked her bicycle to a lamppost, and rang for the concierge who said, "Yes, *ma petite*?" Lisette, much too thin, with watery blue eyes, was doted on by the concierges. She asked to see Annemarie, using her real name, and was taken upstairs, where she delivered her message, which described where and when she was to meet Mathieu.

Then Lisette was off again, carrying the next delivery in the student's briefcase in her bicycle basket.

It was late afternoon on the eighteenth of April when Mathieu, Annemarie, and Sgt. Kalisz left Paris from the Gare du Nord, taking the local train north toward the Belgian border. There had been great scurrying around to acquire the proper documents but it had been managed, the process made easier because Kalisz, after eleven months with the RAF, spoke a rough-and-tumble pilot's English, so he could communicate with Annemarie and Mathieu.

Annemarie and Kalisz were now, according to their papers, newlyweds, he from the Polish émigré community that worked the coal mines up in Lille. Both blonde, they made a pretty couple:

Kalisz in white shirt, tie, and blue suit—to impress his new bride's relatives—while Annemarie wore her mocha raincoat, well-fitted flannel slacks, and lace-up shoes, looking prim and proper on her way to a family gathering. Mathieu sat in the same compartment but pretended not to know them, and would intervene only in an emergency.

It was gathering twilight when they left the train at Nanteuil-le-Haudouin, set among wheatfields some thirty-five miles from Paris, and found themselves in a small village of stucco buildings and cobbled streets, with towering grain elevators on the railway track just beyond the station. A few steps away, the Café de la Gare, and the usual crowd: men in *bleu de travail* work jackets and trousers, women knitting and gossiping while their dogs lay at their feet, and two bulky men leaning on the bar and drinking beer. They were army veterans of the 1914 war, these two, once *paysans,* then soldiers, now *paysans* once more. Annemarie and Kalisz sat at a table while Mathieu joined the men at the bar and identified himself. After formal greetings, they went back to their beer and talk of the weather and the wheat crop.

Twenty minutes later, from outside the café, came the heavy beat of an unmuffled engine that chuffed like a locomotive. The men at the bar drank up the last of their beer, called out goodbys to their friends, and went outside, followed by Mathieu and the newlyweds. Just beyond the door stood a very old tractor with black smoke pumping from a pipe on its hood and huge wheels with iron rims, hitched to a farm wagon with a flat wooden bed. Stacked at the forward end of the wagon, bundles of firewood cut into narrow staves. The two *paysans* greeted the driver, using his local nickname, Flamand, which meant *the Fleming*. Mathieu could see why—with thick black hair cut across a low forehead and ruddy coloring, he looked like a Flemish pikeman in the background of a seventeenth-century painting. When he invited the travelers from Paris to climb on, Annemarie did not hesitate, braced her hands on the edge of the wagon and hoisted herself up, now sitting on a thin layer of dirt and dried cow manure. The *paysans* joined them, Flamand pushed the gear lever forward and they were off, iron rims bumping hard over the stone cobbles. "It will take an hour or so, maybe more," one of the *paysans* said to Mathieu.

It was almost dark when they turned off the road onto a narrow path, the last of the setting sun trailing long, red streaks in the western sky. By the time they reached the landing zone, a wheatfield surrounded by forest, night had fallen and one of the *paysans* used a flashlight so they could see to unload the firewood. Directed by Flamand, they carried the wood to one end of the field and built three piles, with kindling as the bottom layer, to serve as signals. When they were done they returned to the wagon.

Now it was very quiet, rain had fallen earlier and the air smelled of wet earth. Mathieu sat next to Flamand on the edge of the wagon and, in low voices, they began to talk. He and the two *paysans,* Flamand explained, were all members of one family: two brothers and a brother-in-law. "This is our sixth landing," he said, "but your man is a little different. The plane can take only one passenger and it's always been a certain type: briefcase, raincoat, city hat. And they don't talk much. Important people, no doubt, the English don't send an airplane for just anybody." He took out a pocket watch and squinted at the numbers in the moonlight. "We have some time to wait," he said. "We won't light the fires until nine-fifteen."

"Can we help?" Mathieu said.

"No, we'll take care of the fires, you three just get ready to run to the plane, the pilot won't stay on the ground long, your man will climb aboard, then you can help us turn the plane around so it can take off again. You have somewhere to spend the night?"

"We might stay at a house in the village, there was a *pension* sign in the window. Or we'll sit in the station and wait for the morning train back to Paris."

Flamand nodded, then looked up at the sky.

Precisely on time the fires were lit and minutes later they could hear the plane as it circled the field, then the sound of the engine grew louder and the Lysander came in for a landing. It hit the field hard and bounced, a gust of wind caught the wing and the plane came back down at an angle, sheared off the end of the wing, collapsed one of the wheel wells, spun halfway around and finally stopped, the end of the damaged wing resting on the ground.

Mathieu, Annemarie, and Kalisz ran toward the plane. When they reached it they could smell gasoline, there was a starred hole in the glass of the windshield and the pilot lay still, his head against the side of the canopy. Kalisz ran up the wing and, teeth clenched with effort, forced the canopy open, grabbed the pilot by his flying jacket, hauled him out, dropped him to the ground and jumped after him as the first flames began to climb the edge of the cockpit. Mathieu knelt by the pilot, there was blood trickling from his hairline. *"Merde,"* Mathieu said, feeling for a pulse.

"Is he gone?" Kalisz said, breathing hard.

"No, he's alive, but look at his leg." The pilot's foot was bent in an odd position.

The *paysans* now arrived, running as fast as they could. "We better pull him away," Kalisz said, and, with Flamand helping, they dragged the pilot into the field. Just in time. The plane blew up, orange flames shooting into the sky. One of the *paysans* said, "Well, they'll see *that* in Nanteuil."

"Are there Germans in the village?" Annemarie said.

"No, there's a gendarme post in Senlis, about eight miles from here," Flamand said. "They'll hear about it soon enough and, come daylight, they'll have to investigate."

They walked back to the tractor and laid the pilot carefully in the wagon, one of the *paysans* folded up his jacket and slid it beneath the pilot's head. Annemarie took a handkerchief from her shoulder bag, tore it in half, then half again, knotted the pieces together and tied the improvised bandage over the wound in the pilot's scalp. By the light of the burning plane they could see that he was very handsome, a matinee-idol type with ginger-colored hair. "Poor bastard," Flamand said.

Annemarie, kneeling next to Kalisz, sensed there was something wrong with him and he was trying not to show it. Slowly, wincing with pain, Kalisz started to take off his jacket, the inside of the left sleeve was charred and crumbling away.

"Leave it on," Mathieu said. "You're burned, aren't you."

Kalisz nodded, his face taut with pain.

"That needs to be treated," Flamand said. "We're going to have to take the pilot to the doctor in Nanteuil, so we'll take him too." He paused, thinking things through. "And we'll drop you two off at my farm. We can't all go to the doctor's house—we're asking a lot of him as it is. And, after what happened tonight, better not to be a stranger in the village."

"It's not so bad," Kalisz said. "I've been burned before, all it needs is a bandage and some salve."

"That's in Nanteuil," Flamand said. He started up the engine and switched on a dim light mounted on the front of the tractor.

When they reached an ancient stone farmhouse by the edge of a plowed field, the *paysans* said goodby to Mathieu and Annemarie. At the house, Flamand introduced them to his wife and eldest son—there were four other children, already asleep—then left for the journey into Nanteuil. Flamand's wife put out a ham covered in white fat, a heavy loaf of brown bread with a hard crust, a slab of white butter, a bowl of lentils, and an earthenware jug of red wine. "Come and sit at the table," she said. "What happened in the wheatfield?"

Mathieu told the story as he ate. He was very hungry, no surprise to him—he remembered how his tank crews had eaten everything they could get their hands on, despite what they'd experienced while fighting the Wehrmacht. When Annemarie and Mathieu had finished their supper, Flamand's wife said, "You two will have to sleep in the barn, we don't have room in the house."

"Very kind of you, madame, to take us in," Annemarie said.

"It's cold out there, but you'll survive the night. My son will show you the way."

The barn was built of stone, with open squares serving as windows. Inside, moonlight flooded over the four cows in their stalls, while the air was heavily scented with soured milk and rotting straw. Mathieu and Annemarie had been warned about the ladder to the hayloft but, before Mathieu could volunteer, Annemarie had started to climb, slowly, testing each rung before she put her weight on it. Watching from below as he held the ladder steady, Mathieu was distracted by a cat, peering around a beam to see what was going on.

It was much darker in the hayloft. When Mathieu reached the top of the ladder, Annemarie was standing on a thick bed of hay and taking her raincoat off, wearing, underneath, only a thin sweater. "This spot is as good as any, I guess," she said. She settled on her back, the hay rustling beneath her, and used the raincoat as a blanket. Mathieu stretched out beside her, covering himself with his jacket. "Have you ever slept in a hayloft?" he said.

"Played in them as a kid," she said. "When we were in the country we used to go to one of the farms we had, to get fresh milk. I liked it there, the dairymaids wore aprons and bonnets."

"Are you too cold to sleep?" Mathieu said.

"I'll manage . . . we will get some heat from the cows." Then she said, "Do you think the pilot will recover?"

"I hope so, but, head wounds . . ."

"What will we do, now that there's no airplane?"

"I'm not sure."

"Is there . . . someone you can telephone? Ask for help?"

"No, there's only you and me so we'll have to figure it out, how to get the pilot down to Spain."

She sat up suddenly and whispered, "What's that?" Something had scurried along the beam above their heads.

"Probably a rat. Barns always have rats."

"Brrr, I don't like rats."

"I don't think they'll bother us."

She lay back down and said, "I'm so tired," then turned on her side, her back to Mathieu.

Mathieu also turned on his side, facing away from her. "We may have to spend a few nights on the trains," he said. "So we should try to sleep."

She yawned. "I won't have to try very hard." She moved around to get comfortable, drew the raincoat tighter and, moments later, Mathieu could hear the steady breathing that meant she was asleep.

Mathieu wanted to sleep but he couldn't, he was too much aware of the woman lying close to him. He knew she had no desire to make love, but, even so, he wanted to see her with her clothes off and he surely wanted to touch her bare skin. Then he was distracted by the problems he would face in the morning: he needed railway schedules for the trip south but they would not be available at the Nanteuil station, the three of them would have to cross into the Unoccupied Zone, using the *passeurs*, and Kalisz had to have a new jacket, the doctor would cut away the sleeve and part of the shirt.

Annemarie moved around in the hay, then went back to sleep. Far off in the distance he could hear thunder, and as one of the cows drank water he could hear her lapping at the trough and the bell around her neck clanked. Then, a brief commotion at the end of the loft. What was going on? It must be the barn cat, he thought, catching one of the rats. He hoped she wouldn't bring it to them as a gift. Or part of it.

At last he dozed. Then Annemarie turned over and touched his shoulder, whispering, "Are you asleep?"

He mumbled, "No." It was so cold he could see his breath, and the end of his nose was damp.

"I'm freezing, Mathieu, my teeth are almost chattering. May I lie next to you?"

"Of course. We'll put both coats over us."

Annemarie moved until she was almost touching him, close enough so that he was aware of her breath on the back of his neck. Mathieu, using one hand, managed to rearrange the coats, making sure she had more than her share of the much thicker jacket, with the raincoat on top. "Oh, thank you," she said. "Much better now." A moment later, she reached around him and pulled herself closer—now he could feel her small breasts, moving around as she settled herself, then pressed against his back. His right hand was beneath his head, his left at first in front of him but this was uncomfortable so he rested it on top of her hip. "Do you mind if I put my hand there?"

"What? Oh, no, I don't mind."

"Are you still cold?"

"Not like before," she said.

As they lay quiet, he realized that the front of him was still thoroughly chilled. Of course, after a while, they could turn and face the other way, but this position would have been, inevitably, provocative. But, he thought, better not. In the world of the Resistance, intimate relations were known to be dangerous and—more than one story was told about it—often led to catastrophe.

Apparently the hay was tickling her face, so she took her hand from his chest and brushed it away, then held him as before, her hand white in the darkness.

Once again, thunder rumbled in the distance, the smell of the hay was sweet, moonlight poured in on the stable below, and Mathieu felt his heart grow warm, warm for life itself. He took a deep breath and let it out, a kind of sigh.

She said, "What is it?"

"Nothing. I'm trying to sleep."

"I thought you sighed, that you . . . I don't know."

"I always do that before I go to sleep."

"Oh, I see. Well, good night, Mathieu. Pleasant dreams."

.   .   .

20 April. A chilly day in Hamburg, a few April snowflakes drifting down from an overcast sky. On a tree-lined street near the river Alster, Senior Inspector Otto Broehm was sitting at the wheel of a much-dented Hamburg police car. Next to him was a certain Magda, in her forties with long hair dyed brick red and a pretty face marred by a knife scar on her chin. But that had happened a long time ago, when she'd been a doorway whore in the infamous red-light district of the Reeperbahn. Now she was the madam of a high-class brothel in one of the better neighborhoods—prominent politicians of the city were known to visit Magda's, as were the wealthy men of the shipping trade, doctors, lawyers, and bankers. One of the latter, a vice-president in charge of commercial loans, could be seen some way down the street, coming toward the car as he took his schnauzer out for a walk.

"Is that him?"

"Yes, that's him alright, the Herr Doktor Schmidt."

Schmidt was built of solid fat, with beady eyes set above plump cheeks. "Tell me again, Magda, what he asked of you."

"To hide money he'd taken from his bank. 'A lot of money,' he said. I could keep it in one of my bank accounts, and nobody would be the wiser."

Inspector Broehm turned on the car's ignition and drove slowly down the street. "Head down, Magda," he said. "We don't want him to see you with me."

Magda crouched, her head beneath the windshield. When Broehm turned the corner she sat back up. "I have to ask you," Broehm said, "why are you giving him to us?"

"He is a pig, Inspector. You know my girls, young and fresh and not yet hard, they are essential to my business. Well, Herr Schmidt likes to spank."

"Is that so unusual?"

"No, my customers have their preferences and that's certainly one of them. We understand such desire, and provide for their pleasure a carpet slipper with a leather sole. The girls know to cry out for mercy and, when their bottoms turn pink, the spanking is over and the customers' appetites sufficiently sharpened. But with Schmidt it's different, he makes the girls scream, loud, no acting, and he doesn't stop until he sees tears, real tears, and the girls are bruised. My customers don't wish to see that."

"You've told him to stop?"

"Oh yes, told him more than once."

"And what did he do?"

"He laughed at me, he knows he's too important to obey the wishes of a madam."

"Very well, thank you, Magda, we will work with the bank for a time, and, once we know what he did and how he did it, we'll arrest him."

"Will I have to testify at a trial?"

"You won't. You have my word."

"That's all I need," Magda said. "We're lucky to have someone like you in Hamburg, Herr Inspektor."

Broehm let her out of the car and headed home for dinner. At fifty-three he was of average height with a comfortable paunch, slumped shoulders, and thinning gray hair. His grandfather had been a policeman, so had his father, and Broehm had joined the force on the day of his twenty-first birthday. He was a good cop, no, better than good, he was—and this was often said—the Inspector Maigret, the Hercule Poirot, of the Hamburg police. He worked long and hard, was a glutton for details, and something about him encouraged people to speak openly, to tell him things.

Stopped at a streetlight, he filled his pipe and lit it, then drove off when the light changed. When he turned into the pleasant little street where he lived he saw, parked at his door, a Grosser Mercedes automobile with swastika flags mounted on the front bumpers. "Now what could this be about?" he said to himself.

Entering his house, he found two men in the parlor, older, well dressed, who were making polite conversation with his wife. They introduced themselves, saying they were "from the Foreign Ministry," and told Broehm that they were taking him to Berlin for an important meeting. "Not to worry, Frau Broehm," one of them said. "We'll have him back later this evening."

Once they were under way, Broehm sitting in the backseat, the three talked as the car sped down the broad highway known as the autobahn. Berlin was a hundred and eighty miles from Hamburg, they would be there in three hours or less.

"Berlin was bombed again last night," the man in the passenger seat said.

"Was it very bad?" Broehm said.

"Not so bad, not as bad as April ninth, when they bombed the opera house and the Unter den Linden Boulevard. You know Goering's remark: 'If a single bomb falls on Berlin you can call me Meyer.' Well, he was Meyer last August, or Isidore or Chaim. And the Fuehrer was enraged back then. Anyhow, yesterday's attack was the last straw, and every ministry has to submit a plan of action."

"Nobody thought the RAF would do it," Broehm said.

The driver shrugged. "Over six hundred raids on Germany so far this month, but, Berlin, you know, that's different."

Broehm was not shocked; when the civilians of Britain were bombed, what did the Reich expect in return? "Yes, Berlin is different," Broehm said carefully.

"We must propose some kind of action against the RAF—for the Foreign Ministry that's not so easy, we're not the Luftwaffe, we're not the anti-aircraft battalions, thus we've determined to focus on the British aircrews. Those who are shot down over Germany are captured, if they survive, and put in POW camps. But when the flyers land on French territory, we can only get our hands on some of them, others escape with the help of people who call themselves 'the French Resistance.' And these criminals are the responsibility of the French police."

"Are the police effective?"

"They say they are," the passenger said. "They have penetration agents who infiltrate the escape lines, then, when the police are ready, they arrest the whole lot, try them, and send them to French prisons—that is the agreement between us and the Vichy administration in the Occupied Zone. But, in the French courts, different laws apply in different cases, and some of the criminals serve only a year or two."

"You must have someone who makes sure the French police are doing their job," Broehm said.

"We do," said the driver. "A diplomat in Paris, who talks to his Vichy counterpart."

"Yes, they talk," the passenger said. "They talk and talk, then it's time for lunch, and they talk some more."

"This situation cannot continue," the driver said. "The RAF airmen who escape back to England return to the skies over Germany and bomb us again."

For a time, there was silence in the car as the pine forest of northern Germany flew past the windows. Then the passenger said, "We have read your dossier, Inspector Broehm, and it appears that you speak French."

At the vast Foreign Ministry on Berlin's Wilhelmstrasse—the administrative heart of the Third Reich—Senior Inspector Otto Broehm was shown to an office with walls of polished mahogany panels, a mahogany desk, mahogany chairs, a large portrait of Adolf Hitler, and a smaller portrait of Joachim von Ribbentrop, the foreign minister. Across the desk from Broehm, the vice-minister was sleek, smooth, and perfectly groomed, like a man, Broehm thought, in a magazine advertisement. Before him lay Broehm's open dossier.

"Ah yes," said the vice-minister, skimming a page in the dossier as he ran his index finger down the margin. For the next page, a "Hmm" of approval, a vigorous nod for the third page, and a smile as the dossier was closed. "You are the man for us, Herr Inspektor. We need a bloodhound, not a lapdog. Do you really speak French?"

"I studied it in school, and I can speak and understand it, but if the person I'm talking to speeds up and starts using argot, I'm lost."

"It's the same with me—I speak the French of diplomacy, but, beyond that . . . Anyhow, I ask because we will be moving you to Paris."

"And what will I do there?"

"Oversee the French effort to destroy the escape lines. This sounds like an administrative job, doesn't it, but that's not what we have in mind—we want you to work with the details, we want you to involve yourself at the most basic level, you know, get your hands dirty. Much as you have done, very successfully, in Hamburg."

"Will the French detectives take direction from me?"

"Those who are serious about their work will. The others should be transferred."

Broehm pretended to think it over, but he knew it would not be wise to refuse officials in Berlin. "These investigations take some time," he said.

"We know they do," the vice-minister said. "But you'll have help. There is a small Gestapo office in Paris, on the Rue des Saussaies, not very active at the moment, which is as the Fuehrer wishes. He has, so far, been easygoing with the French—most of them have been asleep since the Occupation, why wake them up? We don't need another Poland, with children shooting at us. But now we must tighten the screw, so we've begun to strengthen operations in France: more investigations, better security. You just cannot, in an occupied country, have people running about and doing whatever they want, so there will be arrests and interrogations, and, as we catch them, more criminals will be sent to camps in Germany. Of course you'll find the Gestapo eager to take part in this effort."

Broehm disliked the Gestapo, the secret police of the SS, bellowing Aryan brutes who were torturing and executing their way across Europe. Broehm spoke carefully, saying, "I'm sure they will be useful."

"There if you need them," the vice-minister said. "I should tell you that they were interested in recruiting you, but we told them you were going to work with the Feldgendarmerie, the army's military police. You'll have the rank of major, and retain your position and salary on the Hamburg force." Then he said, "So, Inspector, what will it be? You can say yes, or, on the other hand, you can say yes." Followed by a laugh—*just joking*. But he wasn't.

Broehm knew the Feldgendarmerie. Operating against resistance in occupied countries they were known as the *Heldenklauer,* hero-snatchers, but that was better than working for the Gestapo. "I will be pleased to accept the assignment . . . honored," he said.

The vice-minister stood, shook hands with Broehm, then gave the stiff-armed salute. Which Broehm returned.

It had been an uneventful journey from Nanteuil to Paris—Annemarie, Mathieu, and Kalisz were at the Gare du Nord a few minutes after nine in the morning. Mathieu led Annemarie and Kalisz to a small hotel near the station, then took a Métro to the Sixth and walked along the Rue Dauphine to the Saint-Yves. In his apartment, he prised up the floorboard and removed a thick wad of occupation francs as well as dollars for the long trip down to the border. He then picked up the Beretta automatic, and, after a moment of reflection—the possibility of being searched weighed against the means to fight his way out of trouble—decided to leave it where it was. Meeting Mariana's gaze—she was alert to the floorboard, knew that something important was kept there and always watched intently when it was pulled up—Mathieu now changed his mind, and secured the Beretta in the waistband of his trousers, where it would be hidden by his jacket.

Next he went to the office of his other life and spent the rest of the day there, a foreign place to him now, and dealt with business. The people in his office were good to him, solicitous, speaking in soft voices, assuring him, without words, that they could carry on until he returned. In a way, they knew what he was doing, well, they knew but they didn't know, which was the best Mathieu could do to protect them—just in case. At five he said goodby to his employees, their *adieux* warm and sentimental, as though they might never see him again.

A note had been left at the Saint-Yves, asking him to contact Ghislain, so, when Mathieu left the office, he found a *bureau de poste,* called Ghislain at the Sorbonne, and found him still at his desk. "Can you meet me at the Notre-Dame de Lorette Métro station?" Ghislain said. "Outside the entry."

"I can be there in twenty minutes," Mathieu said.

The Notre-Dame de Lorette church, and the Métro that served it, were in the Ninth Arrondissement; a sombre, run-down quarter with low rents for the white-collar working class, and commercial buildings where long hallways were occupied by cheap travel agencies, confidential agents—private detectives, pebbled-glass doors that said IMPORT-EXPORT, and, on street level, narrow shops where the merchandise was new but looked used and was forever on sale. Daylight was just fading when Mathieu reached the Métro entrance, Ghislain showed up ten minutes later. Mathieu was glad to see him arrive because he'd caught the attention of a policeman. "Let's walk," Mathieu said.

"Did all go well at Nanteuil?"

"It did not. The plane crashed as it landed."

"*Merde,* what happened?"

Mathieu told the story, then said, "The pilot and Annemarie are at a hotel, we'll start out for the south the day after tomorrow."

"Where we're going is across the street from the church," Ghislain said. "We've now acquired what's called a *mailbox,* a place where messages can be left and picked up."

"I see. What will we do with Lisette?"

"She'll continue to deliver things on her bicycle, but the mailbox will make it easier on her."

Mathieu nodded. "At one time we left messages with Jules at the Café Welcome."

"The café is just for recruitment, at the moment, and I should tell you that Jules is getting anxious. He worries about this and that, and now he says that some strange-looking fellow has been hanging around, asking to see Mathieu."

"Strange looking?"

"That was all Jules said—you'll have to see for yourself."

"Maybe tomorrow," Mathieu said.

The mailbox, across the street from the church, was a shop that sold religious articles. A bell over the door jingled when the two entered, and a woman called out, "A moment. I'm in the back." The shop smelled like sandalwood incense, and displayed crucifixes, fancy and plain, Saint Christopher medals, candles, bibles of all sorts, religious paintings—saints with halos, Madonna-and-Child scenes, martyrdoms, crucifixions—and statuettes of Mary and Jesus. The proprietor appeared a moment later. She was bent over, hunchbacked, in her sixties, and radiantly beautiful, her long, thick white hair wound in a bun, her eyes a startling bright blue. "Mathieu, allow me to introduce our new friend, Madame Vigne," Ghislain said.

"Pleased to meet you, Mathieu." The light in her eyes seemed to grow brighter as she looked at him.

"And *we* are pleased that you are willing to work with us, madame. Is there any particular reason you agreed to help?"

"Well, your friend Ghislain *asked* me to, so I said I would. After all, one must do one's bit, I think, and it's easier for me because the Nazis deny the spirit of God. That is an evil way to act, so . . ."

"It could put you in danger, Madame Vigne, if you are found out you might be arrested."

"I would suppose so, they might even kill me." She smiled and shrugged. *What will be will be.*

"Madame Vigne," Ghislain said, "may my friend and I speak in your office?"

"You are welcome to it, messieurs, now, any time at all."

As the two walked toward the back of the shop, Mathieu spoke confidentially. "Ghislain, where did you *find* her?"

"Her spirituality is not exclusive—she does tarot readings and holds séances. Before my wife died she became a regular attendee and Madame Vigne was a great comfort to her."

The office, cramped and dusty, had an easy chair with stuffing leaking from its cushion, while its single decoration was a yellowing astrological chart tacked to the wall. Mathieu took the easy chair, Ghislain sat behind the desk. "This mailbox arrangement will be easier for Lisette," Ghislain said. "It was her mother who telephoned me, and said that Lisette was growing ill with exhaustion." They had both known Lisette's mother, a hospital nurse, before the war and it was she who had originally been considered as a courier, but she was a fervent leftist and known to the police, so her daughter had volunteered in her place.

"Also," Ghislain said, "Lisette worked so much that the other students had a good idea of what she was doing, particularly a boy who liked her, and kept asking to join up."

"Yes? Well, even so, I expect she wants to continue."

"She would not have it any other way, but using the shop will cut down the time she travels after school."

"She needs food," Mathieu said. "Steaks. Calves' liver."

"It was suggested, but she won't even consider anything from the black market—why should she eat well when others cannot? Anyhow, the story goes on. Last week, the boy, Lisette's friend, was summoned to the office of the *directeur* of the *lycée* and questioned about several students, Lisette included. That's what her mother told me."

"What did the boy say?"

"He pretended to be puzzled, what did the *directeur* think they were doing? Why was he being asked questions? The *directeur* wouldn't say why—he was obviously being pressured by the police but he would never admit that to a student."

"Not bad," Mathieu said.

"But not over, I fear."

. . .

21 April. Midafternoon at the Café Welcome, Mathieu and Jules were in the small kitchen, looking from time to time through the grease-flecked glass of the portholes in the door that led to the café proper. There was no sign of the "strange-looking man," so, as Mathieu waited, Jules cooked him a sausage, and put a dab of hot mustard on the rim of the plate.

"A good sausage, Jules," Mathieu said.

"Real pork, the butcher is my brother-in-law." Jules shook his head. "These days, you can't be sure what you're eating."

The afternoon wore on. Mathieu kept looking at his watch— Annemarie was out buying a new jacket and shirt for Kalisz and he wanted to find out if she'd been successful, as they had to be on a train early in the morning. Jules chattered away, ran his fingers through his sparse hair, his conversation too often punctuated by a nervous laugh. You couldn't tell about people anymore, he said, they might be police informers or blackmailers or anything. Over time it became clear to Mathieu that Jules wanted out, fear had overtaken him and he wanted them to stop using his café as a contact point but was too proud to say so. Still, when they returned from the south, Mathieu realized, a new café would have to be found.

Mathieu was about to give up when Jules said, "Ah, here he is!"

Mathieu went to the other porthole and saw what was indeed a strange-looking man, or, rather, a strange-looking boy, barely in his twenties. Standing at the bar and drinking a glass of wine, he had dark skin and dark eyes, wore a buttoned-up overcoat that was both much too tight and much too long, a hat with a wide, flat brim and a low crown, also flat, to which he'd added a bow tie that might once have belonged to a café waiter. With a pencil line of a mustache that traced his upper lip, he struck Mathieu as a boy dressed up to play his father.

"Well?" Jules said. "You can leave by the back door, if you like."

"He used my name, you said?"

"He did, more than once. He likes to talk."

"I better find out who he is." Mathieu's fingers, as though by themselves, brushed the handle of the automatic in his waistband.

He went out into the café proper and sat close to the bar, wanting to see if the boy recognized him. But, if he did, he showed no sign of it and was now trying to start up a conversation with the barman, who apparently didn't like him and busied himself drying glasses with a towel. Mathieu didn't like him either, just didn't, the boy was the sort of person that people didn't like. Finally, Mathieu walked over to the bar and stood next to him. "Are you the fellow who's been asking about Mathieu?"

The boy stared, his face immobile. "Are you him?"

"Let's say he's a friend of mine."

"I would prefer to speak with Mathieu himself. Tell him that, will you?"

"I'll give him a message, it's the best I can do."

"Is it? Are you sure?"

"Why don't you just say what you want? Always best in the end."

"I want to help the Resistance, tell Mathieu I said so, he should be interested."

"Help. Help how?"

"Maybe he needs somebody to . . . watch out for him." The boy smiled, almost a smirk.

"Alright, I'll let him know. What's your name?"

"I am known as the Spider."

"Are you. And why is that?"

"My enemies know why. Not the sort of spider who hangs from the ceiling, the sort of spider who hides, then strikes, and you'll feel the sting for a long time."

"Oh, now I understand."

"Say, you're Mathieu himself, aren't you."

"No, I'm somebody else."

"It's dangerous, the Resistance, maybe good to have somebody around who can handle himself in a fight, no? And I've got friends . . ." He drank down the last of his wine and said, "Mmm, that's good, I think I'll have another. And I'll let you buy it for me."

"Not today, my friend, and not tomorrow. I'll just bet you'd like Mathieu to pay you off, make sure you keep your mouth shut, am I right?"

"Not such a bad idea—it's the way things are done around here."

"Is that so? I didn't realize." Mathieu turned the boy's empty glass upside down on the bar. "Now you're done drinking, and don't come back here, understood?"

"You shouldn't be that way, it might not be good for your health."

"Oh? Well, I'll tell Mathieu what you said."

Then he turned and left the café, but the boy followed him, stayed ten feet behind, his hands now in the pockets of his overcoat. Mathieu ignored him, walked downhill on the Rue de Tournon, headed for the Odéon Métro. When he reached the station, the boy stood close by, so he could board the same Métro car. Now Mathieu tired of the game. There was a policeman standing by the tiled wall, Mathieu approached him and said, "Good afternoon, Officer."

The policeman responded by touching the brim of his cap with his index finger. Mathieu said, "Can you tell me if the trains are still running?"

"Yes, monsieur, as near as I know, they are."

"That fellow"—Mathieu extended his arm and pointed at the boy—"says they aren't, but I guess he's wrong."

Mathieu thanked the officer and, when he turned around, the boy had disappeared.

At seven in the morning, Mathieu collected Annemarie and Kalisz at their hotel and made for the Métro that stopped at the Gare de Lyon, where trains left for the south. Kalisz was now wearing a gray, pin-striped jacket with the trousers of his blue suit—the jacket baggy, well used, and a little too big for him. "Where did you find it?" Mathieu asked Annemarie.

"The used-clothing markets were stripped bare. I was desperate, so, in the end, I stopped a man on the street and bought his jacket. I had to offer him a great deal of money, but there was no other way."

The Gare de Lyon was crowded but the police at the control would not be hurried, making sure that the permit photographs matched the faces of the travelers using the documents. When the three finally reached the platform, they had to run, climbing onto the step of a railcar that was already moving down the track. Annemarie and Kalisz sat together on a bench in the third-class car, with Mathieu directly behind them.

The local train was headed for Bourges, some hundred and fifty miles away, where they would take a two-car tram to the village of La Guerche-sur-l'Aubois and then, with the help of the local *passeurs*, cross into the Unoccupied Zone. He knew that the journey which lay ahead of them would be dangerous but, for the moment, he relaxed, by watching the countryside rolling past his window. Outside, a windy changeful day as the villages south of the city were replaced by plowed fields, with an occasional church steeple in the distance.

In time, they reached the house in La Guerche where they would meet the *passeurs* and be guided past the border control into the Unoccupied Zone. There were two travelers waiting in the parlor but eventually they were led away and a local *passeur*, a middle-aged man with a full beard, showed up and, after formal greetings, took them into the oak forest at the edge of the village. As they approached a fast stream bridged by a tree trunk, the *passeur* held up a hand and put a finger to his lips. Mathieu looked around but could see nothing threatening; the forest was deep in shadow, with a silence broken only by the sounds of singing birds and rushing water. Then the *passeur* whispered, "Do you hear them?"

Mathieu and the others concentrated until, at last, they heard dogs barking, their voices faint in the far distance. "Those are not local dogs after a rabbit," the *passeur* said. "Those are pursuit dogs, tracking dogs." He grabbed Mathieu by the shoulder of his jacket and hurried him into the stream as the others followed. "We'll use the stream, no scent for the hounds," the *passeur* said. "It will take us back to La Guerche."

They were moving upstream and the water, some two feet deep, turned to frothing foam as it parted at their knees. It was difficult to fight the current, taking one step at a time, the spring flow was icy and, as their feet went numb, they had to fight for balance. The *passeur* plunged forward, breaking his fall with his hand. "All this be damned," he whispered. "My wife told me to quit, but did I listen?" Kalisz swore under his breath, rich Polish oaths, one after the other. When Annemarie spread her arms and started to fall, Mathieu reached out to steady her and they both fell backward, Annemarie landing on top of him. When they'd struggled to their feet, Annemarie said, "Sorry, Mathieu," as she wiped the water from her face.

"It's alright, I . . ." He was going to make a joke of it but an angry "Shhh!" from the *passeur* cut him off.

After they'd been in the water for twenty minutes—the barking dogs still far away but getting closer as they waded upstream—the *passeur* beckoned them to follow and stepped onto a narrow bank at the foot of a hill. "Are you the leader?" the *passeur* said to Mathieu, who nodded that he was. "Come with me, we can see the control from the hilltop." When the *passeur* and Mathieu reached the crown of the hill they lay flat and, peering over the edge, could now see the control below them.

A hundred yards away, a country road appeared from the edge of the forest, crossed a weedy field, then climbed a low hill. Halfway up the road, the border between the Occupied and Unoccupied Zones was marked by a yellow metal sign that said ARRÊT!—halt, a striped crossbar that could be lowered to block the road, and a wooden hut with a tin roof and a French flag. An open, khaki-colored vehicle, a command car, was parked by the hut behind two motorcycles, and standing next to the command car were two gendarmes in army-style uniforms with their pistols drawn. Facing them, three civilians stood with their hands raised: a couple, perhaps man and wife, the man heavy and dignified, the woman wearing a hat and veil that had been knocked askew. By the woman's side, a young man dressed as a *paysan* wore a beret pulled down to his forehead. Behind them were three more gendarmes, two of them restraining German shepherd dogs on long leads. The dogs pulled hard and barked furiously—their prey was right in front of them—until one of the gendarmes shouted at them and the dogs stopped barking and sat down. As Mathieu and the *passeur* watched, the other gendarme manacled the hands of the three prisoners then walked them toward the command car.

"Good God," said the *passeur*. "Do you see who they are?"

Mathieu saw; here were the travelers who had preceded them—by a half hour—from the house in La Guerche.

The *passeur* crawled backward from the crest, then hurried down the hill as Mathieu followed. When they reached Annemarie and Kalisz, Annemarie said, "What happened?"

"The couple who left before us were caught in the forest and arrested."

"By *gendarmes*," the *passeur* said. "This control used to be manned by local policemen working as border guards. No longer." He thought for a moment, then said, "We'll stay here until nightfall, then take a path through the fields back to La Guerche, and you can stay at my house until we figure out what to do next."

"Now that they know what goes on in La Guerche," Mathieu said, "will they search your house?"

"They might, they do anything they want. But we'll be warned if they're around—all the people in La Guerche know me, in fact I'm the village mayor." He looked rueful, then said, "Ahh, what a mess, the *passeur* they arrested is my wife's cousin."

. . .

By moonlight, the steel rails glowed like polished silver as they crossed a field. At the edge of the railbed, a small trackwalker's sign spiked to the gravel had numbers that showed the distance to somewhere. First they heard the sound of the approaching train, then they saw the light on the locomotive that cut a path through the nighttime ground mist. The mayor of La Guerche squinted at his watch and said, "Here it is. And on time." The locomotive rumbled past them, followed by a long row of freight cars. As the train slowed to a stop, the couplings of the freight cars clanked and rattled, then, with a long chuff of steam from the locomotive, the train halted—the last car standing opposite Mathieu and the others.

The mayor shook hands with each of them, repeating "Good luck to you" each time. "Here are some sandwiches for the journey," he said, handing Mathieu a package wrapped in newspaper. "You will be in Paris sometime tomorrow, at the La Chapelle freightyards. You must get off there, because this is an armaments train and is headed for Germany."

"Thank you for everything you've done," Mathieu said.

"Remember me," the mayor said. "I'm not done fighting."

The door of the railcar slid open and a man wearing a railway uniform looked out and said, "Good to see you, Mayor Gerard."

"Hello, *mon vieux*," the mayor said. "Here are your passengers."

"Climb aboard, my friends."

The three entered the car, then made space for themselves amid mounds of canvas mailbags as the train pulled away. With the door closed it was dark in the mail car. Annemarie stretched out on one side of Mathieu, Kalisz on the other. "When is supper?" Kalisz said.

Mathieu opened the newspaper-wrapped package and handed each of the others a sandwich then started on his own—a slice of sweet onion between thick slabs of bread smeared with margarine.

Kalisz chewed slowly, relishing each bite. From Annemarie, an "Mmm" of pleasure, then she said, "I have eaten very good food in very good places but it was not nearly as good as this."

The long train moved slowly through the countryside, now and then passing unlit, deserted stations in darkened towns. Done with the sandwich, Mathieu settled back on his mailbags. Beside him, Kalisz began to snore. "He is very tired, our pilot," Annemarie said.

"We all are," Mathieu said.

"True," Annemarie said. "It's hard, all this . . ."

"Well then, good night," Mathieu said, closing his eyes. But he could not go to sleep, he had to calm down a little, unwind; it had been a long day, only luck had saved them. The image of the three people with their hands raised kept returning, though he tried to make it go away. Lying beside him, Annemarie was sound asleep, breathing audible. As he watched her face, he could see that she was dreaming.

28 April. At four in the afternoon on a cloudy day, Mathieu waited at the Rue de Rivoli entry of the ancient and wondrous department store, BHV—*bay-osh-vay* to Parisians, the Bazaar of the Hôtel de Ville, for his younger sister Natalie and his favorite niece, Simone, for an annual ritual these past few years, the buying of Simone's birthday present. There had been dolls and toys in the past, but this year Simone was twelve, and Mathieu wondered what she might want.

Natalie was three years younger than Mathieu and when their father, the mayor of a small municipality just north of Paris, died of influenza in 1910, Mathieu had become, even at the age of nine, Natalie's protector, taking her to school, bringing her home, very much the caring older brother. Now he was an affectionate uncle. Simone and Mathieu liked each other, perhaps because there was more than a little of Mathieu in his niece: the way she watched the world, a certain fearlessness, and she had the same hair and eyes as he did.

At four, Simone now home from school, she and Natalie came hurrying down the street for an eager and lengthy embrace as the crowd of BHV shoppers flowed around them. "Happy birthday, sweetheart," Mathieu said, holding Simone back to have a look at her. "How does it feel to be twelve?"

Simone shrugged. "The same, pretty much," she said.

"She is a beauty," Mathieu said to his sister.

"Isn't she, the boys are already following her around."

"Don't, Mom," Simone said.

"Let's go shopping," Mathieu said.

The interior of the BHV was classic, a great staircase ascended up the middle of the store, revealing shoppers at work on the floor below, wandering across the old, wooden floorboards from display to display. This April 28, the crowd was about two-thirds German officers, and one-third Parisians with enough money to buy the expensive—for the French—merchandise. At the foot of the staircase, Mathieu said, "So, what is it to be this year, *chérie*?

"I think this year it ought to be a sweater, because it was so cold last winter."

As Mathieu stared at the store directory, Natalie said, "The kids' clothes are on the second floor." Clearly, the two had prepared a strategy. As the three climbed the staircase, Simone took one of his hands, Natalie the other. On the second floor, Natalie stood before a counter showing cardigan sweaters. "Oh these are very good," Natalie said. "The wool is good, and warm."

"It *is* spring," Mathieu said.

"Yes, but she has plenty to wear for the summer."

"Plenty?"

"Enough. Now, dear, look these over and see what color you like."

Mathieu wandered off a little way and called out, "Oh you should see *these*."

Simone and Natalie joined him and he held up a cashmere short-sleeved sweater with a tiny bow at the neck. "Um, this is *cashmere*," Natalie said. "Very dear."

But Simone was rapt, she reached out and ran a delicate hand over one of the sweaters, a pale lavender. She then held the sweater to her shoulders and stood before a mirror, and a certain look came into her eyes.

Natalie looked at the price tag and said, "Really, this is . . ."

But Mathieu kissed his sister lightly on the cheek. "It will be so pretty on her."

With her prize in a small paper bag that said BHV, Simone hurried down the stairs, eager to be home. She had just the right skirt.

On the third of May, Parisians left their umbrellas at home and, as they walked out into the street, turned their grateful faces to the blue, blue sky. The real, true spring had arrived, the chestnut trees were in blossom, and the Boche could do nothing about it.

As Mathieu reached the lobby of the Saint-Yves, the proprietor, as usual behind the reception desk, had a beaming smile for him. "Ah, monsieur, it is here at last," she said. "*Le printemps!*" Outside the door, a faint breeze on the Rue Dauphine; Mathieu felt it warm his skin and his heart as well, but he realized that the pleasure of the day would have to be postponed until he'd completed a difficult task—he was off to the Café Welcome to tell Jules that the use of his café as a contact point would have to be ended. *It can't go on forever, too many people know about it, and they talk,* he thought to himself, rehearsing the line he would take with Jules.

He could have used the Métro but this was no day to be underground so he walked to the Rue de Tournon. The usual crowd of bicyclists was in the streets but the weather had affected them; they'd slowed down and stopped ringing their bells at each other, and the women had celebrated by wearing whatever spring colors they had—dusty rose, or lilac, or lemon yellow.

As the Café Welcome came into view, Mathieu saw that Jules was out in front, sweeping the sidewalk—likely a welcome chore in the midday sunshine. But, as he neared the café, he saw that Jules was not sweeping up dust and bits of paper, he was sweeping up shattered glass, the remains of the café window.

Jules stopped when he saw Mathieu approaching. "Look what they did to me," he said.

"Jules, what happened?"

"Some fascist kids smashed my window, is what I think."

Mathieu took the dustpan from Jules's hand and said, "Let me help you." Kneeling on the sidewalk, he held the dustpan level and, after Jules had filled it with glass, headed for the kitchen garbage can that had been moved out to the street. Meanwhile, people passing by, faces grim, shook their heads and detoured around the sparkling fragments.

As he swept, Jules mumbled angrily to himself.

"Tell me, Jules, did that 'strange-looking' boy ever come back here?"

"No sign of him. You think he visited last night?"

"It's possible. Likely."

"Well, I'll have to board up the window—you can't find glass these days."

"Your customers won't mind, everyone in Paris knows this goes on. And, as for a new window, we'll find a way to get you one, and then we'll pay for it."

Jules looked down at Mathieu, holding the dustpan. "If you can, Mathieu, I would appreciate it, but this isn't your fault, I won't hold it against you, and I'll continue on . . . to work for you and our friends."

So much for the rehearsed lines, Mathieu thought. When they were done, Jules invited him in for a glass of wine.

At ten-fifteen that evening, Mathieu was sitting with Max de Lyon at his table in the Le Cygne nightclub. De Lyon ordered a bottle of cognac and lit one of his brown cigarettes. *"Salut,"* he said, raising his glass to Mathieu. "What brings you out tonight?"

"Troubles. I need advice, Max."

"Something gone wrong?"

"We're trying to move this Polish pilot down to Spain. The British sent a plane for him but it crashed in a field, then we tried to take him into the Unoccupied Zone and ran into, not the usual border guards, but gendarmes with dogs and motorcycles, and we almost got caught."

"The war is changing," de Lyon said. "The British are building warplanes day and night, the size and number of the bomber raids are increasing and some of them are going to be shot down. That means more work for the escape lines, which the British themselves mean to run; that's why Edouard showed up here. Meanwhile, there are too many fugitives getting through and the big shots in Berlin don't like it. They put pressure on Vichy, Vichy sends in the gendarmerie. Will it work? Not for long. The Wehrmacht will have the job next, and, in time, you can expect to see the SS and the Gestapo here. So, if you think you have troubles now . . ."

Mathieu finished his cognac, de Lyon refilled his glass. "I don't know," Mathieu said, defeat in his voice. "I really don't, maybe we should just keep trying . . ."

"Maybe not," de Lyon said. On the bandstand, the pianist, using only his right hand, was playing *Paris Sera Toujours Paris*— Paris will always be Paris, a hopeful, popular song from 1939, while his left arm was around the waist of a dancing girl who stood by the keyboard. Finally, de Lyon said, "Do you remember my friend Stavros?"

Mathieu nodded that he did. One of de Lyon's gangster associates, he was a swarthy bear of a man with oiled hair who wore a baggy silk suit—Stavros the Macedonian.

"Maybe he can help," de Lyon said. "Tonight he's entertaining an old friend, a fellow Macedonian. He's the captain of a tramp freighter so . . . who knows, there might be something there for you. Do you want to meet him?"

"Yes, I'll try anything."

"They've taken a room at the Ritz, why don't you go over there? You have time until curfew."

"The *Ritz*?"

"Uh-huh. Stavros likes to treat his friends to a good time. Tell you what, I'll telephone the hotel, they'll know what room he's in." De Lyon grinned. "Will they ever."

Mathieu finished his cognac and was preparing to leave, then he said, "One more thing, if you don't mind."

"Me? No, I don't mind, ask me anything you want."

Mathieu told de Lyon about the "strange-looking" boy who called himself the Spider and had tried to blackmail him. By the time he was done, de Lyon's good spirits had vanished, replaced by a darker mood. "Not good, these types can be really hard to deal with—kids who want to be tough guys. In fact you can't deal with them, that only encourages them, so . . ." He let it hang there, as though Mathieu knew the rest, then said, ". . . you may have to solve the problem the old-fashioned way, *if* you can find him before he denounces you."

"The old-fashioned way . . ."

"You know what I mean, Mathieu."

"Yes, I know."

"Now, get going, see Stavros at the Ritz. If nothing else you'll have a good time, forget your troubles."

There was a coal-fired taxi waiting in front of Le Cygne and Mathieu was at the Ritz in minutes, entering the elegantly furnished lobby with a group of men in tuxedos and women wearing diamonds. When he asked at the desk for Monsieur Stavros, the clerk studied the register, then said, "Unfortunately, monsieur, we have no guest with that name. Perhaps another hotel . . . ?"

Then Mathieu described Stavros and the clerk knew right away who he was. "That would be room forty-seven, monsieur, shall I telephone that you're on your way up?"

"You needn't bother, he's expecting me."

Mathieu shared an elevator with a monocle-wearing German officer who determinedly did not, given Mathieu's everyday clothes, choose to see him. They both got out on the fourth floor and, when Mathieu knocked at the door of room 47, the officer was not far behind him. Close enough so that when the door opened, and a great cloud of cigarette smoke came billowing out, the smoke flavored with champagne fumes, heavy scent, and hashish, Mathieu could see him speed up, running away from whatever went on in that room.

Stavros, wearing only drawstring underpants that came down to his knees, greeted him with a powerful, sweaty hug. "Mathieu! My friend, Mathieu! Welcome," Stavros said, his words slurred, his body swaying. Once Mathieu was in the room, Stavros said, "Meet my friend Bogdan, the ship captain." Bogdan, also in his underdrawers, was big and beefy, his nose with the bump that meant it had been broken, probably more than once.

Like Stavros, Bogdan spoke a primitive form of French. "Happy to meet Stavros friend," he said.

Further into the room, three women, two blondes and a brunette, also in their underwear, were sprawled out amid the tangled sheets and blankets on the spacious bed. Prostitutes? Not quite, Mathieu thought. A classier version of the breed, Parisian ladies out for a night to make money. Tomorrow, proper bourgeois women. "Come have a champagne," Stavros said, shoving an arm and a leg out of the way so they had room to sit on the edge of the mattress. Stavros poured champagne into the toothbrush glass from the bathroom—a silver tray on the floor held what remained of a few delicate champagne flutes, a few more had been thrown into the fireplace.

The brunette sat up suddenly, eyes unfocused, modestly holding a pillow across her lap—the frilly, red panties on the bedpost, Mathieu guessed, likely belonged to her. "Why is *he* dressed?" she said, pointing at Mathieu before collapsing back on the bed. Bogdan and Stavros looked at Mathieu who, with a tolerant smile, took off his clothes, keeping only his new-style boxer shorts. "Hey!" Stavros said, grabbing Mathieu's bicep. "You play sport?"

"Not for a long time," Mathieu said.

Bogdan put the champagne bottle to his lips, took a long drink, mumbled something in Macedonian, and drew the back of his hand across his mouth.

"Poor Bogdan," Stavros said.

"What's wrong?" Mathieu said.

"He has ship in Marseilles, but he can't go back to his own port. Salonika, you know?" The Germans had occupied Salonika in early April. "Maybe now, the Boche take the ship."

"No!" Bogdan said, with the sudden anger of the very drunk. "I fly Venezuelan flag! Neutral, *neutral.*"

Stavros caught Mathieu's eye—his friend the sea captain didn't know the Germans. "That's right, Bogdan, I forgot about the flag."

"Does the ship have a cargo?"

"In ballast," Bogdan said. "Where do I go now? No charters from Salonika, the company maybe finished."

One of the blondes woke up, wiggled to get comfortable, rested her leg across Mathieu's thighs, then went back to sleep. "Hey, *you* . . . ," Stavros said.

"It's alright," Mathieu said. Turning to Bogdan, he said, "Would you take a passenger?"

"Where you go?"

"Not me, a friend of mine wants to get to Spain."

"He's in trouble?"

"On the run," Mathieu said. "If you'll take him to Spain, I can pay you for the voyage."

The brunette rolled off the bed and, still holding the pillow across her middle, staggered toward the bathroom.

"Pay?" Bogdan said. "Is twenty-five thousand dollars."

Mathieu's heart sank, they had nowhere near that amount of money.

Stavros watched him for a moment, then spoke quietly to Bogdan in Macedonian, spoke for half a minute. Finally Bogdan answered him, then said to Mathieu, "Is now, for friend of Stavros, five thousand. Always good to help Stavros and his friends because maybe, sometime, you need them to help you. So, mister, you got five thousand dollars?"

"I do."

Stavros licked the palm of his right hand, made a fist, then smacked it into the palm of his other hand. It meant, in certain parts of Europe, that a bargain had been struck. That done, he grinned and said, "Now we drink on it!"

He looked around for more champagne and found a bottle—on its side under a pillow—that still had half its contents, the bedding had absorbed the rest. He topped off Mathieu's glass, then drank from the bottle and passed it to Bogdan, who finished it, yawned, said, "Lie down now," wedged himself between the two blondes and, almost immediately, began to snore.

"Here's to you, Stavros," Mathieu said, gesturing with the toothbrush glass. "Tell me, how did the captain get to Paris?"

A puzzled Stavros said, "By train. The express from Marseilles."

"How did he cross the border?"

Now he understood where Mathieu was going and said, "He has a German paper."

"Can I see it?"

"It's in his room." He pointed down the hall.

"Tomorrow I'll be back here with the money and I will need to borrow the paper for a day. Then he'll get it back."

"Sure, Mathieu, that's alright. You're going to the forger, heh? Have him make a paper like it for your friend?"

"I am. And, thanks to you, my friend can go home."

As Mathieu retrieved his clothing from a chair, Stavros said, "Say thank you to Max, he can get things done. You want to stay? Have one of the girls?"

"Not tonight, Stavros. Next time."

. . .

Mathieu did not make it home before curfew but there were no patrols out—the Rue Dauphine was deserted; he could hear his footsteps echo as he walked. Above him, ranks of blacked-out windows and a curved sliver of the new moon, which shone up at him, reflected by a puddle on the cobblestones in front of the shuttered umbrella shop. Then he stopped, just by the entry to the Saint-Yves, and tried to see if there was light at the edge of the blackout curtain in Joëlle's room, but he saw none. So, she was asleep.

Mariana was waiting for him, just inside the hotel vestibule, and gave him a long, inquisitive sniff—*What have you been doing?* In his apartment, she lay on her side, tongue out, and watched as he prised up the floorboard. When he'd counted out five thousand dollars, and a few hundred more for expenses, he said, "We need to find more money, girl." Ghislain's crowd—lawyers, businessmen, a few children of wealth—had been generous, and would be again, but . . .

The only alternative was the dreadful Edouard. "Really, the British ought to pay for their pilot, no?" But that money came with strings attached. He found himself going back over de Lyon's theory about the expansion of the German effort to destroy the escape lines, and decided it was a good theory. Not only that, but his bargain with Stavros's friend the sea captain had a lesson for him if he cared to see it. Yes, Stavros had done him a favor, but he ought to have been able to pay the twenty-five thousand dollars. "Should I have a talk with Edouard?" he said. Mariana knew what a question was and answered always in the same fashion—a double thump of her thick, flowing tail. "I'm afraid so, girl." He put the floorboard back in place, and, exhausted, lay down on the coverlet. *It's just for a minute or two,* he told himself, *then I'll take off my clothes and get into bed.* Mariana knew better and, now on guard for her sleeping master, settled on the threshold in front of the door.

The following day he stopped at the Ritz, handed the money to Bogdan who, red-eyed after a strenuous night, paged through the documents in a fat, leather passport wallet until he found the *Ausweis* and handed it to Mathieu. "Your friend is First Mate, I think," he said. Then Mathieu was off to the two-story hotel in the Marais where the forger worked. Next, he sent Chantal to see her friend at the Préfecture, to secure a permit for Kalisz to leave the city. Finally, he made his way to the Café Welcome, its window now boarded up, where he found Jules behind the bar.

"Dark in here, now," Jules grumbled, setting a cup of occupation coffee in front of Mathieu.

"Not the same without the window," Mathieu said.

"No, it isn't, there's no street to look at. No people."

"As soon as possible, Jules, we'll change that. Tell me, have you seen the boy who calls himself the Spider?"

"He hasn't come around."

"He may reappear, now that we've been taught a lesson, to see if we've changed our minds. Or, he may even telephone."

"Some lesson."

"Let's pretend it worked," Mathieu said. He reached into his jacket and counted out five hundred occupation francs he'd taken from beneath the floorboard. "If he comes in here, give him the money, from 'Mathieu's friend,' and tell him to come back in a week for another payment."

"You know best, chief," Jules said, a dubious eyebrow raised. "Sometimes one might as well just pay the money."

"And if he telephones, tell him that Mathieu's friend left something for him. No, not something, an *envelope*, he'll understand that."

Jules put the money in his pocket. "An envelope, I'll tell him."

"And make the delivery for a certain time on a certain day."

From Jules, a look of alarm. "Mathieu, please, not in here."

Mathieu hesitated, then said, "We may take him from here, then we'll go somewhere quiet."

"He'll fight, Mathieu, right here in the café. The *flics* will show up."

"Do you have, what's it called . . . *chloral* something."

Jules scratched his head, said, "What . . . ?" Then said, "Do you mean a Mickey Finn?"

"Yes, a free glass of your finest wine, with a little powder in it."

"I don't have anything like that. Why would I?"

"We need a pharmacist, or maybe we can just buy it, I'll have somebody try."

"Mathieu, maybe we *should* just pay, heh?"

"At least we have to have a long talk with him, in private, and scare the piss out of him. At least."

Jules was relieved. "That's better, that's a *good* idea, give him a fright."

"I think you're right, that's exactly what we'll do," Mathieu said, with sincerity, as though it were true.

When he'd finished his coffee, he left the café and returned to the Saint-Yves, wrote, on a scrap of newspaper, *Would you like to come up and visit tonight? Or tomorrow?* and put it in Joëlle's mailbox by the registration desk. Then he went out to the Rue de Buci market stalls, stopped at a *crémerie,* showed Madame a hundred francs, accompanied her to the storeroom, and discovered, to his delight, a ripe vacherin; soft, smelly, cow cheese produced at mountain dairies.

5 May. At nine-thirty that evening, Mathieu and Joëlle stood in the kitchen, he in boxer shorts, she in bra and panties. She was, he thought, good to look at with her clothes off—dark, slim, and lithe, with a supple waist, almost a sprite. They had each had a taste of the vacherin before wrapping it up in its newspaper so she could take it home. Mariana, now on her folded blanket in the corner, where she stayed when she wasn't wanted in the bedroom, also got a taste—those pleading eyes could not be resisted. Mathieu poured out two glasses of red wine, and he and Joëlle went into the bedroom. The window was open, blackout curtain drawn, a candle burning on the night table.

For the pause that preceded lovemaking, they had discovered that underwear and a drink went together very well, and sat close enough so that one of them could keep a hand on the other. Reaching over to the night table, he turned his radio on and waited for it to warm up. "Sometimes at night . . . ," he said, fiddling with the dial until the signal grew stronger, "you can hear jazz on this station, I think it comes from England." Amid the static, a slow piano backed by a bass and a drummer using brushes. "It's called *Willow Weep for Me,*" Mathieu said.

He lay back next to her and she rested her head on his chest. "It's sad, this song," she said.

"Lost love, if you know the lyrics."

Outside, some vehicle with a siren sped past the hotel. When it was gone, Mathieu said, "Joëlle, do you want to wash up?"

"I had warm water in my room tonight. A miracle!"

"Good old Saint-Yves."

He kissed her lightly on the forehead, then, with a finger crooked beneath the waistband of her panties, slipped them off.

"So," she said, snapping the elastic band of his boxer shorts, "let's have a look at you."

He took his shorts off, she leaned down and gave him a tender kiss. "Now see what you've done," he said. After a moment he said, "With this candle, I worry about the blackout curtain, we don't want the police blowing their whistles at us."

"Why don't you fix it?"

"Maybe you should."

A sexy walk to the window for Mathieu to watch—Joëlle's splendidly white bottom shifting with each step. At the window, she said, "I know what you want, you fiend, you just want to look at my ass." She swung it left, saying, "Is it *this* side of the curtain?" Then back the other way. "Or *this*?"

When she was again lying close to him she said, "I'm glad you sent me the note, I was thinking about you."

"Good thoughts?"

"Oh, you know, reminiscing, one could say . . . having fantasies."

"Ah, those." He began to stroke her, knee to upper thigh, then back. "Was I doing this, in the fantasy?"

"Sometimes. I dream up all kinds of naughty things, you would be surprised."

"It's the same with me. With everybody, I suspect."

"Yes, sometimes I imagine doing it with someone I've seen on the street, sometimes a lover of long ago." She smiled, amused by what came to mind. "There was a woman who taught at my *lycée*—lord, what I didn't do to her. And she loved it, at least in the fantasy she did. What a frisson when she came!"

"Was she fair? Or dark?"

"Fair, I would say, pale, and well fed."

"Did you undress her?"

"Oh no, in my fantasy I made her undress for me. She had great hauteur, a severe woman, and a snob, always her nose in the air, so I was very stern with her; made her pose, made her dance, made her crawl on her hands and knees so I could see everything and, when she didn't want to crawl anymore I encouraged her with a leather belt. Then I lay on my back and raised my knees and she . . . well, you know what she did, it's something you like to do. Of course she knew exactly the right place, the right touch . . ."

"Well, she should have, after all it was you." He rested his fingers on her shoulder, slid them down her arm until he held her hand, then put it between her legs. Idly, at first, she moved two fingers back and forth. As her breathing deepened and sped up, she held her breast, then, with two fingertips, her nipple. Down below, he laid his hand atop hers. After a time, she held a final breath, then gasped.

Eventually, he said, "Did she enjoy it, the teacher?"

"Yes, Madame X was very hot tonight, more than ever, she must have known I wasn't by myself and it excited her." She paused, said, "Bad boy," pulled him to her, kissed him lavishly, then said, "I love that about you. You're so . . ."

"What?"

"I guess it's that you have a wicked mind."

"Just me?"

"No, me too. But most men don't think women are like that."

Mathieu laughed. "Women are just as wicked as men, even worse, once they feel free. What was her name, your teacher?"

"I'd never tell you that, my God, you might *know* her."

They were silent for a time, content to lie on their backs and gaze up at the ceiling, then, a sudden gust of wind blew under the blackout curtain and the candle flickered and died. Mathieu, half awake, swore, went to the window and yanked the curtain aside. "I hate this thing," he said. "It keeps the world out." The warm evening air felt good as it filled the room, and the Rue Dauphine was busy; a dog barked, a couple came by, talking in low voices, their words indistinguishable but their tone intimate, a bicycle with a squeaky wheel passed slowly below the window and a woman called out, "Oh, Yvette, come back, I forgot . . ."

"Alive on a spring night, our Paris," Mathieu said.

"Funny, it's just life going on but, when it isn't there, you miss it." She turned on her side and began to play with him.

"I'm still feeling your nice kiss," he said.

As her mouth closed around him he remembered a certain gleam in her eyes as she described her fantasy lovemaking with the teacher. She'd had, at that moment, a touch of the dominatrix about her, more than liked being in command, especially over a woman who, during schooltime, had command over her. How had she described her? Fair, she'd said, and pale, with great hauteur. Probably wore a stiff brassiere and girdle, or perhaps a corset, nothing frilly or seductive, armament beneath her teaching dress. A black corset, he imagined, no, a *beige* corset, which, after it was taken off, revealed a fulsome body of pale flesh, like a nude in a Rubens painting. And then, soon enough, impatient little cries of desire as hauteur gave way to passion . . .

Afterward, Joëlle said, "I can guess what went on in your mind just now."

"Can you?"

"A visit with Madame X, perhaps?"

"Are you psychic?"

"Oh no, I'm just Joëlle, but she knows how you work."

The warm air and the small sounds of the street were hypnotic and soon he put his arm around her and began to doze. For an hour? More? He wasn't sure but when he came fully awake he heard the airplanes coming from the direction of the Channel. Not over Paris, this time, to the north, but still audible, as were the thuds of the anti-aircraft cannon. Mathieu waited for the flight to vanish into the distance but it didn't. Not for a long time, it didn't.

The gunfire had woken Joëlle. "Did it scare you?" he said.

"It woke me." Then, after a pause, "Well, maybe a little. I was dreaming about you, love."

"Mmm, tell me, all of it, everything."

"No, not that sort of dream. You were kissing me, in a romantic way, and you meant it. From the heart, *that* kind of kiss."

"Maybe, if you go back to sleep, the dream will continue."

From Joëlle, a small laugh. "I don't think it works like that. I was dreaming about *us,* about what I want for us."

He answered by pulling her closer, meaning that he felt the same way. What she'd said was good to hear, better than good, but in his response there was also fear. He didn't want her to be in love with him because it was possible that some night he wouldn't come home and she would never see him again and he knew what that would do to a woman who loved you.

THE
SECRET
AGENT

17 MAY. S. KOLB HAD GIVEN MATHIEU A CONTACT ADDRESS, A HAVAS travel agency in Neuilly. Mathieu sent a wireless telegram to the address, heard back immediately, and a meeting with Edouard was arranged for five in the afternoon at a *hôtel particulier*—private mansion: a grand house with a gated entry courtyard in front and a garden in back, built centuries earlier when the nobility ruled the country. This *hôtel particulier,* known as the Hôtel de Quercy, stood on a narrow street near the Marais. Barely stood—the lovely, ancient building was crumbling away and looked to have been abandoned for years. As Mathieu approached, the late afternoon sun threw long shadows over the cobbled courtyard.

Following instructions, Mathieu walked to the back of the mansion and entered through a tall gate that squeaked on rusty hinges and led into a garden gone wild long ago: overgrown shrubs that reached out to block the gravel paths; a statue of a nobleman—the statue had lost its head as, perhaps, the original nobleman had; a huge, gnarled, dead oak tree; and a few resident cats. The back doors of the mansion were ajar, Edouard was waiting for him when he arrived.

He was as Mathieu remembered him—*rich English bastard from Mayfair,* Mathieu had thought at the time—with a neat blonde mustache and a prim set of the mouth, as though he were offended by the world around him. "I am so glad you have decided to meet with me," Edouard said, a hint of triumph in his voice. "Let's go upstairs, shall we?" He gestured toward a staircase and followed as Mathieu, not so comfortable with Edouard behind his back, climbed to the second floor. Where they entered a vast room: floorboards that creaked with every step; tall windows, wood paneling on the walls. An enormous table—large enough for dinner for forty—stood at the center of the room with a few spindly, old chairs pulled up to it. Mathieu chose one, Edouard another.

"I expect you've been a very busy fellow," Edouard said, in his near-perfect French.

"That's true, I have couriers and escaping airmen all over the place."

"Yes, big raids now. Big, *big* raids, new bombers coming off assembly lines day and night."

"True of the Luftwaffe as well, I expect."

"Indeed, a slogging match. We're at stalemate today but wait until the Americans get into it. So then, to business. We will provide funds, as I said before, thirty-five thousand dollars for a start. Have a look." He slid the briefcase across the table and Mathieu opened it, revealing packets of hundred-dollar bills bound with rubber bands. "Do count it, Mathieu, always a good idea, with money changing hands."

Mathieu transferred the packets to his briefcase, saying, "I'm sure it's all here."

Next, Edouard took a typewritten page from his briefcase

and placed it on the table in front of Mathieu, saying, "And, of course, we must have a little something for the dear people in the London accounts department." The paper was written in English and Mathieu read it slowly: legal language, a receipt for the money Edouard had given him. "So," Edouard continued, "sign and date on the bottom of the page, you will find a line there." He paused, then said, "Your true name, please."

Mathieu hesitated, looking up from the document this receipt was dangerous. If the Germans got hold of it . . . "How does this paper reach London?"

"By diplomatic pouch, from a neutral embassy. Safe as can be, old man, the Germans don't read their mail, though I can't imagine why not."

Mathieu signed, and Edouard, with brisk satisfaction, put the paper in his briefcase and buckled it shut. "Now then, some details," Edouard said. "We know you're busy, Mathieu, but we do have a little job for you, date to be determined, but soon. A beach reception, up in Normandy, for two of our agents coming in by submarine. These are people who managed to leave France after the Occupation and make their way to General de Gaulle's Free French headquarters in London, where we recruited them. De Gaulle would surely, to put it mildly, like to command all French resistance himself but, for the moment, he hasn't the means, so he cooperates with our special operations people. Your job will be to meet our agents and get them safely to Paris, where they will be on their own and your operatives are not to see them again."

"Who are they?"

"A sabotage instructor and his wireless operator. Their gear— time-pencil detonators, fuse cord, plastic explosive, and all that sort of thing—will be in two duffel bag–sized metal containers. So you'll want a vehicle to carry it."

"Can you tell me where, exactly, your agents will be?"

"Can't tell you what I don't know, but I'll have the details in a day or two. Do you have a drop-and-receive mailbox in Paris?"

Mathieu told him about Madame Vigne and the religious articles shop across the street from the Notre-Dame de Lorette church.

"Then that will be all for today," Edouard said, and so Mathieu was dismissed from his presence.

I shouldn't have done it. The regret was powerful and there was no point in denying it to himself. True, he'd had no alternative and he knew it, but still his mind hunted for some possibility he'd missed. After a few minutes of this, he realized he had no idea where he was going, then saw that he'd entered the Marais, the Jewish quarter, the poor Jewish quarter, and now found himself walking up the Rue Elzévir. The population of the neighborhood had swollen as war drove the refugee Jews west and Mathieu walked past knots of people engaged in animated conversation—arguments in French, Yiddish, and Polish—about what might happen next, and what was the right thing to do, and was there anything they *could* do.

The Saint-Yves lay across the river from the Marais and when he reached the Seine he took the Pont Marie, a bridge he especially liked. Pausing to look down at the river, Mathieu saw a man called LeBeq, an acquaintance from his other life who worked for an insurance company. Mathieu tried to turn away but he was too late, LeBeq hailed him then greeted him like a long-lost friend. "Where the devil have you *been*? Somebody said you'd left the country."

"No, here I am, but I've been busy, I haven't seen any of the usual crowd."

"Are you managing alright? You didn't renew your policy . . ."

"It escaped me, somehow, too much on my mind."

"Anyhow, if you decide to renew, you know where we are. By the way, did you know that Annette and Paul have separated?"

"Them? That's a surprise, they were very much the loving couple the last time I saw them."

"No more. The pressure of the Occupation, that's what it is, it makes small things seem very important and people fight over the tiniest details."

"Well, I'm sorry to hear the bad news."

"Would you care for something to drink? I know a café near the end of the bridge."

"Thanks, but I have to be on my way, I'm meeting . . . somebody."

"Ah, the life of a single man, I envy you," LeBeq said, with a conspiratorial smile. "Why not telephone sometime? We'll go out for dinner, my wife's cousin has a little restaurant in Montmartre, he'll take care of us, if you understand me."

"A good idea," Mathieu said. He shook hands with LeBeq and crossed the bridge, not far from home now and wanting to sit quietly and think about what he'd done and what it might mean for the people who worked with him.

19 May. Otto Broehm—formerly senior inspector of the Hamburg police department, now major in the Feldgendarmerie—walked from his apartment in Paris to his office on a cloudy, spring morning. This took only a few minutes as, eager to be at his desk, he'd set off at a brisk pace, and the office was only a few blocks away. He was now installed at the Kommandantur, the headquarters of the German occupation forces based at the Majestic Hotel, on the very fancy Avenue Kléber, a close neighbor to the Arc de Triomphe and the Avenue Champs-Élysées. Broehm, accustomed to the no-nonsense furnishings of Hamburg police stations, was still a little startled when he opened the door to his office—an elegant room that had, a year earlier, been home to guests at one of the grandest grand hotels on the continent.

Broehm was alone in Paris—his wife had chosen to remain in Hamburg, amid family and friends—but he found this a useful arrangement, for he intended to give all his time and energy to his new job: destruction of the escape lines taking downed RAF airmen out of France—and that meant long hours and no distractions. As he reached his office, his aide, Leutnant Fichter, sprang to his feet and saluted. Fichter, stationed just outside the office door, always made a great show of effort. He had yearned to join the SS but, at five feet five inches, his height fell four inches short of the SS standard. It doesn't matter, he would tell himself, he would show the world what diligence and zeal meant in an officer of any service.

Broehm sat at his polished mahogany desk and had a glance at his schedule for the day, his first appointment with one Madame Passot, an employee of the Vichy office that worked with the military police—the Wehrmacht's Feldgendarmerie. Disruption of the escape lines had been the responsibility of the Vichy office but they hadn't done very well at it. Now, that would change.

His telephone rang, it was Leutnant Fichter. "Madame Passot is waiting to see you, sir, the dossiers you'll need are on your desk."

"Please send her in," Broehm said.

Madame Passot was a lifelong civil servant: a thin, sour woman who wore eyeglasses attached to a chain around her neck. Broehm greeted her, then said, "It seems you've done your job quickly."

"I have, Major. I limited my investigation to the Paris area— there are cases of people working for escape lines all over the Occupied Zone—and I have completed five interviews: three wives, one mistress, and a mother, who all lived with men convicted of offenses—for instance use of false papers—committed while helping RAF airmen to avoid capture."

"Not aiding the enemy?"

"France, despite Berlin's urging, has not declared war on Great Britain, so aiding the enemy doesn't apply."

"And your approach?"

"I said I was employed by the office that issues ration coupons, and it was my job to make sure the domestic situation was as stated on the registration form."

"And were the subjects compliant, when questioned?"

"Oh, yes—they are all frightened of the government, as well they should be, what with their loved ones serving time as criminals. They are also, because of that confinement, very short of funds, though all of them assured me that their present allotments are quite sufficient to their needs. I asked one of the wives what the family would be having for dinner that night, her answer was 'Turnips and a potato.' "

Broehm nodded with satisfaction. "Then my research was correct. The censor's office at the Santé prison reports that the subjects' letters to the prisoners are filled with complaints—'life is hard without you' and so forth—which is no doubt the truth and why these particular women were selected."

Broehm squared up the dossiers before him and said, "We will start with these, Madame Passot, and see what can be done. Don't be in a hurry, take your time, I'm sure you took notes, but I will welcome all the details that occur to you as we go through the interviews."

"Yes, sir. I will begin with the wife of prisoner eight-four-six, Roche, Louis, who was apprehended while trying to pass through the document control at the Gare Saint-Lazare railway station."

The following day, Major Broehm was driven to La Santé—a soot-blackened brick building erected in 1867, in the Fourteenth Arrondissement. His first impression on entering the prison was twofold: a strange, eerie silence, a silence that seemed to echo—talking was forbidden at certain times of the day—and the eye-watering smell of the disinfectant bleach known as Javel water.

The prison administration had made available the basement room used for interrogation, a kind of dungeon—gray walls stained with moisture, a single bulb in a wire cage hung from the ceiling, and a table and three chairs, two on one side, and one, bolted to the floor, on the other.

The first prisoner he would see that day was called Roche, a schoolteacher from a village on the southern edge of Paris, who had been caught taking an RAF tail gunner out of the Gare Saint-Lazare. Manacled at the wrists and ankles, Roche was escorted into the interrogation room by two prison guards.

"Take those things off him," Broehm told the guards.

Dutifully, the guards did as they were ordered, left the room and closed the door. Broehm, reading over the prisoner's dossier, let Roche stand there for a time. He was a small young man, pale from life in a prison cell, who, his eyeglasses stolen on his first night at the Santé, squinted as he stared at Broehm. Who was not an intimidating presence: he was of average height with a comfortable paunch, slumped shoulders, and thinning, gray hair. When Roche entered the room, Broehm was smoking his pipe. "Number eight-four-six?" Broehm said, looking up from the dossier. "That is, Louis Roche?"

"Yes, sir."

"Monsieur Roche," Broehm said—the usual form was "prisoner," not "monsieur," followed by a number—"please sit down. Would you care for a cup of coffee?"

"Yes, sir, I would like a cup of coffee."

Broehm went to the door and asked the waiting guard to bring them a mug of coffee, with sugar. Then Broehm returned to the table, studying Roche's dossier and making notes until, a few minutes later, the coffee arrived. As Roche took his first sip, Broehm said, "Did they put in the sugar?"

"Yes, sir, the sugar is plentiful."

"Not so good to be in prison, is it, Monsieur Roche."

"No, sir, not very good in here."

"Do you regret what you did?"

Roche nodded, but did not speak.

"I understand patriotism, of course, but it can be costly. How is your family doing?"

"Not too well, sir, they haven't enough to eat, and they were cold in the winter—they had little money for heating."

"You know, I believe that's the hardest part of serving time, the effect on the family. How long have you been here?"

"Five months and a few days, sir."

"And how much time will you have to serve?"

"Another three years . . . the sentence was forty-two months."

"Three years!"

"Yes, sir, three years."

"Would you like to get out earlier?"

"Of course, sir, who wouldn't?"

Broehm shook his head, slowly, a gesture of sympathy. "If there is such a person, I don't know him. You are never the same, you know, after a term in prison, it changes a man." Broehm's pipe had gone out and he relit it with a wooden match. "Tell me, Monsieur Roche, do you suppose the English appreciate your sacrifice?"

"I wouldn't know what they think, sir."

"Well, there are those of us who find them cold-blooded—you helped *them,* but I doubt they would help you." He paused, then said, "And do your friends come to visit you?" "Friends" was said in such a way that it suggested fellow conspirators.

"No, sir, only my family."

"I'm surprised," Broehm said. "Perhaps they don't like the idea of showing their documents to prison officials, could that be it, do you suppose?"

"I can't say, sir, you would have to ask them."

"I'd be happy to ask them, if you'll make a list of their names and addresses."

Roche looked down at the floor. After a time, he said, "I wouldn't know who to name, sir—I believe the police interviewed some of the other teachers at my school, but I don't really have many friends, I used to spend all of my spare time with my family."

"You said you would like to be released before your sentence is up. What would you be willing to do in exchange?"

Now Roche seemed honestly puzzled. "What would you *want* me to do?"

Broehm waited, letting the silence gather, giving Roche time to consider an answer to his question. But the prisoner simply sat quietly and stared down at the floor. When, after three or four minutes, Roche had found nothing to say, Broehm spoke again, his tone regretful but far from angry, almost affectionate—*I'd like to help you but you refuse to be helped*. "Finish your coffee, Monsieur Roche, then I'll call the guard and you can go back to your cell." He drew a business card from his pocket and handed it to Roche. "Louis, take some time to think it over, think about the people who need you, who suffer because of what you did. And then, think about the people who talked you into breaking the law—they can't help you now but I can, and my offer stands. If you decide you want to speak to me again, give the card to someone in the warden's office and simply say that you would like to meet with me."

Roche raised the mug and finished his coffee, holding the card in his other hand—the prison uniform had no pockets. Courteous and diffident, he said, "Thank you, sir, for the coffee." Later that day, a guard found the card on the floor of a corridor.

Oh well, Broehm thought as he left the prison and its silence. He'd had hundreds of such interviews, most of them failed to produce results and over the years he'd become philosophical about that. In this instance, he'd been hunting for a wolf and had turned up a rabbit. But a brave rabbit, when all was said and done, who had acted on his ideals and resisted the Occupation. In fact, the information that Roche declined to give him didn't matter; Madame Passot's office had informed Broehm that the escape line Roche had worked for no longer existed, its leader, along with most of its couriers, had been arrested. Broehm had interviewed four other prisoners, from various resistance cells, with much the same results. One of them had wavered, tears in his eyes, but, in the end, held firm.

Outside the prison, another world: everyday life in a busy neighborhood; work over for the day, Parisians went about their business, waiting in line at the markets, sitting in the cafés, pedaling home on their bicycles. Walking along the Boulevard Arago, he noticed that the people in the street did not look at the prison. Was there, in this crowd, someone he could use? Likely not, he thought. *But I only need one.*

A certain type—he knew them all too well from years of experience as a detective, he knew how they acted, how they spoke, how their minds worked. These were people who would do anything to win at what they saw as the game of life, who had no allegiance to anyone or anything beyond themselves, who were gifted liars, who could scheme their way into almost anyone's confidence, then betray them without hesitation. If they were criminals—and that species of the breed was the most familiar to Broehm—they believed in their hearts that *everyone* was a criminal, everyone was a hypocrite. To such people, the only thing on earth that mattered was their own existence; what happened to their victims, and they left a trail of victims, counted for nothing—it was their own fault, too bad for them.

This was what Broehm needed, a predator, a monster. So then, where was he?

The following day, Broehm drove out to the gendarmerie post in the town of Senlis, not far from the village of Nanteuil-le-Haudouin where, on the eighteenth of April, a Lysander aircraft had crashed as it attempted to pick up a fugitive RAF airman. A captain of gendarmes, a stolid, cautious, veteran officer, had been ordered to meet with him and together they drove to the wheatfield where the Lysander had crashed and burned. Broehm tried to secure the captain's confidence but his attempts at amiable conversation were, politely, rebuffed.

The burned-out airplane had been taken away soon after the crash and all that remained, as Broehm and the captain reached the site, was charred earth, plowed after the accident, with wheat stalks probing up through the ground. Walking across the field, Broehm saw a fragment of cloth half buried in the dirt and stooped down to pick it up. Old habit—there was nothing to be done with it, still, he put the bit of cotton into his pocket. When he looked up, he saw that the captain was faintly amused. "Tell me, Captain, did you take part in the investigation of the crash?"

"I did, and a report was written. If you'd care to read it you're welcome—it's in a file at headquarters."

"And did you find out who was responsible for the escape?"

The captain shrugged. "We had our suspicions, but the local *paysans* don't really talk to us. An old tradition in rural France—they talk to the authorities but they say nothing."

"Yes, I know about that," Broehm said.

"In Germany, that would be."

"Yes, in Germany."

"Mmm."

And that said it all, that "mmm."

Still, Broehm persisted. "How was this managed, do you think? Who arranged the pickup of the pilot?"

"Probably an office in London," the captain said.

"And the link between the local farmers and the English officials?"

"We have no idea, Major. Obviously the London office was in contact with the chief of an escape line, but who the individual was, that we don't know. And, I suspect, the local people don't know either; a name was used, but it would have been an alias, a nom de guerre."

"Very well, there's nothing further to see here. We might as well return to Senlis."

Together, they walked back across the field and, when they were seated in the captain's command car, Broehm lit his pipe. They drove in silence for a time, bouncing along the rutted dirt path, then Broehm said, "Well, there wasn't much to see, but I want to thank you, Captain, for your cooperation."

"I'm glad to be of help," the captain said, with not a hint of sarcasm in his voice.

He would, Broehm thought, read the report when they reached Senlis. That was his method—follow every lead, take nothing for granted. But he knew the report wouldn't help him, just as he knew the captain wouldn't help him, and, he now began to understand, the French police wouldn't help him.

. . .

28 May. Deauville.

There were twenty arrondissements in Paris, Deauville was sometimes referred to, in jest, as the twenty-first. It was, on the Normandy coast north of Paris, a magnet for the Parisian upper classes. *Oh, we'll be up at Deauville for the weekend, staying at the casino.*

As was Mathieu. He stood at a hallway window outside an office on the top floor of the Grand Hôtel et Casino Régence and looked out at the view: a version of the scene beloved by artists of a certain sort—*La Plage à Deauville* was a much-used title—that showed bathers, striped umbrellas, usually a dog or two, children with pails and shovels, and, almost always, the French tricolor flag flying in the wind so you could see the blue, white, and red. The view from the window was not unlike the paintings—seen from above, golden sand spreading into the distance—only there were no children, there was no flag, and these were not Parisians, splashing in the surf, these were Germans. Officers, he thought, tall and well built, lying on colorful beach towels, playing with a soccer ball, swimming as though in competition.

"Hello, I'm Frankel, sorry to keep you waiting."

The voice came from behind him and Mathieu turned to discover the man he'd come to see, Monsieur Pierre Frankel, owner of the hotel-casino. He was a short man in his sixties, with thick-framed eyeglasses, who wore a tan summer-weight suit cut in a way that might be called *sharp*—too square at the shoulders, too wide at the lapels. Frankel, standing next to Mathieu, looked out at the scene and said, "Enjoying the view?"

"Not much."

"How they love it up here! This is what they fought for, after all, *la belle France*."

"They won't have it forever," Mathieu said. "Only until somebody makes them go away."

"'Somebody' is a hundred miles across the water: England. That's where it will come from, when it comes, the invasion. So the

Boche is sensitive about their beach—if you're not in uniform, best not to be seen with a camera."

"Where are the people who used to have houses here?"

"They're around, but they stay away from the beach. When the Occupation began, the Germans proclaimed a fifteen-mile Forbidden Zone along the entire French coast, but, you know how we work, this one wangled an exemption, then that one, so now they call it a Restricted Zone, and most of the people who owned homes before the war are back. But, only Boche officers at the Régence."

"Do they like to gamble?"

"They love it. They get drunk, they gamble, they lose, what's new. And some of the big losers connive at having their debts canceled. Which we're happy to do, in return for the occasional favor. I am a Jew, as it happens, so I have to be exempt myself. And, since the Wehrmacht doesn't run casinos, I'm a good Jew to have around."

"You were recommended to me, Monsieur Frankel, by the lawyer who works for us, a friend of a professor at the Sorbonne."

"Yes, he telephoned. Carefully, of course. Let's go into the office—we'll want a little privacy."

The office was spacious and airy, a sea breeze blowing in through the open window, Mathieu could smell the salt. Frankel opened a drawer in his desk and rummaged through the papers until he found what he needed. "You can take this to the local police station and have it stamped."

"I will need two more forms, for a man and a woman."

"Forms I have, so let's start with you." Frankel found a dotted line and said, "So, you are going to be a croupier, what name would you like to use?"

Mathieu gave him the name he'd used on his false papers. "A croupier," he said, smiling at the idea. "Pulling in chips with that little rake they have, calling out *Banco!*"

"Are you a gambler?"

"Boxing, bicycle racing, horses—I'm not much for cards."

"Just as well, it gets expensive . . . fickle Lady Luck, all that. You don't plan to actually work at the tables, do you?"

"No, I just need a paper to show if anyone asks."

"They might, they're planning to build some kind of defensive system up here, I've talked to one or two of the engineers. And, lately, we're seeing Gestapo, they've taken a house in the town, kicked the owners out and made themselves at home. Anyhow, these are people you want to avoid—any little thing and they're liable to explode."

"Still, you can't avoid them forever, can you?"

Frankel shrugged. "They don't come to the casino . . . and, truth is, for the moment I'm not at risk, my fix is high up. High enough, I hope."

"We'll be here for several days, is there a place we can stay?"

"We have a few shared apartments in town, some for men, some for women."

"That's good—we'd rather not register at a hotel."

"As you wish. Let me fill out the papers for your friends." When he was done he said, "I have no idea what you're doing, I only hope you do it well, because if you are caught you will have to deal with the Gestapo."

"If things go as they should, nobody will ever know we came here. By the way, my understanding is that there is also a casino at the village of Ouistreham, down the coast from here, can we use these papers there?"

"You can. It's a small hotel and casino, but active. Your woman friend will be a secretary, and the man will also be a croupier."

Mathieu stood up and offered his hand to Frankel, who also stood, and said, "*Give* it to the bastards, *Monsieur le croupier,* give it to them with my best wishes." Frankel, having shaken hands with Mathieu, patted him on the shoulder—*good boy*—saying, "I am proud of you, son."

.   .   .

The couple—Mathieu and Chantal—had afternoon tea at the Ouistreham hotel. The restaurant was just across the hall from the gaming room, where German officers were playing roulette, shouting with glee or frustration as the silver ball rattled into a slot. *"Ach! Verdammt Rot!"* Someone had bet on red and lost.

"Very frisky, aren't they," Chantal said. "And always in a group, have you noticed that?"

"They are occupiers of someone else's country, so as much as they swagger and strut they can never be comfortable, too much aware that the day may come when we rise up and cut their throats."

"Tell me when, Mathieu, I'll be there."

"Then you'd better have the last *petit éclair,* you'll need your strength."

Chantal used the silver tongs to put the éclair on Mathieu's plate. "I can see it in your eyes, *chéri,* desire . . ."

Mathieu smiled with gratitude and the pastry was gone in two bites. Then he finished his tea and said, "Well, my sweet, would you care for a little walk on the beach?"

"You romantic old thing . . . what about my shoes? High heels not so good in sand."

"You shall carry them in your hand, that will make a tender impression on the local crowd."

They looked very much the couple at a beach resort; both wore newly purchased straw hats, Chantal's cotton print dress floated around her, and she'd tied a pretty scarf to the strap of her sensible shoulder bag. They left the casino by the French doors that led out onto the beach, where the wind was blowing hard off the sea and, despite the late afternoon sun, Mathieu felt the chill.

Some way down the beach, a German officer and his French girlfriend were lying on a blanket, snuggling, waiting for the privacy of nightfall. Even so, the German wished them a good afternoon, though the young girl beside him looked away, pretending she wasn't there. Mathieu took Chantal's hand in his, while Chantal, with her other hand, swung her shoes back and forth, which made her seem happy and carefree, out for a walk with her man.

"How far is it to the reception site?" Chantal said.

"From here? Maybe thirty miles or so—today I just wanted to get a sense of the shoreline. According to the instructions left at Madame Vigne's shop, there's a fishing village outside of Arromanches, then I have to find a black rock formation on the waterline at low tide. By the way, do you have the spare batteries for the flashlight?"

Chantal patted her shoulder bag, saying, "They're in here, as I told you when you asked this morning."

Mathieu was about to apologize when they heard a shout and turned to see the German officer trotting to catch up with them. He waved his hand down the beach and said, *"Nein, nein,"* waggling his index finger as though to naughty children. Saying *"Verboten,"* he pointed at an empty sentry post, a wooden hut open to the sea set high on a grassy dune. Then he smiled with regret and spread his hands—*What can you do, that's the rule.*

Mathieu said thank you and the two headed back toward the casino. The officer walked along with them and, as they approached the blanket and the waiting girlfriend, tried to say something in French. Mathieu, who hadn't understood a word of it, replied by saying, "Oh yes? Well . . . ," his voice barely audible above the crash of the waves but the answer seemed to satisfy the officer.

When they were beyond the blanket, Mathieu said, "Any idea what he was trying to say?"

"Can't imagine . . . they do have such a hard time with the language."

Mathieu laughed, amused by a memory. "I was in a café somewhere, and a German asked directions to the *salle de nains.*"

From Chantal, a bark of laughter, then she pressed her hand to her mouth. The German had wanted to visit the bathroom, the *salle de bains,* but *nains* meant dwarves, so he was headed to the dwarves' room.

"Oh that's funny," Chantal said. "I can see them, the dwarves in the Snow White cartoon, all in a row, sitting on the pot."

"Yes, and maybe a couple of them would need new names."

Mathieu and Chantal waited in the casino parking lot until the bus for Deauville showed up—not a wood-fired bus, since the traffic between the two casinos was mostly German, gasoline-powered transportation service had been arranged. As the bus rattled along the beach road, the German officers began to sing—loud songs that sounded like marching music—while their French girlfriends looked out the window. Raising her voice above the song, Chantal said, "How is your apartment?"

"Crowded, four beds to a room, so there are twelve of us. The croupiers spend a lot of time on their looks, shaving and powdering and snipping off the stray hair. I'd guess the casino bosses insist on that—if someone takes your money, they at least ought to be well groomed, therefore trustworthy, and not too handsome, no gigolos. What about the women?"

"They're young, a lot of them from Paris, who spend the summer season working as maids, and they like to have a good time when they aren't cleaning rooms. Women in a group with no men about don't have to be so ladylike. The girls lie around in their underwear, cursing, smoking, drinking whatever they can get their hands on—mostly by flirting with the bartenders—and they tell dirty stories about men they've known and laugh like hell."

"Well, after tonight we'll move to our hideout."

"How did you find it?"

"Ghislain, always Ghislain, what would we do without him. He forever pursued, before the war, elevated social connections, one of those professors who collects fancy company—aristocrats, lawyers, merchants, the idle rich. But this sort of climbing turns out to be very useful in a country with a resistance underground."

"Can we have dinner at the casino?"

"I wish we could, but the less we're seen the better."

"Oh well, the food in the apartment isn't so bad, there's plenty to eat, a lot of it stolen from room-service trays. Last night I had some little lobster legs from behind the claw, a chicken wing, and veal in tomato aspic—most of the veal had been eaten but the aspic was good."

When the bus stopped near the apartment where Mathieu was staying, he kissed Chantal on both cheeks, *goodby* Parisian-style, and said, "Ten in the morning, tomorrow, we'll meet here."

The next day, Mathieu met the couple who owned the house that would serve as a base of operations. They came by taxi to collect Mathieu and Chantal and the first time he saw them his interior warning alarm lit up: not red, but certainly amber.

He had intended to use Daniel for the landing reception but, three days after Daniel's escape from Rouen, Mathieu had received a letter at the Café Welcome. In very oblique language, Daniel had let him know that there had been "some trouble, a bicycle accident near the Carmelite convent north of Rouen," and he went on to say his return to Paris would be delayed, and the friend he'd come to see in Rouen was still there. Mathieu had telephoned the convent, to learn that Daniel had contracted pneumonia, probably from the immersion in icy water during his escape, and would be in bed for some time. Four days before Mathieu took off for Deauville he called again and Daniel was in Paris a day later; but he was still pale and weak, in no shape for the beach operation. So, Mathieu had to improvise, and decided to use Émile, Ghislain's friend who owned the house at Deauville. Émile was now seen climbing out of the taxi to open the door for his wife, Claudette.

The de Boiselliers. Mathieu had heard about them more than once: the most charming couple, *tout Paris* adored them. Seen, before the war, at the best restaurants that nobody yet knew about, where the chef would come out to greet them after the meal. They attended the most exclusive dinner parties, with the politician or intellectual of the week telling confidential stories at the table. They played tennis—well, they skied, they had a box at Longchamp for the horse races.

Émile was a partner at a prominent Parisian advertising agency. Likely he never wrote an advertisement but was brought out to lunch with important clients and he was good at it: he listened graciously, he told funny stories, and it did not hurt that he was an incredibly beautiful man, with extraordinary green eyes, a golden green, set off by the dark complexion of southern Europe, and fine features. He dressed with perfect taste, tending away from formality, and had the softest, most welcoming smile, which made him seem comfortable with whatever was going on around him. What he did to women would not bear description, and it was not so different for men, who are often drawn to the handsomest among them.

And then there was Claudette, who wore her chestnut-brown hair cut short, close to her head, a style complemented by tiny gold-hoop earrings. She had brown eyes, a suntanned face, with lips emphasized by dark red lipstick, all of it perfected by the magicians at the beauty salons of the Sixteenth Arrondissement. Seductive, Mathieu thought, as he watched her glide out of a taxi, but a handful. What word had Ghislain used? *Barracuda,* as Mathieu remembered it. Shaking hands with Mathieu, she looked hungrily into his eyes, mouth partly open. Yes, she was married to a Parisian god but here was something rougher, something rather interesting.

In the small Renault taxi, four people and the driver made for close proximity—Chantal in front, Mathieu in the backseat, a de Boisellier on either side, his cologne and her perfume heavy in the air, her body, thigh and shoulder, much closer to him than it needed to be, her eyes looking innocently out the window but for a conspiratorial glance when the driver took a curve too fast and she was thrown against him and said, "Oh-la-*la.*"

On Mathieu's left, Émile started a conversation. "I want to tell you—Mathieu, right?—how grateful I am to . . ."

Mathieu nodded his head toward the driver—meaning *Let's not use that name in public*—while Chantal cut Émile off by saying, "Oh that's a lovely statue! Do you know who it is?"

"A statesman of the last century," Claudette said. "I'm sure he had a name, but . . ."

When Émile cleared his throat and started to complete his earlier statement, Mathieu cut him off. "Let's wait, Émile—we'll have a good, long talk when we get to your house."

Émile said, "Ah, yes, the house . . . we shall have a glass of wine . . ." As Mathieu had turned his head when Émile spoke, the Parisian god gave him a wink.

It took some time to reach the de Boisellier house, in the countryside south of Deauville, set among orchards and grazing land. Now Mathieu, in his other life, had visited some stately and spectacular homes—sometimes a château, sometimes a grand apartment—but never anything like this. As they rounded a curve in the boxwood-hedged driveway, and the house came into view, Émile saw that Mathieu was impressed and said, "A miracle it's still here—built in the sixteenth century."

As they left the taxi, Claudette meant to push against the leather seat in order to stand up but, by happenstance, her hand found Mathieu's thigh. *"Pardon,"* she said. Had, Mathieu wondered, Émile seen this? Or did he not care? No reaction from Émile, holding the door and taking his wife's hand to help her out of the taxi.

It was a proud couple who gave them the tour: the half-timbered Norman farmhouse with a steeply pitched roof was only fourteen feet wide, with one room leading to the next. There was a double fireplace, to warm a room on either side, and, since there wasn't much space for furnishings, the de Boiselliers' decorator had covered the walls, and the sofas and chairs, with fabric, cotton toile—a rustic scene in cornflower blue and cream.

They settled in the small parlor and Émile produced a bottle of Échezeaux and four crystal glasses. "Shall we drink to our success?" Émile said. After they'd had a sip of wine, he said, "Ghislain didn't go into the details of . . . of what you will want from me. I work in an office in Paris and I know how to do that, but this . . ."

"It won't be so difficult," Mathieu said. "You and I will reach a rendezvous point about two-thirty in the morning—it's just west of the fishing village called Arromanches. We'll wait for a signal from a Royal Navy submarine, then we'll confirm the signal and we'll bring two people, secret operatives, back here and wait for daylight, when Chantal and I will escort them to Paris."

"It doesn't sound, complicated. Do you always have two people, doing these . . . things?"

"These operations, yes, always."

"The way it sounds, well, it could be done by one person."

"There will be heavy duffel bags, we will help to carry them."

Émile nodded, that made sense. "I've never done anything like this in my life, you know, I just hope I don't make a mistake."

"That's not unusual, we've all had to learn as we go, and we'll be helping our country."

"I expect," Chantal said, "that the man who built this house had to bear arms for the king."

"I'm sure you're right," Émile said. "Drink up, everybody, there's another bottle waiting."

Scared, Mathieu thought, but then who wasn't. Changing the subject, Chantal said, "Tell us how you found this wonderful house."

The couple brightened and, taking turns, began to tell a complicated and amusing anecdote, while Mathieu and Chantal—native Parisians, thus adept at conversation—laughed or exclaimed in all the right places. Which led to other avenues of small talk, and so they entertained themselves for an hour and a second bottle of the magnificent Échezeaux. Then, true to the unwritten law of the visit to the country house—they may have gathered at a secret hideout but it was still a visit to a country house—Mathieu and Chantal excused themselves and were led to a guest room. As Claudette stood in the doorway, she said, "I'm going to take the sun on the terrace, would anyone care to join me? Mathieu? Chantal?"

"Thank you," Mathieu said, "but I think we'll stay here."

When Claudette had gone, Chantal said, "That pretty man is one very frightened man, Mathieu, can we rely on him?"

"He will do what needs to be done, frightened or not. And remember, Chantal, he's *French*—not so much afraid of dying as afraid of doing something wrong."

The guest room—walls and coverlets in blue-and-cream toile—had two narrow beds and two windows: one with a view of an apple orchard, the other of a stone-block terrace. While Chantal sat on the room's only chair, taking off her shoes, Mathieu stared out the window. "Look who's here," he said. Chantal joined him and they stood side by side as Claudette, wearing a tiny two-piece bathing suit, walked across the terrace, holding a towel in one hand, a book and eyeglasses in the other. She then commenced to organize herself for sunbathing; spreading the towel, setting book and glasses next to it, taking off her bathing suit, then lying on her right side, facing away from the window. She put on her glasses, found her place in the book, and began to read; a few seconds later, she drew her left leg up, then rested her bent knee on the towel. As the window was open, and Claudette was only thirty feet away, Chantal spoke in a whisper. "Now we have it all, don't we."

Mathieu nodded and said, "We do indeed."

With her clothes off, Claudette had grown smaller, her shape well proportioned, her skin smooth and perfectly tanned. From somewhere beyond the house, cicadas had started up, whirring in the afternoon calm. Claudette turned a page.

"Should I close the curtain?" Mathieu said.

"Not for my sake," Chantal said. "Surely you are enjoying this."

"I am, yes. I never tire of an interesting view."

"Perhaps there is more to come," Chantal said. "Perhaps it is a stimulating book—one wouldn't want to miss that."

Mathieu turned toward Chantal, who had a knowing, woman-of-the-world smile on her lips. When he again looked out the window, Claudette was smoothing her hair back, then her hand disappeared.

"Alas," Mathieu said, "now we'll never know."

"Oh we'll know alright. One's hips move in a very particular way when one is engaged in . . . whatever you like to call it."

"Is it me she wants?" Mathieu said. "Or you? Or both?"

"Perhaps both," Chantal said. "An afternoon treat."

"Have you ever . . . ?"

"I haven't, though I will confess I've thought about it. You?"

"No, more from lack of opportunity than reluctance."

"It's the same for me."

Neither of them made a move to leave the window. Mathieu sensed that Chantal was excited, and wondered how he knew. He was close enough to her that he could hear her breathing, which seemed normal. "Are you also enjoying this, Chantal?"

"Naughty boy, you're not supposed to ask a lady about things like that."

"Even so . . ."

"You'll never know," Chantal said, teasing him, meaning *Yes, I am.*

A few minutes passed, Claudette turned another page, the cicadas whirred. Then Chantal sighed and said, "I guess I've had my moment as voyeur, now I'm going to take a nap, a nap in my underwear, so you will be twice blessed today, Mathieu." She patted him on the arm, then walked over to the narrow bed.

Late that afternoon, Émile telephoned for a taxi, which showed up in a few minutes. As Mathieu climbed into the back, he checked the name and address he'd received in the instructions from Edouard. "The Boucherie Borbal," he told the driver. "In Honfleur, on the Rue de . . ."

"I know where he is, monsieur." This was the same driver they'd had on the previous trip. Shifting up through the gears, then speeding along a country lane, he said, "Nice people, the de Boiselliers."

"They are," Mathieu said, not encouraging conversation.

"Generous people."

"I'm sure."

The driver gave up and, twenty minutes later, they reached

Honfleur. Across the Seine estuary from Le Havre, Honfleur was a fishing village with tourist hotels spread along the waterfront. The Boucherie Borbal, on a market street in the town behind the port, had a gold-painted horse's head above the entry, signaling a *boucherie chevaline,* a horsemeat butcher. Inside, the shop smelled like old meat and had abundant flies, despite well-visited strips of fly-paper dangling from the ceiling. Behind the counter, Borbal himself, Mathieu guessed, a giant of a man with ears flat to his head, a thick neck, red face and red hands, who wore a bloodstained apron. Mathieu waited for him to finish serving a customer, then said, "Are you Monsieur Borbal?"

"That's me. What can I get you? I've plenty of offal, some sausage, and, as you see, rabbit." Skinned rabbits, a fresh pink, with fur left on the feet to prove that the rabbit was in fact a rabbit, hung from hooks above the counter.

Mathieu used the identification protocol specified in Edouard's instructions: "Do you sell newspapers here?"

Borbal was lost for a moment, then, as recognition dawned, said, "Ahh, so it's *that* sort of affair." He closed one eye and tapped his index finger on the side of his nose—*You and I share a secret*—then said, his voice lowered, "Let's go out back."

Parked in a courtyard behind the shop, a butcher's van: a small, boxlike vehicle with a blunt hood, tall enough to appear unstable, that was colored a grimy white and had BOUCHERIE BORBAL painted on the side. Borbal took a jerrycan from a shed built against the wall of the courtyard and began filling the van's gas tank. "How long will you want it?"

"Tonight and tomorrow night. Maybe longer."

"Well, you can have it for a few days, but I'll need it later in the week. The price for two days is ten thousand francs—more if you keep it longer. And, I'm telling you, *mon ami,* take care of it. I won't ask where you're going."

Mathieu reached into his pocket and, from a fat wad of francs, counted out ten thousand, some two thousand American dollars.

The butcher wet his thumb and counted the money. "Expensive, this kind of secret *merde*," he said, "but that's how it is. Slow around the corners, heh? This old lady will turn on her side if you go too fast."

Mathieu held out another thousand francs and said, "I will want the use of your apron, Monsieur Borbal."

"What? Look at it, it's . . ." Then he shook his head and said, "Stupid old Borbal! Of course you must have it." He undid the string tied twice around his middle and handed the apron to Mathieu. Who thanked him and slid into the driver's seat—caved in by the butcher's weight—turned on the ignition and shoved the tall gearshift into first gear. "Easy on the clutch!" Borbal shouted as Mathieu drove off.

When, a half hour later, Mathieu reached the de Boisellier house, he wondered if he should turn around and drive off: a BMW motorcycle was propped on its kickstand by the front entry. But he had a lot to do before nightfall, so parked the van and knocked on the door. Émile answered the knock right away, eyes wide open, face taut with anxiety. "Oh, it's Monsieur *Richard,* dear." He came down hard on the fake name, warning his wife, his voice noticeably higher than usual.

Claudette, now wearing a white sundress, in a cotton thin enough to more than suggest what was underneath, hurried to the door. "What a nice surprise—another visitor!" Mathieu followed the couple to the parlor where a German officer rose to his feet, ready to be introduced.

"Allow me to present Monsieur Richard," Émile said. "This is our friend, Hauptmann Fischer, who has come to pay a visit."

"Pleased to meet you," Mathieu said, shaking hands with the officer—a muscular fellow with coal-black hair, very dark, colorless eyes, and a face—heavy bones, thick features—just short of brutal. His hand was bigger than Mathieu's, his grip powerful.

"We're having a whiskey," Émile said, moving to an array of bottles on a wicker drinks cart, where he poured a generous splash of scotch into a glass, added soda water from a siphon, and handed it to Mathieu. "Klaus is stationed in Le Havre," Émile said.

"And do you like the city?" Mathieu said.

"Not so much. It's a dump—docks and cranes, sailors' bars." His French was slow but precise, language-school French. "Tell me, Monsieur Richard, how do you come to know Émile and Claudette?"

"Émile and I are in the same business, advertising, though I'm at a smaller agency."

"Work friends," Fischer said. "It's the same with us, me and Émile. Before the war I was an advertising manager with the Opel company and I would always see Émile and Claudette when I came to Paris." Something about the way he pronounced her name drew Mathieu's attention.

"A satisfying job, I would think—Opel makes excellent cars."

"You have a place up here?" Fischer said.

"Wouldn't I like that but no, I stay at the Régence." *You must get away from here,* Mathieu told himself, *before Fischer sees the van.* And he wondered where Chantal was hiding.

"Do you play the tables?" Fischer said.

Polite conversation, but Mathieu sensed he was probing for information. "Now and then, but mostly I enjoy the ocean bathing."

Claudette appeared from the kitchen, carrying little silver bowls of toasted almonds on a tray. When she stood in front of Mathieu to offer the tray he could smell the strong scent she'd used and he thought she had somehow—he had no idea how—changed her makeup. "Will you join us for dinner, Monsieur Richard?"

"I'm afraid I can't—I'm down here to see friends and I thought I'd stop by since I was in the neighborhood."

Émile, trying for a new topic in the conversation, said, "Klaus works with the Civil Affairs Bureau in Le Havre."

"Oh? What's that like?"

Fischer shrugged. "Frankly? It's boring, military life isn't much my style but when the war started I had to enlist. However, lucky for me, I wound up near the de Boiselliers."

The small talk continued, back and forth, this and that, until Mathieu, with his acute sense of social time, felt that the requisite forty-five minutes had passed and then, with regret, stood up to leave.

"Very nice to meet you, Monsieur Richard," Fischer said. "Perhaps when I get to Paris I'll telephone and we can have lunch. What is the name of your agency?"

Mathieu gave him the name of a Parisian agency that had closed after the Occupation.

The van didn't start on the first try. Mathieu closed his eyes, counted to ten, said something close to a prayer, pulled out the choke and, after a few shuddering coughs, the engine came to life. He turned the van around and drove out the country lane until he reached the main road, then, a few miles further on, pulled off the pavement and parked on the weedy shoulder, thanking heaven that he'd decided not to wear the bloodstained apron.

30 May. After midnight, Mathieu and Chantal were in the kitchen with the de Boiselliers, preparing for that night's operation. Émile was bright and talkative. As he stood at the kitchen counter, pouring Échezeaux into a thermos, Mathieu saw that he held the lip of the bottle against the rim of the thermos because his hands were shaking. Chantal and Claudette stood at the kitchen table, making sandwiches of ham on thickly buttered baguettes. Chantal, reminiscing about the afternoon, said, "If this happens again, I'll have to find a better place to hide. Your closet is not the place to spend three hours."

"Under the bed?" Claudette said. "When you fix up a house, you don't think about places to hide."

"The cellar is no more than a dirt floor and stone walls," Émile said. "Maybe the attic . . ."

Mathieu was sitting across from the sandwich makers at the kitchen table, loading a spare clip for the Beretta automatic. "I'm sure the closet was bad enough, but I had to pass the time parked by a road and some farmer's dogs came to the van to see what smelled so good—they barked and barked and scratched at the doors and they wouldn't go away."

"Nothing we could have done," Émile said. "Fischer telephoned from somewhere outside Deauville and we had to invite him over."

"Well, we survived it," Mathieu said. "But I wouldn't trust Hauptmann Fischer if I were you."

"He's just lonely," Claudette said. "In a foreign city, nobody he can talk to . . ."

"How sad for him," Chantal said.

"The thermos is full," Émile announced, screwing the metal top on. "We should save some for the agents, Mathieu. 'Welcome back to France.'"

"Would you like to have some coffee with you?" Claudette said. "We can put it in a wine bottle."

Émile laughed. "I don't think I'll need coffee to stay awake, not tonight." He left the kitchen and returned a few minutes later wearing a worn and faded *bleu de travail* outfit, jacket and trousers. "How do I look?" he said.

"Where did you find *that*?" Claudette said.

"In the garden shed—it's what Henri wears when he works in the garden. It's not a proper butcher's costume but it will have to do."

Mathieu looked at his watch and said, "Time to go, Émile."

The mood in the kitchen changed. As Émile and Claudette embraced, she whispered something in his ear. For Mathieu and Chantal, a Parisian-style farewell kiss. "You be careful," Chantal said, her eyes shining. "Did you hear me?"

He took her hand as he said, "Yes, we will be careful, Chantal, as much as we can."

• • •

By the time they passed the casino at Ouistreham, the weather had changed: a drizzling rain, an overcast sky, with no sign of the waning moon. The operation's planners would have been pleased—for them, the darker the better. The sentry hut that Mathieu had seen stood high on a dune, at road level, and the sentry, when he saw approaching lights, walked out onto the road, rifle slung over his shoulder, and held up a hand. Foreseeing this eventuality, Mathieu had consulted a German phrase book and cobbled together a sentence, which he had memorized: "We are going to Saint-Aubin-sur-Mer"—a fishing village west of Ouistreham—"to pick up a horse that died." The sentry managed to untangle Mathieu's version of his language, saw the name on the van and the bloody apron, then gestured to Mathieu to drive on.

The headlights cut two furrows in the darkness. Mathieu leaned close to the windshield and squinted down the road—the windshield wipers were almost useless, leaving wide streaks as they swept across the glass. And, after the road passed the casino, it narrowed to little more than the width of one car, its surface—ancient, cracked, macadam paving—bearing deep potholes. Every time they hit one, Mathieu feared for the tires. To his right, the sea, he could hear the pounding of the waves, the windows left open to the rain because of the smell in the interior of the van.

Émile lit a cigarette for himself and one for Mathieu. "I am sorry about Fischer showing up, I hope he doesn't cause you trouble."

"Likely he won't, but, I should tell you, this is no time to be friends with a Boche."

"He's more Claudette's friend than mine." Émile let that hang for a moment, then said, "And nobody tells Claudette what to do. She's from a wealthy family, her grandfather owns an olive-oil mill down south, at Nyons."

"Do they make your life comfortable?"

"Oh yes. They love their little girl and she must have everything she wants."

"And has she other . . . friends?"

"Yes, as do I. The first few years we were married, everything was as it should be, then . . . how to put it, we got bored."

Going around a curve, the van slid on the wet surface, the right rear tire spun in the sand by the road and, with power only in the left rear tire, the van was turned sideways by the time Mathieu got it stopped. He swore, then climbed out onto the road. As he knelt by the tires, Émile joined him. "We can back up," Mathieu said, "but the rear wheels are going to wind up in the sand."

"*Merde,*" Émile said, cupping his hand over his cigarette to keep it dry.

They got into the van, Mathieu started the engine, then shifted into reverse, backing up until the front tires cleared the sand. Then he turned the steering wheel hard left, found the friction point on the clutch, and gave the engine the barest taste of fuel, but the rear wheels spun, and spun faster as an angry Mathieu stamped on the gas pedal. "Fuck this thing," he said. "You drive, I'll push." He circled the van, pressed his hands on the rear doors and shouted, "Now!" Émile tried the inch-at-a-time technique, Mathieu strained, using all the strength he had until, finally, the tires found traction and the van was again on the road.

When Mathieu got his breath back he said, "You did that well, you can drive."

"I used to like to drive, when I had a car—a little MG, a two-seater convertible."

"What became of it?"

"When the Germans were approaching Paris we ran with everybody else, but we only got as far as Fontainebleau. We gave up and left the car in a garage, then we walked toward Paris, and finally got a lift in the back of a truck."

"You think it's still there?"

"Maybe, maybe not. We'll find out when the Germans go home."

They passed through the village of Saint-Aubin, not a light on, and the road got worse as they drove west. "Not much up here," Émile said. "And nobody fixes the roads."

"That's the point," Mathieu said. "The Normandy coast has some good-sized cities: Dieppe, Le Havre, Caen. The people in London who planned this had to find the most deserted beach they could, so that's where the reception will take place—just past a cluster of fishermen's houses outside Arromanches, it doesn't really have a name."

Mathieu looked at his watch and said, "Not long now, another half hour."

"We'll do better on the return trip—this thing is like all the vans, too light in the back. Once we get the duffel bags and the agents, we'll have some weight."

"You've driven a van before?"

"Oh yes, about ten minutes ago."

Arromanches was less of a village than Saint-Aubin and just as dark. Mathieu drove another mile, stopped when he saw a few weathered cottages gathered at the foot of a sagging dock, then turned onto a muddy track that led to the cottages. As the van crept slowly through the mud, a dog let the village know that strangers were about and was soon joined by others. Mathieu found a path that crossed in front of the cottages and stopped at the last one. "Would it be better to park on the beach by the reception site?" Émile said.

"Safer over here," Mathieu said. "There's a German patrol boat that cruises up and down the shore, they would see the van and they might radio somebody."

From the cottage, an old man wearing a sou'wester raincoat over his nightshirt walked toward them, a shotgun held in one hand, a retriever dog by his side. "What do you want here?" he said.

"We're headed for Bayeux," Mathieu said, naming the small city below Arromanches. "We can't drive on this damned road anymore and we decided we'd stop for the night and sleep in the van."

The old man thought it over. "I guess you're welcome," he said.

"Sorry to disturb you, monsieur, but the road . . ."

"Yes, yes, I know, the fat-asses in the province office won't spend the money to fix it. Well, good night to you."

As he turned and walked back to his cottage, Émile had a big grin on his face. "What a mustache! He looked like a walrus."

"A lifetime of fishing will do that," Mathieu said. "Now, let's go for a walk, Émile, the black rocks should be another mile from here." He took off his butcher's apron and left it on the driver's seat.

They set out walking west, away from the fishing village. The drizzle had turned to a steady rain and Mathieu in his thin, cotton jacket and Émile in his work clothes were soon soaked. In the darkness, they could see white combers breaking on the sand. They were silent for a time, then Mathieu said, "What did you say Fischer did in Le Havre?"

"He told us he was with the Civil Affairs Bureau."

"And that is . . . ?"

Émile shrugged. "They deal with the local population, I guess."

"Do you think they're some kind of secret police?"

"Good God I hope not. But, I agree with you, there's something about him, he is forever . . . curious."

"What does Claudette say?"

"She doesn't talk about him. She doesn't talk about any of them—it's her private life."

"I understand, but this goes beyond the chic arrangements of the Sixteenth. He could be using her, to work his way into the confidence of people who won't associate with the occupation forces . . . people who know things the Germans would like to find out."

"You mean a spy, don't you."

"I do. It's time for you to have a talk with your wife, Émile. I know how it is with Parisian couples who have lovers—bad manners to speak openly, everything must be 'understood,' but nonetheless . . ."

At the prospect of such a talk, Émile sighed.

"It won't be easy, Claudette won't like it, this is not the *mauvais quart d'heure*"—a bad fifteen minutes when your mate finds out you're having an affair—"this is serious. If Fischer is what I think he is, life could go very wrong for both of you—it's worth a fight with your wife to avoid that."

They had to work at it, walking on soft sand, breathing hard, surf pounding forty yards away. Mathieu raised his wrist to his eyes and managed to make out the time—a few minutes until two in the morning, he wanted to be at the reception site well before the two-thirty signal time. Once again, he made sure of the flashlight in the pocket of his trousers. "Are we on time?" Émile said.

"We are, but we're moving slower than I thought we would."

"Only a mile, you said, but . . ."

Suddenly, a bright light appeared ahead of them, sweeping slowly in their direction. Émile managed to say "What . . ." before Mathieu grabbed him by the collar of his jacket and they fell full-length together. Mathieu said, "Turn your face away from the light and do *not* move."

Émile did as Mathieu directed, trying to spit sand out of his mouth. As the light crept toward them, Émile said, "What is it?"

"The patrol boat, on its eastern run."

The light came nearer, passed over them as Mathieu held his breath, then returned, lingered for a few seconds, once again headed east, and was turned off. Mathieu could just hear, almost lost in the roar of the surf, the thrumming of a powerful engine some way out to sea. "I think they saw us," Émile said.

"They saw *something*—whatever they thought it was didn't interest them. Still, don't move, they play tricks with their searchlight, turn it on and off." Mathieu gave it another minute, silently counting off the seconds, then slowly turned his head: when the light went back on it was well east of them. Again they walked west, now moving to the hard sand left by the outgoing tide.

. . .

At two-fifteen in the morning, they reached the rock formation. What they had first seen as a ghostly bulk rising in the darkness was, up close, some thirty feet high: smooth, black basalt shining with rain. White foam floated past the base as the tidal ebb ran back to the sea and, in the distance, whitecaps curled over the crests of the heavy swells.

Seeking a vantage point, Mathieu thought that the beachside wall of the formation could be climbed, got his fingers in a crevice above his head and tried to haul himself up, but the soles of his shoes skidded on the slick surface. Sloshing through the water by the wall that met the tide, he tried again, found a narrow shelf that rose fifteen feet above the sand and slithered up on his belly. A moment later, Émile joined him, finding space to flatten out at Mathieu's feet. Mathieu retrieved the flashlight—rubber coated as the planners had specified—and aimed it out to sea. Two-thirty passed, then two-forty. And, at three in the morning, only darkness.

"They're late," Mathieu said, his voice rising above the crash of the waves.

"Maybe something happened . . ."

"If they don't appear, we're instructed to try again tomorrow night."

"Well, dawn is—"

Then, the signal.

A light from the sea, farther out than Mathieu expected and very bright, it shone for three seconds, went out, then returned for another three seconds. As Mathieu confirmed the signal with the same sequence, he could just hear Émile's voice, tight and emotional as he said, almost to himself, "*Vive la France.*"

By the glare of the signal lamp, Mathieu had been able to make out a long, dark shape lying atop the water, a submarine. Something he'd never actually seen, only the cinema version, and he found the real thing sinister, clandestine, deadly. Then an inflatable rubber boat materialized from the gloom, rising and falling with the swells and paddled by two men, one in front of the other. The boat would make land to the west of the formation, so Mathieu and Émile slid down from their vantage point to meet it. Excited, they ran a little way out into the water and waved their arms. When the craft was almost ashore, they grabbed the rope line that circled the inflated pontoons of the hull and dragged the boat up the sand as far as they could.

The two agents, faces darkened with lampblack and wearing rubber suits, climbed out quickly and one of them spontaneously threw his arms around Mathieu, who said, "Welcome home, monsieur, welcome," his voice unsteady. The man who had embraced him said, "I am called Gerard, and this is Jean-Luc."

"I'm known as Mathieu, and my friend is Émile." The four then shook hands as though meeting by chance in a café.

There were two duffel bag–sized metal containers in the boat, Mathieu took hold of one of them and, at first, could barely move it. "Heavy, heh?" Gerard said with a grin, taking the other end and helping Mathieu roll the container out of the boat. Next to them, Jean-Luc and Émile had done the same thing. "Now the boat," Gerard said, pulling a plug so that the pontoons began to deflate, while Jean-Luc jumped up and down on them, trying to force the air out. Both agents wore knapsacks with entrenching tools strapped to their sides and now began to dig, working fast until they had a grave-sized trench some three feet deep. Jean-Luc, breathing hard, threw the rubber shell into the trench, then both agents wriggled free of their rubber suits, tossed them on top, and began to fill in the trench. "We busted our balls practicing this, so last time and not sorry," Gerard said as he worked.

He was about thirty years old, Mathieu guessed, a short, thick-bodied fellow with sandy hair. Jean-Luc was older, balding and lean, and had close-set eyes and a certain cast to his features, as though he were about to become angry—you would not, Mathieu thought, ask him for directions in the street.

They were almost done—they'd left enough space for the entrenching tools, threw these in last, then all four kicked sand over them. "This seems like the proper moment," Émile said, taking the thermos from his jacket and unscrewing the cap. "Some Échezeaux, to celebrate your return to France."

Jean-Luc took a sip and raised his eyebrows in appreciation. "It is kind of you, monsieur, and very good." When the thermos had been passed around, the two agents took cloths from their knapsacks and began wiping the lampblack from their faces. "Where are you gents from?" Gerard said, calling them *mecs,* a working-class usage.

"We are both from Paris," Mathieu said. At this, both agents seemed slightly surprised—they had not expected that the operatives awaiting them would be sophisticated Parisians.

"I was born in a village near Nantes," Gerard said. "But I'm a professional soldier, so I haven't seen home for quite a while. I was in North Africa when the war ended and made a run for London to join the Free French. Jean-Luc is from Brittany."

"Long ago," Jean-Luc said. "I was a colonial police officer in Saigon, when the war started. Served out there for twenty years. Some of the Indo-Chinese—communists, whatnot—didn't want us there and resorted to sabotage. It was my job to learn how they managed their explosives and timers and I became a specialist." After a moment he patted the container and said, "I'm the instructor—Gerard is the radio operator—so now it's my turn to play on the other side." Mathieu recalled Edouard's description of what the agents would bring with them: time-pencil detonators, fuse cord, plastic explosive—and plenty of it, given the weight of the containers.

With their rubber suits off, the agents were now in civilian clothes and had been, Mathieu saw, very carefully dressed—in plain, inexpensive outfits and much-worn felt hats and looked something like artisans of the upper trades, electricians perhaps, on their day off. "Shall we get moving?" Mathieu said, reaching for the strap at the end of one container.

Jean-Luc looked at his watch and said, "Not yet. The patrol

boat is due back in ten minutes, so the best place for us is behind the rocks." They hauled the containers over the sand, then sat with their backs against the formation. They saw the light of the patrol boat from a long way east as it swept back and forth across the beach. Gerard swore at it, "*Espèce de merde,* I hate these bastards."

"You'll see a lot of them," Émile said. "They are all over the place, hard to avoid, particularly in Paris."

"Well, we will be based there for a time," Gerard said. "Then we'll travel . . . recruit and train, that's our job."

"Will you find enough recruits?" Émile said.

"The English spy service has been operating here for a long time, they lost some agents—that's how this work goes—but they found plenty of people who say they want to fight."

In time, the patrol boat passed by and the four set off with the containers. They had to stop and rest twice—Émile was game and did his best but he was in no condition for this kind of effort. Eventually they reached the fishing village and, when the dogs started up, the old fisherman, a woman who Mathieu guessed was his wife, and his retriever stood and watched as the containers were stowed in the van. When Jean-Luc saw the name painted on the side he laughed and said, "A butcher! Well, that's just right for us." He climbed into the passenger seat while Émile and Gerard lay down in the back. Then the fisherman came to the window and said, with some gravity, "I wish you good luck, gentlemen." Sitting beside Mathieu, Jean-Luc remarked on the condition of the road, then looked at his watch. "We're supposed to be in Deauville before sunrise, which is at four-fifty."

"We won't quite make that," Mathieu said, "but it will still be dawn when we arrive. Then, the following morning, we'll go down to Paris."

Mathieu drove with full concentration, hands gripping the steering wheel, babying the van over the puddles and the potholes hidden beneath them. The rain had abated to a thin drizzle, blown against the windshield by the offshore breeze. Above, the sky was clearing, with light from a thin slice of moon reflected on the storm clouds as they floated inland.

When they were almost at the Ouistreham casino, they came around a sharp curve and saw the sentry, standing by the side of the road and talking to an officer, who was leaning on the hood of a command car. The two were smoking and talking and appeared to be relaxed. "The officer's come to pick him up," Jean-Luc said. From the back of the van, having no view of the road, Gerard said, "Trouble?"

"Maybe, we'll see, but prepare to use your weapon."

Mathieu said, "That's the sentry who stopped us on the way out."

"Slow down and wave to him, he might let you drive on." He paused, then said, "But, with his officer there . . . Are you armed?"

"Yes."

"Where is it?"

"In the waistband of my trousers."

The sentry ambled out onto the road and raised his hand. Mathieu put on the brakes. The sentry remembered him and said "Home?" as he pointed up the road.

Mathieu nodded and said yes.

The sentry started to move off, but the officer was curious. Still leaning on the hood of his car, some ten feet away, he said, in phrase-book French, "What do you carry?"

"A horse that died," Mathieu said. "We're taking it back to the shop in Honfleur."

The officer thought it over, then stood up straight and walked toward the van. "I want to see. Open the doors."

Mathieu and Jean-Luc both got out on the road and followed the officer to the rear of the van. As the officer waited for the doors to be opened, Jean-Luc shot him in the back of the head and he collapsed without a sound. Mathieu ran around the van and fired twice at the sentry, who had frozen at the sound of the pistol shot. Mathieu had apparently missed, because the sentry aimed his rifle and fired two rounds. Mathieu shot at him again and this time he cried out and fell backward. When Jean-Luc reached him, knelt down and put his pistol to the man's temple, the sentry mumbled the German words for "No, don't," but Jean-Luc pulled the trigger, next walked to the officer's body and did the same thing. From the rear of the van, Mathieu heard an angry curse from Gerard and when he opened the doors he saw that Émile had been hit. Lying on his back he was lifeless: eyes closed, body completely still, while a thin trickle of blood ran from his hairline and down his face. Jean-Luc brushed Mathieu aside and put two fingers on Émile's neck. "Still alive," he said. "Now what? We can't leave him here, to be captured and interrogated, we can't take him to a hospital with a gunshot wound. We just killed two German soldiers—this area will be *crawling* with field police, Gestapo, SS, so then . . ."

"Then what?" Mathieu said.

Jean-Luc's answer was silence, his pistol held by his trouser leg.

"We'll take him back to Deauville. There's surely a doctor in Deauville we can trust."

"You know this for a fact?"

"You are not going to shoot him, Jean-Luc," Mathieu said. He had not put the Beretta away.

"What are you going to do about it if I do?"

"Get back in the van, we have to get the hell away from here, *now*."

Meanwhile, Gerard had taken a first-aid kit from his knapsack and was using a gauze pad to clean the blood away, then, to stop the bleeding, he pressed the gauze against the wound. "It wasn't fatal," he said. "He's unconscious but not dead. Not yet. The sentry must have fired at an angle, both bullets went through the side panel, then hit the opposite side and ricocheted, and then one of them hit your friend. If he doesn't go into shock he may survive. Do you have a blanket? Keeping him warm helps, with shock."

"We don't," Mathieu said. He gunned the engine and drove off as fast as the van would go.

From the back, Gerard said, "Well, in the future, you should try to have a blanket with you, there's a lot you can do with a blanket—carry a wounded man or a corpse, use it under the tires to get free of snow, all sorts of useful things." His tone was casual, as though what had happened on the road was, to him, nothing new.

In the passenger seat, Jean-Luc lit a cigarette and began to re-load his service automatic. "He's right, you should have a blanket."

It was dawn by the time they reached Deauville, the early light was soft and gray and the birds had begun to sing. Jean-Luc and Gerard carried Émile, Mathieu knocked on the door. Claudette answered—still wearing the white sundress, she had stayed awake waiting for them to return—and, when she saw Émile, saw the bandage with a red bloodstain around his head, she screamed and burst into tears. "What have you done to him?" she wailed, then ran to Émile, fell to her knees and put her arms around him. "Oh God," she said.

"He's unconscious," Mathieu said. "He was wounded by a bul-let that ricocheted inside the van—it's important that he get medi-cal help, as soon as possible."

Chantal took Claudette by the waist and gently eased her away. "Let's go to the telephone, he needs a doctor, Claudette—is there a doctor nearby who's a friend?"

"Yes, I think so."

As Émile was carried to the bedroom, Mathieu ran to the guest room and gathered up both toile-covered quilts. Meanwhile, Chan-tal held Claudette up and walked her to the parlor, where she opened a drawer in the table that held the telephone and found an address book but, hands trembling, had difficulty turning the pages.

Chantal took the address book, saying, "Let me help you, Clau-dette, what is the doctor's name?"

"Laroux."

Chantal dialed the number, handed the receiver to Claudette, and, as they waited for the call to be answered, gave her a clean handkerchief. Dabbing at her eyes, Claudette said, "Oh Paul, thank God you're there. Émile has been in an accident and is badly hurt, please come as soon as possible." She waited the length of a brief answer, then said, "Thank you, thank you."

Mathieu, having dropped off the quilts in the bedroom, reached Claudette as she hung up the phone, put an arm around her and held her tight. "I want you to drink some brandy, to settle yourself, because you'll have to deal with the doctor."

"On the wicker drinks cart," Claudette said. "There's cognac there. Hennessy."

Ten minutes later, the doctor appeared—another Parisian god with an apartment in Paris and a house in Deauville. Mathieu and the two agents hid in the cellar, Claudette stood beside the doctor as he examined the wound. "What did this? Something small, at speed. Could it be a bullet wound?" Claudette didn't say a word and the doctor looked up at her; clearly, her silence meant *yes.* Next he cleaned the wound, sewed it up, put on a fresh bandage, then, preparing an injection, said, "I'm going to bring him back to consciousness, do you want to tell me what happened? An accident? A jealous husband?"

Claudette put her hand on the doctor's arm. "You can't tell anyone about this, Paul. Émile could be arrested . . . by the Germans."

"Very well, then. I understand. Something secret, involving . . . *Émile?* I wouldn't have guessed that he would . . . but life is changing here."

31 May. Late that afternoon, Mathieu used the de Boisellier telephone to call Olivia Brun, an old friend from his former life, and asked her to meet him at her office early the next day. Then, at two in the morning, with Gerard and Jean-Luc, he drove south, timing

the van's arrival in Paris for five-thirty, the end of curfew, when they would join the procession that fed the city: farm trucks, vans, ox-carts, and wagons pulled by horses, all of them headed for the Les Halles market. Once upon a time, German officials had ordered the Paris police to control this traffic but, as much as the Germans liked to make rules, the French liked to break them—the farmers, fishermen, and market gardeners, great believers in *order* but anar-chists at heart, knew how to create chaos and did so. *Oh, look, a bullock has got loose and is running up the Rue Rambuteau!* Thus the *flics* had given up and arranged to be elsewhere.

As the procession moved, at the speed of an oxcart, toward Les Halles, Mathieu turned south, heading up into the Sixth Ar-rondissement until he reached the administration building at the edge of the Jardin du Luxembourg. When he rang the bell, a *gar-dien* came to the door, stood swaying for a moment, then said, "The hell do you think you're going? There's nobody here yet."

"Mademoiselle Brun is waiting for me in her office."

"Mmm, then, well, come in." The smell of wine on his breath was overpowering.

"I know where it is," Mathieu said, climbing the marble stair-case. Olivia was waiting in her office, with a big, excited smile for him when he walked in the door. She jumped up from her chair and kissed him on both cheeks, holding his head in her hands, turning it left and right. A mousy woman in her forties, she helped to man-age the public gardens. She had thin hair pulled back and held by a clip, and wore tortoiseshell eyeglasses, her shoulders a little slumped as though by the weight of the world. She sat back down and said, "When you telephoned I was mystified. I couldn't imagine what you wanted. At six in the morning, no less!"

"Strange as it may seem, Olivia dear, I would like to use one of your greenhouses. And you can't tell a single soul about it."

She stared at him, then said, "*What* are you doing? No, don't tell me . . . if it's something secret . . . have you become a *résis-tant?*"

Mathieu nodded.

"Oh my dear," she said, putting a hand over her heart. "So now I will be one as well." She sat back down and said, "Yes, it makes sense, you are the type. But, dangerous, no?"

"Of course it is. Now, I am driving a van . . ."

"Well, use the service road and pick any greenhouse you like, they're all open. You won't harm the plants, will you?"

"I won't touch them."

"Then, what . . . ?"

Mathieu closed his eyes and shook his head—*Don't ask,* then said, "We will need shovels and a rake."

"There's a shed that adjoins the second greenhouse with an open padlock on the door—the key was lost so often we no longer bother to lock it. All the tools you want in there."

"And I have friends who will be visiting the greenhouse, not often, now and then."

"Just at the end of curfew is best, there's nobody around." After a pause she said, "Or perhaps they are people who know how to evade the police."

"And the *gardien*?"

"You won't need to come into this building, and, anyhow . . ." She made a fist, extended her thumb, put it to her lips and tilted her head back, a gesture that imitated someone drinking from a bottle—"he's always drunk, spends most of his time asleep. Your friends needn't worry about *him.*"

"Then, I'll be going. Thank you for your help, Olivia."

"May I tell Frieda?"

Frieda had been her lover for years, and the two had been friends with Mathieu for a long time. "Only her, nobody else, agreed?"

"That will make it easier for me. We wondered where you were, the last year or so—we had such good times together, laughed and laughed, we miss you."

"These days I have to keep to myself, I hope you understand."

"Yes, of course, a secret life." With a rueful smile—*Maybe I won't ever see you again*—she kissed him goodby.

Walking back to the van, Mathieu felt relief. The operation's planners had directed him to find a hiding place for the containers and he had, after a lot of thinking, decided to use a greenhouse, then realized he had an old friend he could trust who worked at the public gardens, and Olivia had not disappointed him.

It was sweltering in the greenhouse, with thick, humid air scented by dried manure used as fertilizer, and Mathieu, Jean-Luc, and Gerard, bathed in sweat, worked with their shirts off. The beds of blue violets, waiting to be planted by the gardeners, were divided by gravel paths. Mathieu chose one of them, used a shovel to break up the gravel, then was joined by the others as they raked it to one side and began to dig into the exposed ground; exhausting work—the earth, compacted for years, was hard as a rock. But, slowly, enough dirt was removed to allow space for the containers. Before they were buried, Jean-Luc opened one of them and removed a few packets wrapped in oiled paper, which he stowed in a small valise. "Enough to start with," he said, "then we'll have to come back for more."

"And do this all over again," Gerard said, crumbling leftover dirt with his hands and scattering it over the violets. As they walked out the door, Jean-Luc said to Mathieu, "You'll have to get rid of the van, you know, somebody will surely remember seeing it."

"Don't worry about that," Mathieu said. "I have friends with a garage, they'll repaint it and change the name, BOUCHERIE CHEVALINE maybe, and fix the holes, because Monsieur Borbal will need his van back."

Jean-Luc shook his head. "If that's how you do things . . . ," he said.

"I may need it again," Mathieu said, rather than telling Jean-Luc that yes, this *was* the way he did things. "Now, where can I take you?"

Jean-Luc gave him the address—the Hôtel de Quercy where he'd met with Edouard. At the gate of the wild garden in back of the *hôtel particulier,* Gerard and Jean-Luc wished him luck, then Mathieu headed for the garage.

. . .

At last, back at the Saint-Yves, Mathieu was lying half asleep on the sofa, Mariana stretched out beside him as the spring dusk faded away over the Rue Dauphine. Mathieu felt as though he had been away for a long time but it had only been a few days. Staring out his window, he went back over the operation and the people he'd encountered, especially Olivia. He missed her, he missed Frieda and other old friends, they had been important to him, as much as he had of family.

He'd met Olivia and Frieda in his late twenties, on an August night when Paris steamed in its annual heat wave, at a party given by a famously dreadful artist. Dreadful perhaps, but he had a houseboat docked on the Seine and gave the liveliest parties: smoky and loud, with a dense crowd of poets, artists, models, slumming aristocrats, and strays from all over Europe. Now and again, couples would leave, hand in hand, for the privacy of the upper deck. As the party wore itself out, a few of the guests had been invited back to the apartment Olivia shared with Frieda. To Mathieu, it soon became evident that the two women liked to have a *very* good time: champagne was served, hashish smoked, cocaine snorted, and everybody laughed and laughed.

In time, the guests staggered off into the night and Mathieu was the last one left. The three sat on sofa pillows on the floor, smoked and talked, had a little more of this, a little more of that. Eventually, Olivia, fanning herself with her hand, said, "I'm too hot, my friends, so . . ." and took off her blouse and skirt. In bra and panties, she had a mildly excessive low-slung rear end and small, shapeless breasts, but erotic energy flowed from her like scented smoke, like burning incense.

"Well, why not," Frieda said, and did what Olivia had done. She was Swiss, a heavy woman with coarse, curly black hair, a round face, and eyes that sparkled—lit by the pleasure of being alive. She patted the pillow in front of her and spread her legs so that Olivia could sit with her back braced against her. Frieda relit the hash pipe, held her breath, then coughed out the smoke. She smiled at Mathieu and said, teasing him, "Are you shy?"

He wasn't, and stripped down to his boxer shorts. A little later, Olivia dozed off. "Up, up, *chérie*," Frieda said, taking Olivia by the hand and leading her to the bedroom. Looking back over her shoulder, she said to Mathieu, "There's just enough room for you—it's too late to go home." Out the window it was already dawn, with the red-streaked sky of another hot day. Frieda pulled the cover and sheet off the bed, settled on the far side of the bottom sheet, clasped her hands atop her stomach, and closed her eyes. Olivia lay next to her, with Mathieu on her left, close enough so that Mathieu could feel the heat of her body. Lying still, he wondered what, if anything, would happen next. A few minutes later, Olivia's hand came visiting but was not there long, being the recipient of a playful slap as an amused Frieda whispered, "Naughty girl!" From Olivia, a whispered response and a giggle, then Mathieu turned on his side and fell sound asleep.

In the morning, the three went off to a fancy café where the croissants were crisped with honey and ordered *café calva*—coffee spiked with calvados, and they were fast friends for a long time after that, until the Occupation, when they became part of Mathieu's other life. But no longer.

16 June. Otto Broehm—former senior inspector of the Hamburg police department, now major in the Wehrmacht's military police—sat in his office at the Majestic Hotel and idly picked through a stack of papers left on his desk by his adjutant. Most of it meant nothing—the daily output of a grinding bureaucracy speaking to itself. Then he looked over at the telephone, which didn't ring, but, he thought, give it time. Any day, the bigwigs in Berlin who'd ordered him to destroy the escape lines would be calling. Pleasant and courteous to be sure, yet in their voices a note of *pleasant and courteous, for now.*

He returned to his papers: a long list from Madame Passot. She was his official liaison to the Vichy administration and had sent him a carbon copy of a list, originating from the office of the warden of Fresnes prison, with an underlined item: <u>Prisoner Kusar, Stefan—448601,</u> and a handwritten note in the margin, *Major, may we discuss?* Broehm looked up at the heading: *Prison Transfers for the Week of 25 June.* What, he wondered, has she found? He called her office and asked her to come and see him immediately.

She appeared a few minutes later, a thin, sour woman who wore eyeglasses attached to a chain around her neck. "Please sit down, Madame Passot," he said, and lit his pipe. "You wish to discuss this prisoner?"

"Yes, Major Broehm. The warden at Fresnes is an old friend of mine, and I happened to mention to him that your office was seeking a penetration agent. A week later, this list arrived with a note that said, *A candidate?*"

Broehm had a sudden policeman's intuition—*Here is the solution.* The one thing he needed beyond all else was a penetration agent or, as he put it to himself, a *predator.*

"So I telephoned," Madame Passot continued, "and he told me that this Kusar is a Croat, wanted for murder in Zagreb, who's been hiding out in Paris since April of 1940. Then he said we might want to take a look at him, in person, before he's shipped back to Croatia, but it was no more than a hunch."

"How was he arrested?"

"He tried to evade a passport control, then it turned out that the Zagreb police had a warrant out for him and had sent a copy to the Paris Préfecture—they suspected he might be hiding here—and, as you know, the Préfecture is efficient and found the warrant."

Broehm drummed his fingers on his desk, looked out the window at the leafy plane trees on the Avenue Kléber. "Call your friend the warden and have this man brought to my office, and better if he wears the clothing he had on when he was arrested. And, Madame Passot, please thank the warden for his suggestion."

Broehm had lunch in the hotel dining room, then returned to his office and began to respond, where needed, to items in the stack of papers on his desk. At three-thirty his adjutant knocked on the frame of his open door and, when Broehm beckoned him in, said, "Major, an inmate from Fresnes prison is here to see you. He is accompanied by two guards—shall they come in as well?"

"No, I will see him alone. And close the door after he comes in."

Standing at the closed door, Kusar appeared to be in his thirties but was one of those men who is described as *youthful,* and was casually dressed in what he'd been wearing when he was arrested, a double-breasted, dark blue blazer, which would have suited an English country gentleman, and thin flannel slacks. As he stood waiting for Broehm to speak, his face betrayed no sign of tension, an amiable face but closed, not easy to read. His eyes met Broehm's without fear or hostility. "Please sit down, Monsieur Kusar," Broehm said, indicating the chair on the other side of the desk. "Would you care for a coffee? I can have it brought up here."

"Thank you, no, Major."

"You speak French easily, monsieur."

"I have been in Paris for a year, so I had the opportunity to learn it. Then too, in the Balkans almost everybody, of a certain class, speaks two or three languages . . . a necessity."

"You are wanted for murder, in Zagreb. Can you tell me how that came about?"

"An accusation, Major. The police needed a suspect and they chose me." His shrug was accompanied by a rueful, and rather charming, smile.

"Can you be specific, about the accusation?"

"It was said to have happened in a nightclub in Zagreb, one of the customers went to the WC and was standing before a urinal when he was stabbed in the heart."

"Was this a dispute of some kind? Over a woman perhaps, or some political argument?"

"That I wouldn't know."

"And who was the victim?"

"The newspapers said that he was a journalist."

"I see," Broehm said. He wondered if Kusar would now want to expand, to explain, to deflect guilt—Broehm had conducted hundreds of interrogations and this was often the case. But Kusar kept silent and waited, patient, ready to help as best he could. Finally Broehm said, "And now you are to be sent back to Zagreb, what will happen to you there?"

"Oh, they will hang me. I suppose there will be some sort of trial, but it will be only a formality, the decision has been made." He spread his hands and half smiled, *So life goes.*

"What did you do to earn a living, in Zagreb?"

"I sought out opportunities, advised people who wanted to invest in some enterprise or other. I have, or rather had, a wide acquaintance."

"Did you murder the journalist, Monsieur Kusar?"

"No, Major, I did no such thing, why would I?"

"For money."

"Ah, the professional assassin, that's a good business in the Balkans, hatreds and feuds need to be settled. But not by me."

"Do you have any idea why you are here, being questioned by a major in the German military police?"

"No, sir, no idea whatsoever."

"What is your opinion of the so-called Resistance, here in France?"

"I don't know much about it, but these underground conspiracies are nothing new where I come from, they raise hell but in the end nothing changes. In truth, I never met anyone in Paris who claimed to be part of it."

"The people involved here come from the former military, or they tend to be defiant intellectuals. Now, tell me, what would you do to avoid the hangman's noose?"

"Well, honestly, what wouldn't I do? Nothing much I can think of."

"Some of these resistance cells aid fugitives to escape to Spain, would you join such a cell? And keep me informed as to who is involved?"

Kusar thought it over, or pretended to think it over, then said, "Yes, I would."

"Because, if you agree, I can have you released from prison and I can pay you well for your efforts, and, because Croatia is a close ally of the Reich, I can have the charges against you withdrawn. Of course, it will be dangerous, you will have to be patient, and cunning, you will have to understand the people you are dealing with, you will have to say the right things, you will have to be an actor, a *good* actor."

"Nothing new, Major, I have been a good actor all my life. And I have studied people, their behavior, their desires, their weaknesses, with me it's a kind of talent. I don't like to be fooled."

"People will be arrested, you know, as a result of your work."

Kusar shrugged. "They gambled, they lost, life goes on."

Now there was work to be done: Kusar's papers, including his Croatian passport, retrieved from the Préfecture, his poorly forged permits replaced by official documents, arrangements made with the Fresnes prison administration for Kusar's release, a detailed history of Kusar's life taken down by Broehm's adjutant. Meanwhile, Madame Passot's French assistant rented a room at a hotel near the Gare du Nord, the Hotel Magenta—cheap, anonymous, meant for the traveler staying overnight.

So it was late afternoon of the nineteenth before Kusar moved from the prison to his new address, where Otto Broehm, in civilian clothes, was waiting for him. It was a small room with a window that looked out over the busy Boulevard Magenta, its walls, bed covering, and curtains all some version of a nameless color somewhere between the darker tones of brown and gray. As for Broehm, he was both relieved and wary; relieved because he could now tell Berlin that his operation against the resistance escape lines was under way, wary because he'd worked with informers in Hamburg and he knew that Kusar was not to be trusted, none of them were. When Kusar entered the room, carrying the pasteboard valise they'd given him, he greeted Broehm, looked around, then said, "A room for a fugitive. Am I to be a fugitive, in my new role?"

"We will go over your story, at length, until you have it all down, but the answer to your question is yes, you fled Zagreb a year ago in fear of Croatian fascists, the Ustachi, who didn't like your liberal politics. Did you know such people?"

"Perhaps a few, they were everywhere."

"Good, then you can describe them. Where were you hiding, in Paris?"

"It's in the history, Major, names, dates . . ."

"Even so, I want to hear it from you."

"I managed to meet a woman, somewhat older than me, and injured in a railway accident when she was young so she had to use a cane."

"Does she know that you were arrested?"

"No, I could have had her informed, but why. As far as she's concerned I just disappeared."

"And how did you support yourself?"

"She had a good job, working as a clerk in the office of the Renault plant and made more than enough for both of us."

"This for a year?"

Kusar smiled. "There were two or three before her, women often fall for me . . . very useful, the way I see it."

"Could you go back to the woman you were living with?"

"I suppose I could but now I prefer the freedom of being on my own—no explanations, no tears, you know what women are like."

"Then for the time being you will stay here. Your valise has a spare shirt and socks, toothbrush and so forth, as well as five hundred occupation francs. You may need more, because we have a lot to do: work on the details of your approach to one of the escape-line cells, which will require careful investigation. We *will* find them, but, until then, we want you to live quietly and, if some woman falls for you, leave her alone. Understood?"

"Yes, sir, understood."

"And we will be in touch with you as to how you and I will meet. Meet in secret. Anything else?"

"No, sir, I know what you need, and I'm ready to begin the work whenever you say."

The following morning, Broehm telephoned the Zagreb police department and was eventually connected to a senior officer who spoke German and was familiar with Kusar's activities in Zagreb. After a few minutes of professional small talk, Broehm said, "I've questioned this Stefan Kusar and he claims he had nothing to do with the nightclub murder. Could that be true? He was really quite persuasive."

"Yes, persuasive is what he is."

"Then . . ."

"He lies, Major, he *always* lies, he is an excellent liar, and he surely lied about this. There were eyewitnesses who saw him follow the journalist into the WC."

"Was this a business with him? Murder for hire?"

"No, this was a practical killing. He got some rich fool to help him start a life insurance company in Zagreb—they never paid a claim, to our knowledge—and the journalist intended to expose him."

"Are you looking at his dossier, Commander?"

"I am."

"Did he commit other crimes in Zagreb?"

"Suspected, interrogated, but never charged. For fraud, mostly, but we could never get the evidence . . . he's slippery as an eel, Kusar."

"Well, I appreciate your help," Broehm said.

"Call again, if you need us, and be careful with him, whatever you're doing, he is very clever."

21 June. At the Café Welcome, Jules, the proprietor of the café, watched the stream of Parisians passing up and down on the Rue de Tournon; watched because Mathieu had been true to his word and a new window had been installed. It was the late afternoon of a summer day, he'd had a good crowd for lunch, now there were a few customers standing at the bar, drinking whatever Jules could offer in the way of wine or beer, and Jules was relaxed and happy—life did get better, even in an occupied country. He stood before his new window, hands clasped behind his back, and enjoyed the passing scene.

But then, a familiar face.

The boy, who called himself the Spider, dark skin, dark eyes, pencil line of a mustache, who had attempted to intimidate Mathieu into trading money for silence. And he was, Jules saw, accompanied by two thuggish friends and, worse, was carrying something by holding it beneath one side of his overcoat—a spring overcoat now, buttoned up to a point where his waiter's bow tie was visible.

The three came through the door, walking quickly and with purpose. When they reached Jules, the boy put his hand on the window and said to his pals, "Oh look, a new window!"

"What do you want here?" Jules said.

"It's time to pay up, dad." With this, he slid a hammer out of his overcoat and gazed meaningfully at the window.

"Ah yes," Jules said. "I almost forgot, Mathieu left an envelope for you, it's in the kitchen so I'll just go fetch it." That *had* been the plan, never carried out, so there was no envelope. He did go into the kitchen, his mind working frantically on some way not to get his window broken, then he decided to go to the cash register and give the bastard whatever he wanted. Looking back through the porthole in the kitchen door, he realized the boy could see him, and was now, to the laughter of his friends, tapping on the window with his hammer, eyebrows raised in mock inquiry—*Shall I break it here? Or would you prefer I break it over here?* His friends laughed even harder: what an amusing fellow!

That did it. Jules snapped. He came rushing out of the kitchen shouting curses, murder in his eye, a meat cleaver in hand, his arm raised and ready to strike. The boy's eyes widened with fear, for a moment he froze, then dropped his hammer and ran for the door, followed by his friends. Jules chased them out onto the Rue de Tournon, still cursing, and running as fast as he could, face bright red, apron flapping, cleaver held high. A woman screamed, the boys ran faster. Finally, out of breath, his legs weak, Jules stopped. As he watched the boys running for their lives, there was pure joy in his heart.

Denunciations were usually made by mail—the unsigned letter, thus the Spider, humiliated before his friends, would have his revenge. He and his friends stopped at a *tabac,* where the boy bought a sheet of paper, an envelope, and a stamp. Next the three found an outdoor table at a café, where the boy wrote with difficulty, carving the letters into the cheap paper: the Café Welcome on the Rue de Tournon was being used by the Resistance, as a place where people could arrange to meet a resistance leader called Mathieu.

Then he addressed the envelope to the Kommandantur at the Majestic Hotel, put the stamp on, and mailed it.

FUGITIVES

23 June. A heavy, humid day, the Parisian sky pale, the surface of the river flat and listless. At one in the afternoon, Joëlle left work, returned to the nearby Hôtel Saint-Yves and took Mariana for a romp. From the street that bordered the Seine, where the booksellers had their stalls, a stairway descended to a cobbled quay at the edge of the water and there Mariana—tongue out and panting on a hot afternoon—and her dog friends took turns chasing each other about. Joëlle often chatted with a woman down there who had a collie called Charlemagne, Mariana's favorite among the dogs that visited the quay. Joëlle said hello and complained about the weather, the woman said it would storm, come evening. At their feet, a terrier was pestering the two bigger dogs who, for the moment, ignored it. "I heard something interesting this morning," the collie's owner said. "The Germans have attacked Russia."

"Really? I thought they were allies."

"They were, but now Adolf has decided otherwise."

Joëlle shrugged. "Is that good for us?"

"I really don't know. Maybe."

The two women put their dogs back on lead and walked them up the stairway to a café across the street where a waiter brought them a bowl of cold water. On the corner, a crowd had gathered as a news vendor tacked the headline page of the latest edition to the side of his kiosk. All the newspapers in Paris were managed by the Germans, so nobody ever believed what they printed, but the headlines, thick and black, were likely true that day. *Operation Barbarossa,* the attack was called, and a man close to the kiosk read the news aloud to those too far away to see the print. There was a photograph, tanks crossing a field.

Mathieu knocked at Joëlle's door at nine that evening, inviting her to share a large tin of sardines, a baguette, and two bottles of beer. The predicted rain had not appeared and the air, awaiting the storm, was thick with humidity, so Mathieu and Joëlle, accompanied by Mariana, went up to the roof of the hotel in search of a breeze. Mathieu rested his back against the chimney, Joëlle did the same. With patience and strong fingers, Mathieu inserted the metal lip of the tin into the key, then rolled the top all the way to the other end. "Bravo," Joëlle said. Mathieu tore off a piece of the bread, used the blade of a clasp knife to spear a chunk of sardine, dipped the bread into the oil, spread the sardine on, and offered the open sandwich to Joëlle, hand-fed some sardine and bread to Mariana, and made himself a sandwich. He then found the protruding edge of a brick in the chimney and, using the heel of his hand, popped the caps off the beer bottles. He handed one of them to Joëlle, said, "To our roof picnic," and the two clinked bottles. The beer was warm and thin, but he enjoyed it anyhow. "You know about the German attack on Russia?" he said.

"Yes, it was in the papers. Is it true?"

"I think so, we'll go down and listen to the BBC at ten."

Joëlle finished her sandwich and let Mariana lick the oil from her fingers.

"Another?" Mathieu said.

"In a minute." She sat forward and turned so she could face him. "I have been wanting to ask you a question," she said. "A personal question, do you mind? I know you don't much like to talk about yourself."

"Ask me . . . anything you want."

"There's something you don't want me to know about, you have some kind of secret, I can sense it, and it worries me when I think about you."

Mathieu was silent. He had known this would happen and now it had.

"Very well," Joëlle said. "I'll mind my own business."

Mathieu lit a cigarette and offered one to Joëlle, who shook her head. "I think I have to tell you what's going on, I don't want to, much safer not to, but . . . the truth is that I have to live a secret life."

"Which means, I suspect, that you are in the Resistance."

"Yes, where I am known as Mathieu."

"I'm not surprised," she said, "and if I can help, you only have to ask."

"Maybe someday I will, maybe I will have to, but my instinct is to keep you from danger, to protect you."

"To protect me, yes, that is your nature, that is who you are. But if the day comes when it all goes wrong and you can't protect me, you should know what will happen, because on that day I will stand with you and, if need be, I will die with you, and that is who *I* am." She sat back against the chimney and moved closer to Mathieu so that her shoulder was pressed against his. "And now," she said, "I am ready for another sandwich."

Just before ten they returned to Mathieu's apartment, where he turned on the radio and worked the tuner until he found the French service of the BBC. He had to keep the volume low, so rested the radio on the sofa, and the two lay on either side of it, heads close to the Bakelite case. On the stroke of ten o'clock came the first notes of Beethoven's Fifth Symphony, corresponding to the Morse code dot-dot-dot-dash, which was the letter *v*, as in V for victory. There followed the voice of the announcer: *"Ici Londres! Les Français parlent aux Français."* London here, the French speaking to the French.

The French announcer was not dramatic—here were the facts. On the International Bridge, which spanned the river border between Germany and Soviet-occupied Poland, it was customary, at the changing of the guard, for the German and Russian sentries to salute each other. But, at three in the morning on the twenty-third of June, the German sentries didn't salute, they shot the Russian guards. The following German attack was massive: three million troops, six hundred thousand vehicles, seven hundred and fifty thousand horses, more than five hundred tanks, almost two thousand aircraft, spread across an eighteen-hundred-mile front that ranged from the Arctic to the Black Sea. The attack was fast moving and successful, the Wehrmacht overwhelming all resistance and advancing at speed across the Ukraine. Winston Churchill had been quick to promise to do all possible to help the Soviet Union, Britain's new ally in the fight against Hitler. When the announcer had signed off, there followed a program of swing music from London: Ellington, Artie Shaw. "Will the Russians surrender?" Joëlle said.

"I doubt it. They will fight hard for their homeland, and it's a long way to Moscow. Remember what happened to Napoleon; there is a two-sided sign in the Lithuanian city of Vilnius. On the western side of the sign it says, 'In June of 1812, Napoleon Bonaparte passed this way with six hundred thousand men.' On the eastern side of the sign it says, 'In November of 1812, Napoleon Bonaparte passed this way with six hundred men.' So, we shall see."

Later on, sometime after midnight, Mathieu and Joëlle were awakened by something going on in the Rue Dauphine, just down the street from the Saint-Yves. Mathieu went to the window and opened the blackout drapes, Joëlle followed, both still naked from the evening's lovemaking. They leaned out of the window and saw two men, wearing the work outfit of Métro laborers, all of whom belonged to one of the Communist unions. They were swaying in the street, having drunk a good amount of wine that night and, arms around each other's shoulders, they were singing *La Marseillaise*. A spirited rendition and, as they walked off in the direction of the Seine, perhaps for an encore on another street, people at the windows of the apartment buildings on the Rue Dauphine applauded.

24 June. In a note left at the religious articles store the previous day, Edouard had asked Mathieu to stop by the Hôtel de Quercy, the crumbling mansion that the Englishman used as a secret meeting place. They sat in the immense dining room, sun pouring in through the cloudy glass of the tall windows. "I have some bad news," Edouard said.

"Yes?"

"About the men you picked up in Normandy, Gerard and Jean-Luc."

"Have they been arrested?"

"They're dead, I'm afraid, rotten luck."

Voice hushed, Mathieu said, "What happened?" He had been shaken by the news and he showed it.

A little too much emotion for the stiff-upper-lip Edouard. "Now, now," he said, in an English nanny voice. "They died bravely, they died to save the mission, they could have surrendered, but that would have meant Gestapo interrogation, so . . ."

"Were they betrayed?"

"No. A German wireless detection van was in the neighborhood while Gerard was sending messages back to London. From the power station the Germans turned off the electricity, block by block, until the sending stopped. As they searched the buildings in that block they discovered Gerard and Jean-Luc hiding beneath a stairway and, when the Germans demanded the two come out with their hands up, they came out firing their revolvers, but the Germans had those beastly machine pistols and that was that."

Mathieu shook his head, *this war.*

"They will be replaced, by Lysander this time and you, and one of your people, will be the reception committee. *Not* the same chap as last time, the one with the, umm, wife, use somebody else. Your job will be to find the new agents a place to hide in Paris, and then lead them to where the containers are buried. I will have the details for you, place and time of the plane's landing tomorrow. Meanwhile, since yesterday, the situation has changed . . ."

"The invasion, you mean," Mathieu said. "And now there will be a Communist Resistance in France."

"Well, it has begun," Edouard said, lighting one of his machine-rolled cigarettes. "This morning, a machine fitter at the Renault works shot a German naval officer on the platform of the Barbès Métro station. The Germans are putting up posters announcing the reprisal, a hundred prisoners, 'Communists, terrorists, and Jews,' as they put it, to be shot."

"That won't stop them for a minute," Mathieu said.

"Indeed. Reprisal doesn't worry them—it is a recruiting tool, the way they see it, such brutality will inspire hundreds of people to join them. These workers are not like you and your cell, the Communist labor unions have spent years organizing clandestine activity, ever since the Bolsheviks took over in 1917. They are disciplined, are experts at sabotage, and they know how to fight."

"Will you, I mean Britain, arm them?"

Edouard hesitated, smoke from his cigarette curling up the shafts of sunlight, then said, "To be decided."

From Mathieu, a quizzical stare.

"When the Occupation ends, whenever that may be, there will be civil war here, the Communists mean to have France for their own, so if we give them arms, they will, in time, use them to shoot at us."

Chantal left her apartment at six in the evening, rode her bicycle over to the Rue de Tournon, and locked it to a streetlamp. Lisette had brought her a message from Jules; some fellow asking about the Resistance at the Café Welcome, and it was her job to look him over and collect his name and address. He would then be contacted and told where to meet Mathieu.

The café was crowded, air thick with cigarette smoke, conversation low and private—as it often was these days when the subject was politics, and that night the café's patrons were trying to figure out what the German attack might mean for them—for France, for Paris, for a wife's cousin in Kiev. Jules was working behind the bar. Chantal stood at the far end, greeted Jules, and congratulated him for the defeat of the boy who called himself the Spider. As Jules served her a glass of wine, he said, "I don't know what got into me, maybe everything, the Occupation, the rationing, and this *espèce de merde* demanding money." Smoothing his thin hair back, he said, "I'm not a violent man, Chantal, but I would've killed him."

"Has somebody been asking about you-know-what?"

"At the table in the far corner, with the coffee and the book."

Chantal turned sideways, leaning an elbow on the bar, and had a good long look: somewhere in his thirties, hair neatly cut and carefully parted to one side, he was freshly shaved and had, she thought, used talcum powder afterward. When he looked up from his book to have a sip of his coffee, she saw that he had very dark eyes, almost black, and a rather prim mouth, and his face had no expression whatsoever, was curiously still. He was sitting down but Chantal could see that he was of less than average height, with narrow shoulders and a soft body. Beneath the table, his shoes were polished to a high gloss. Chantal, holding her wineglass, walked over to his table and said, "May I join you, monsieur? I don't like to stand at the bar."

The man closed his book and, courteously, rose to his feet, saying, "You are welcome, madame, please," as he indicated an empty chair.

A nice voice, smooth and confident, French decent, not native. "A good book?" she said. "You seemed absorbed, I hope I'm not disturbing you."

"It's by Honoré de Balzac, *La Cousine Bette.*"

"Ah yes, Balzac, keeps you reading."

He sighed. "Hard for me, I have to work at the French, and I don't have a dictionary, so I guess."

Now a sudden, charming smile. As a woman speaking with a man for the first time, Chantal sensed him reaching for her. "Are you a regular patron here? I don't recall seeing you before."

"My first time. I live in a hotel room up by the Gare du Nord, so I do a lot of walking . . . well, that's true, as far as it goes, but I came here . . ."

Uncertain, not sure how to go on, tried to lie and failed. "Yes?" Chantal said, with a pretty smile.

"How to say this . . . would you care for a cigarette, madame?" He took from his pocket a very thin, hand-rolled cigarette, bent slightly awry from its stay in the pocket.

Taking the plunge, but hesitant. Scared? "I may have one later. You were saying . . . ?"

"I was told I might meet somebody here . . . somebody . . . somebody who is familiar with, opposition to the Occupation."

"You know, I've heard that too, people talk . . ."

"Any idea who it might be? I've been observing the patrons, but it could be anybody."

Chantal thought it over. "Well, I have an acquaintance who is said to know about such things, if you were to give me your name and address, perhaps somebody will be in touch with you."

"My name and address . . ."

"If you'd rather not . . ."

"No, no, this is my adopted country and I've felt for a long time that I must stand by her. My name is Stefan Kusar, and I live at the Hotel Magenta, room seventeen."

Chantal opened her shoulder bag and hunted about in it, finally coming up with a small slip of a receipt and a pencil, then writing the address. "Can you spell 'Kusar' for me?"

He did, then said, almost apologetic, "It is a name from the Balkans." Then, "Thank you, madame, for your help."

For Chantal, time to leave. She glanced at her watch and said, sounding disappointed, "Oh dear, I fear I must be on my way . . . an appointment."

29 June. On the Route N13, a narrow road lined with plane trees, a hearse drove slowly through the summer countryside, headed toward Paris, some twenty miles away. There was, as the chauffeur knew, a Wehrmacht document control at the edge of Saint-Germain-en-Laye and, when the hearse came to a stop at the lowered crossbar, the chauffeur rolled down his window. "Your papers, please," the officer said. The chauffeur, in dark cap and suit, with a Vichy Francisque—Frankish battle-axe—pin on his lapel, handed the officer his documents, then reached over to the widow in the passenger seat and collected hers. She was attractive, with ash-blonde hair, wore a traditional black-crepe mourning dress and a black pillbox hat with a veil, a handkerchief held crumpled in her hand.

As the officer scanned both sets of papers, he said, "Where are you coming from?"

"From Évreux, sir, we are taking the deceased for burial at a cemetery in Paris. They were madame's nephew and his wife, who died in a road accident."

The officer walked to the back of the hearse, opening the door to reveal two expensive coffins. He then returned to the chauffeur's window and handed over the documents, saying, "You may go ahead," and signaling that the crossbar could be raised. Once the hearse was well beyond the control, Mathieu said to Annemarie, sitting by his side, "I'm going to pull over and make sure they're alright." After he'd picked up the hearse and the coffins at a Paris funeral parlor, he had drilled two airholes in each of the coffins. Now he pulled off the road, parking the hearse between two plane trees, and began to loosen the lid of the first coffin, saying, "Are you getting enough air?"

"I don't like it in here," was the answer.

"Not long now, maybe a half hour."

As he worked on the second coffin, he said, "Everything alright?" When there was no response, he rapped on the lid and said, "Hello?"

"Sorry, I fell asleep."

Passing through Saint-Germain-en-Laye, they were soon on the streets of Paris, the bicyclists making way for the hearse—at least most of them did. Mathieu drove the hearse past the doorway of the Le Cygne nightclub, then turned into an alley and stopped by the metal-covered door of the nightclub's service entry. The door, which had been left unbarred, opened to a hallway with a staircase that led first to Max de Lyon's office, then to the spare room above it. Next, Mathieu returned to the hearse, opened both coffins and, waiting until the street was clear, hurried the two agents into the building. "You were quick about that, Mathieu, probably a good idea," Annemarie said. "Somebody sees two men climbing out of the back of a hearse, well, somebody's liable to get a bit of a shock."

"Not these days—somebody will know exactly what's going on."

In conversation a few months earlier, de Lyon had mentioned a spare room above his office, so, when the Lysander operation in Normandy was imminent, Mathieu had asked for the use of it. Now he took the two agents to the room, which was bare but for two straw mattresses with blankets thrown over them, then went back downstairs to de Lyon's office.

De Lyon was sitting at his desk, account book open before him. When Mathieu entered, de Lyon looked at his watch and said, "You made good time, did you meet the Lysander by yourself?"

"I had Annemarie with me, she's taking the Métro back home."

"So, all went well?"

"Yes, the plane landed in a field near Aubergenville—the pilot looked like a sixteen-year-old, but he was *good,* set that little plane down with not a bump, much better than the last reception. The agents got out in a hurry and he was *gone,* waggled his wings at us and was off into the night."

"Likely he was eighteen, the RAF is scrambling for pilots."

"How goes the nightclub business?"

De Lyon laughed, then lit one of his brown cigarettes, and said, "Mathieu, you should have been here last night, we had a fucking *conga line*—naked dancer, German officer, naked dancer, and so forth, the Germans were shouting, laughing, having the time of their lives. I think for a conga line you're supposed to have your hands on the hips of the dancer in front of you, right? Well, the Germans had their own version of *that.*"

"A new dance is born," Mathieu said. "It needs a name."

"I'm afraid it's going to become a regular feature of the show. The girls weren't all that pleased, they don't like being grabbed at."

"Happy Germans, lately, they expect to have summer homes in the Ukraine."

From de Lyon, a bark of laughter. "They'll stay in the Ukraine, alright, in its—how do they say?—in its 'rich black earth.' Why that little weasel in Berlin decided to fight the *Russians* I don't know. Yes, he beat the French and the Dutch and the rest, but they aren't Russians, fighting for the motherland. The Russians will fuck him over but good." He paused, then said, "My new guests are in the spare room?"

"They are, likely dead asleep by now, they had a long night."

"They'll want food, I'll bring something up for them."

"I guess you can't send a waiter—nobody's supposed to see them."

"Nobody will, only me. Who are they?"

"One's a Belgian mining engineer, nom de guerre of Fabien, he's the instructor. The radio operator, Arnaud, is young, English, educated, he grew up in Chartres, parents owned a hotel there. They got out the day before the invasion."

"Have you found a place where the agents can work?"

"I'm looking . . . anywhere but here. They'll be safe in the room, can stand a passport check if they have to, the detonators and the explosive and the radio will be elsewhere."

"I hope the people they teach can start work soon."

"Me too, Max, me too."

Eight-twenty in the evening, the summer twilight fading fast. In the Tenth Arrondissement, east of the vast marshaling yards that served the Gare du Nord and the Gare de l'Est, was the Canal Saint-Martin. Crossed by ancient iron footbridges, bordered by cobblestone quays, the canal was at the center of a lost *quartier,* a peaceful place with cheap little hotels, more *pensions,* boarding houses, than hotels, their rooms occupied by factory and railroad workers. Set above the canal, the Hôtel Victoire: two windows wide, a bar in the lobby which was also used as the reception desk, had a dozen battered tables and tin ashtrays, the air scented with tobacco smoke and the smell of old cooking grease. Mathieu sat at one of the tables and read a newspaper.

He was impatient to meet the new recruit, had spoken with Chantal about her impression of this Kusar. "For some reason," she'd said, "I couldn't read him all that well, I think maybe because he's from the Balkans. A French man or woman, I know who I'm talking to, but not this one. He seems innocent, somehow, unso- phisticated. Anyhow, it's up to you."

To help him decide, Mathieu had Ghislain sitting at the next table, reading a thick, scholarly tome with a faded cover and making notes with his fountain pen. His job was to listen to the conversation. He and Mathieu were not the only patrons interested in Stefan Kusar: sitting at separate tables were two French detectives from the Sûreté—national police, one of them was a young man, scruffy and down-at-the-heels, his hair too long, who sat gloomily staring out the window, while the other was a well-dressed older gentleman, reading a newspaper and sipping at his coffee. The two detectives had been recruited by Madame Passot, who had made sure of their loyalty to the Vichy regime, then assigned them to work for Major Broehm's office. Their job that evening was to watch Kusar, then follow whoever came to see him until they discovered where the individual lived. No more than that. Major Broehm had made it clear that this was a waiting game—no arrests until they had the entire cell.

Kusar was prompt, Mathieu recognized him from Chantal's description, *youthful,* in a well-worn blue blazer. Kusar had not been given the name Mathieu—Broehm had kept that information for himself—and could not ask for him, so he looked over the patrons in the bar, wondering which one might be the person the woman at the café had mentioned. He had received a note, unsigned, slid under his hotel-room door at night, that directed him to the bar at the Hôtel Victoire, with day and time specified. That was all. Mathieu let him stand for a time, then beckoned him over to the table.

Kusar said, "Good evening," and waited to sit down until invited to do so.

"You are Stefan Kusar?" Mathieu said. "Who wants to join a resistance group?"

"I am," Kusar said. He sat with back straight and hands clasped in his lap, as though he were a pupil being questioned by a teacher.

"Tell me, Monsieur Kusar, how did you come to hear about the Café Welcome?"

"I used to get bored, alone in a hotel at night, so I would go downstairs and talk to the desk clerk and, eventually, we talked about the Occupation—he said it was a terrible thing, and that there were people who worked against it. I asked how one would go about joining such a group and he mentioned the Café Welcome, so I went there and spoke with the proprietor and soon met a woman who said she had an acquaintance . . ."

"What makes you want to join the Resistance?"

"I am from Zagreb, in Croatia, but I was chased out by the fascists and fled to Paris. From the frying pan into the fire, one might say, because a month after I arrived, the fascist Germans came to occupy the city. These people are my enemies and, in time, I decided I would try and fight them."

"So, a political decision? An anti-fascist decision?"

"Yes . . . I am an anti-fascist. In Zagreb I got into trouble by writing letters to the newspapers, and having the wrong friends—left-wing journalists, for example."

"I see," Mathieu said. "Now tell me . . ."

Kusar leaned forward, unclasped his hands, and said, in a confidential voice, "I don't mean to interrupt you, sir, but there is more, a personal reason. In Croatia, before I came to Paris, I was engaged to be married. Unfortunately, when I left the country I couldn't take her with me as she had to stay and care for her elderly parents. For a time, I was alone here until one day fortune smiled on me and I met a beautiful young shopgirl and we fell in love and, for a few weeks, we were happy together. Sadly, it didn't last. One day, in tears, she said she would have to leave me and go to live with a German officer. He had seen her in the shop and returned several times, finally he said he liked her and she would have to come to live with him. He frightened her, he threatened her parents, then he just . . . *took* her. Like a *slave*." Kusar paused, got control of his anger and said, "So that is my reason, I don't know if it's a good reason for joining a group but it's mine."

"A sad story, but there are worse to be heard here."

Kusar nodded.

"Do you think about the danger, of joining a resistance group?"

"I have, but there's something inside me . . . I knew in Zagreb I should just shut up like everybody else and leave the politics alone, but somehow I *couldn't,* a kind of anger in me wouldn't let me do that. It's the same with the girl I met in Paris . . . nobody should be allowed to do what that bastard did, and if I don't find a way to fight back this will eat at me for the rest of my life."

The conversation continued. Ghislain had unearthed a story from Zagreb—through a university colleague who read Serbo-Croatian—about a crime much trumpeted in the press: bandits had ambushed an armored car, murdered the driver and the guard and made off with a vast amount of money. Eventually the bandits were caught and put on trial at a time when, if Kusar was telling the truth, he was still living in the city. Mathieu asked him about it, Kusar knew of these events, he knew the names.

Mathieu was uncertain, could he trust Kusar? Or not? Still, he needed people. What to do? He let the interview wind to an end, then told Kusar he would be contacted at his hotel. "Soon, I hope," Kusar said, and left the bar. Mathieu sat for a few moments, made eye contact with Ghislain—*We'll talk later*—and walked out the door. The two detectives gave him some time, then, first one, then the other, left the Victoire and, at a distance, followed him. Mathieu wandered along the quay, crossed the canal on an iron bridge, and found himself on the busy Rue Louis Blanc, his mind concentrated on the various problems he faced. In time he descended the stairway to a Métro station and, running, just got through the doors before the train departed.

3 July. The summer heat wave now took hold of the city, leaves on the street trees hung lifeless in the still air, men out on the Rue de Tournon had loosened their ties and taken their jackets off, carrying them slung over one shoulder with their fingers in the collar. As for the women, they wore thin summer dresses and, stopping to talk to a friend, fanned their faces with an open hand, a gesture lamenting the heat. At the window of the Café Welcome, Jules watched them as they talked.

Now, a midafternoon customer, an ordinary-looking man, who

stood at the bar and waited to be served. With a sigh in his heart, Jules abandoned the women and moved to his place behind the bar. "Yes?" he said. "What can I get for you, monsieur?"

"Maybe a beer would be good . . . it's a real furnace out there."

Jules filled a glass and slid it across the zinc bar.

"Nice place you have here."

Jules thanked him for the compliment with a gracious nod.

The man sipped at his beer, then turned halfway around and had a look at the patrons sitting at their tables. When he turned back to face Jules he said, "Has Mathieu been in today?"

It took Jules a moment to reply, was this some friend of Mathieu's he hadn't met? Then he recalled that the last time this name had been used in his café it had been the Spider who'd used it. *Oh no, not again.* Finally he said, "I don't think I know a Mathieu, anyhow not one of my regulars."

The man took another sip. "He said he might meet me here."

"Well, keep an eye on the door, maybe he'll show up."

"I'll do that," the ordinary-looking man said.

Mathieu sat in Ghislain's office at the Sorbonne: books and papers everywhere, piled on a table, on the spare chairs, on the floor. A nineteenth-century map of Melanesia, in bright colors, with names rendered in swirling script, was tacked to the wall above Ghislain's desk. "Well then," Mathieu said, "what do you think?"

"About Stefan Kusar?"

"Yes."

Ghislain lit a cigarette, so did Mathieu. As Ghislain shook out the match he said, "Strange bird, isn't he."

"I kept thinking, he isn't like any of the people who work on the escape line. And, what he said about the stolen lover, did you believe it?"

"Such things happen, Mathieu, we've both heard the stories. What's going on now is that the Resistance is growing, gathering new people, some of whom will be different than those who volunteered in April. Meanwhile, the British raids are increasing: more bombers and fighters, more of them shot down, more airmen trying to escape the country. Which makes life difficult—hard to tell a volunteer 'Sorry, we don't need you,' when we can't tell some fugitive 'Sorry, we're too busy to help you.' "

Mathieu sighed. Usually, his decisions came quickly, intuitively, but not this time. He'd heard that other resistance cells used foreigners—Spaniards, Armenians, Serbs, and others—who were both brave and careful, and loyal to the country that had sheltered them. And, testing himself, Mathieu could see nothing wrong with Kusar—he did not seem dangerous or crafty, he seemed pleasant and his story, the stolen girlfriend, made sense. At last he said, "*Merde,* I'm not sure what to do."

"You need more information. Why not try him out? Don't take him into the group, he's not one of us. Yet. Send him on a mission, perhaps with Chantal, who he's already seen, at the café. Then see how he acts under pressure. Chantal will know to stop the operation if she has any suspicions."

Mathieu thought it over. "We've got an RAF Canadian, waiting to be picked up, who's down in Provins. It's a short run on the train, likely safe enough, and we'll have Chantal bring him back to Paris. Depending on what she thinks, we can send him on another mission or just say goodby." Mathieu paused, then said, "Ghislain, do you think Kusar is a spy?"

"I don't think he is. But, if he's any good at it, there's no way to know until it's too late."

6 July. Chantal and Kusar took the night train to Provins, a local scheduled to arrive after ten in the evening. But, twenty miles from Paris, the train slowed to a crawl, then, with one last chuff from the locomotive, it went silent and the train rolled to a stop. One of the passengers made his way forward to the next car, found a conduc-

tor, and demanded an explanation. From that car, a minute later, came shouting. When the passenger returned he announced, his voice rich with disgust, "Something's gone wrong with the locomotive, we'll be here for two hours. And damn the whole damn railroad to hell!" A few passengers applauded.

It was warm in the compartment, Kusar looked at his watch, yawned, made a pillow of his jacket, leaned back against it, and closed his eyes. Glancing out the window, Chantal saw that some of the passengers had left the train and were sitting by a tree in a field. "I'm going to get a breath of air," she said to Kusar, took her shoulder bag, left her small valise in the rack above the seat, and headed for the door.

The heat in Paris had not abated—the nights were worse than the days, but not down here, not in this field, where a soft breeze stirred the leaves beneath a crescent moon and pinpoints of starlight, and Chantal found her own tree to lean against and let the cool night air wash over her. She had to fight the urge to sleep, lately she was tired, weary, all the time, tension did that to you, she thought, the tension of day-after-day work for the escape line, tension not relieved as it had been before the war—a book, a dinner, a bath, a friend—that was all gone now. *It's subtle,* she thought, *it works on you slowly, then you're exhausted and you wonder why.* And it didn't help that she was lonely; she needed a lover, she needed to be touched, in her dreams she made love and was disappointed when she awoke, alone in bed. She stared up at the sky and let reverie take her where it would.

She woke up suddenly and discovered she'd been asleep for twenty minutes, and worried she would be left behind if she closed her eyes again. So with regret she stood and headed back toward the darkened train—the lights in the coaches had been turned off. Some thirty feet from the track she saw a shadowy profile in what she thought was her compartment. Kusar? She counted windows, five of them, and realized she'd been right—that was where they'd been sitting. Peering through the gloom, she now saw that Kusar was standing on the seat, his arms reaching forward, his hands out of her view. *He's searching my valise!* What was in there? No papers, no address book, only a change of clothes, spare shoes, a nightshirt, and a small bag of cosmetics.

Kusar, who had among his many talents a thief's intuition, spun suddenly toward the window. Chantal tried to get out of his sight but failed; he'd seen her, and had to know that she'd been watching him as he searched. But Kusar was game. When Chantal entered the compartment, he was in the same position as when she'd left the train and was pretending to be asleep. After she sat down next to him, he waited a moment, then opened his eyes.

"Oh, sorry to wake you," she said. "A good nap?"

"Yes, I always sleep on trains."

"Have some more then, don't mind me."

No sleep for Chantal, she was wide awake and thinking hard. The operation could not continue—someone else would have to retrieve the Canadian airman. But that had happened before: by the time Mathieu had made a second try to rescue the RAF photography specialist hiding in a Rouen hotel, the specialist had disappeared. And his lover, the woman who owned the hotel, had disappeared with him. What now lay ahead of Chantal was a night in a Provins hotel with Kusar, and then, when they returned to Paris, she would tell Mathieu what had happened, and that would be the end of Stefan Kusar's service to the Resistance.

Provins had been an important trading center in the Middle Ages, so, to preserve its ruins—battlements, part of a tower—the railroad track had been routed around the town's medieval center. Even so, the hotels were only a few minutes' walk from the depot.

"May I carry your valise?" Kusar said.

"Thanks but you needn't, only a few things in there."

At the first hotel they reached, Chantal had Kusar stand by the door, then she went inside, waited for a minute or so, and emerged looking disappointed and irritated. "Not there," she said. "He left yesterday."

"Why would he do that?"

"Fugitives are easily frightened, then they try to hide somewhere else."

"And now?"

"Now we go to our hotel room, spend the night, and return to Paris in the morning."

"Will we try again?"

"We might, we'll let you know."

Chantal had reserved one room, the two were traveling as a married couple—she had intended to have a mattress brought up for the Canadian airman. Standing outside the hotel, she said, "After we register, you go to the room while I stop at the desk to see if I can get us something to eat."

"Too late for food, I would imagine."

"Oh, you never know . . ."

When Chantal rang the bell on the exterior door, the *propriétaire,* in her bathrobe, let them in and wrote their names in the register. As Kusar climbed the stairs, Chantal asked the woman if there was anything, anything at all, to eat. The woman led her to the kitchen and chattered as she collected a piece of bread and some cheese. Meanwhile, Chantal, intent on surviving the night, snatched a small, serrated paring knife from a worktable and put it in her shoulder bag.

In the room, two narrow beds were set against opposite walls, some ten feet apart. To change into her sleeping outfit, she went into the WC and emerged wearing a shirt that came down to midthigh and covered her panties, where she'd hidden the paring knife. During the brief walk from the WC to the bed, Chantal felt Kusar's eyes on her and had to suppress a shiver. She believed that, rather than being exposed as a thief, he would try to kill her but first, making sure she didn't scream, meant to rape her—why waste a chance to bed an attractive woman?

Once the lights were turned out it was dark in the room, no light from the street, and very quiet. Meanwhile, Kusar prepared for sleep, got into his bed, and wished her good night. For what seemed like a long time, Chantal stayed awake, the knife in her hand beneath the pillow, but, in time, she fell into a fitful doze, then the brush of a bare foot on a wooden floorboard—a light, furtive step, followed by another, brought her fully awake. She could see him, a pale shape in the darkness, his body tense, prepared to strike. *If he reaches the side of my bed,* she thought, *I will use the knife.* However, Kusar the hunter was sensitive to prey, stopped halfway across the room, and whispered, "Are you asleep?"

"No, go back to your bed and stay there, Monsieur Kusar."

With a whine in his voice, Kusar said, "I only wanted to give you a kiss good night . . . you are a beautiful woman, Chantal."

"Thank you for the compliment, but if you come anywhere near me you may be sure I will cut you, guess where."

Kusar muttered something deflective and went back to bed.

The following afternoon, Kusar received a message: he was to report to Major Broehm, in the back office of a men's clothing store on the Avenue Kléber, not far from the Kommandantur. Broehm was waiting for him, sitting at a bookkeeper's desk and smoking his pipe. "Well, how did it go . . . the operation in Provins?"

"Not very well, Major. The fugitive had fled by the time we got there so we spent the night at a hotel and took the train back this morning."

"Did anything unusual happen?"

"No, sir."

"Now I'm going to show you a drawing. When you met with the resistance operative at the bar by the Canal Saint-Martin, we had detectives there. They have worked with a sketch artist, who produced this likeness. Does it look like the man you met with?"

Broehm handed Kusar a sheet of drawing paper and waited

while he studied it. "That's him," Kusar said. "That's his face. For the rest he is built like an athlete, with big shoulders and hands. And he carries himself a certain way, poised, confident."

"We believe this man is Mathieu, the leader of the escape line. When you go on your next operation, perhaps mention the name to the agent who accompanies you, this Chantal or anyone else, and see if you get a response. But, Kusar, go about this carefully, be your most clever self. Am I understood?"

"Yes, sir."

"Very well, you can leave now. When you are given a new assignment, signal me immediately, day or night."

Back at his office, Broehm met with Madame Passot. "We are making progress," he told her. "We had detectives waiting for them at the Gare du Nord, and after the female operative left Kusar, we followed her home. Now we know where she lives, the woman who uses the name Chantal, we know her real name, and we have taken her photograph."

From Madame Passot, a rare smile. "Good news!"

"It is, and there's more: Kusar confirms that the drawing of Mathieu is a good likeness, now all we have to do is distribute mimeograph copies, and prints of the woman's photograph, in case she tries to disappear, but only to dependable detectives, committed Vichy people, otherwise they'll be warned."

In the bar by the Canal Saint-Martin, Kusar had claimed that he heard about the Café Welcome from the night clerk at the Hotel Magenta, now Daniel went to the hotel reception desk and showed the clerk a detective's badge. Daniel played the detective as world-weary, a *flic* trudging through yet one more night of routine footwork. Daniel asked the clerk, an old man with thick hair dyed reddish brown, a series of easy questions, then said, "There's a fellow up in room seventeen, Kusar he's called, from somewhere in the Balkans, ever talk to him?"

"Kusar, you say, in seventeen? I've never spoken with him, is he wanted for a crime? Is he dangerous?"

"No, don't worry about him. He's a witness in an important case, so we have to make sure he's a dependable sort. Otherwise, well, you know, lawyers get up to tricks. And, if you ever do happen to talk to him, don't say anything about our discussion, alright?"

"You can be sure of that, I'm a friend to the police."

Daniel rode his bicycle to Madame Vigne's religious articles shop and left a note for Mathieu: however Kusar heard about the Café Welcome, it wasn't from the night clerk at the Hotel Magenta.

On the tenth of July, four men dressed as itinerant laborers stowed their bicycles in the baggage car of a local leaving the Gare de Lyon, then, sixty-five miles from Paris, left the train at the village of Esternay and pedaled off to the west. This location had been chosen because it was isolated and empty—the Île-de-France: tiny villages set far apart; fat, white, cumulonimbus clouds towering into the sky; and the endless wheatfields that had fed Paris for centuries.

It was Fabien, formerly a Belgian mining engineer, now sabotage instructor, who led the line of bicycles. He was followed by two cousins, both stonemasons from one of the workers' towns southeast of Paris, who had been recruited, just as the war ended, by clandestine British operatives. Last in line was Arnaud, the young, handsome radio operator. Just beyond Esternay, the fields sloped gently toward the horizon and Fabien toiled away, the ride not made any easier by a small suitcase roped to a shelf, a metal grid, behind the seat. Fabien was a tall, thin fellow, looking taller by way of a long, narrow head with flat ears and hair shaved high on the sides, who wore glasses and a close-cropped beard.

They rode single file, sweating in the afternoon sun and silent, saving their breath. When the riders came upon a section of the road lined by plane trees, Fabien signaled a halt—they would stop and rest in the shade. The four sat on the ground, Fabien opened a packet of sausage sandwiches and passed them around, to be washed down by a few sips of water from the men's canteens. The sandwiches had been delivered early that morning, by Edouard, to an abandoned broom factory at the far edge of the Nineteenth Arrondissement. Mathieu had found the factory—now both hideout and classroom—and bought it from the grateful widow of the factory owner.

When the supper had been eaten, they lit cigarettes and relaxed. One of the stonemasons looked up at the rounded masses of cloud and said, "That will mean rain, maybe thunder and lightning."

"It's about time," Arnaud said. "I've had about all the heat I can stand."

"Did you hear about the escape?" the stonemason said. "Somewhere down below the demarcation line."

"We stay out of sight, at the factory," Fabien said. "And we don't talk to anybody."

"Well, you won't read about it in the Vichy newspapers, now all the news is by word of mouth but it gets around. Seems the police captured an important resistance leader, a woman, who ran one of the big escape lines, served by former soldiers, mostly, and the *flics* grabbed her and put her in a cell at the local Préfecture.

"That looked like the end of her, because the Gestapo was coming for her the next morning, but she did manage to get a note to her friends and, as night came on, a bribed guard brought her a bottle of olive oil."

A good storyteller, he made his audience wait for a time while he lit another cigarette. "So, she spent her last day at the window, which was just above the street and, as she'd been thin all her life and hadn't been getting much to eat, she wondered if she could wriggle between the bars—she knew that if you can get your head through, the rest of you will fit. But the space between the bars was too narrow, until she decided to try them all and realized that two of the bars were set slightly, very slightly, wider than the rest."

Again he stopped, and his cousin picked up the story. "What she had discovered was 'the mason's bar,' that's what we call it. Since a long time ago, masons have been known to be anarchists— opposed to the state and its methods of control, like locking people up in jail cells."

"Not *us*, of course," his cousin said with a certain smile. "We're good boys."

"I'm sure you are," Fabien said, with a similar smile.

"When those anarchist masons set bars in the windows of prison cells, they made one space just a mite larger than the others, wide enough that a prisoner could get his head through. So, after midnight, the woman prisoner took off her clothes, covered herself with olive oil, and worked her way between the bars, then she ran down the street bare-ass naked to where her friends were waiting in a car."

Arnaud said, "Is that really true? It's a good story, but . . ."

"It's the truth, my friend, it happened," the first mason said. "I heard about the escape from people I *know*, people who can be trusted."

Fabien looked at his watch, stood up, and said, "Well, we've still got some riding ahead of us, so . . ."

Slowly, the others got to their feet, climbed on their bicycles, and rode off through the wheatfields. By nightfall they were close to their objective, an abandoned branch line of railroad track that had once served a remote village where, years earlier, the village well had dried up and the people had gone away. Now Fabien stopped pedaling and, with one foot on the ground, lit a match, consulted his odometer, and said, "We're close." A few hundred feet further and there it was, not far from the road: well-rusted rails, the creosoted ties weathered by time but still in place. Following Fabien's example, the men laid their bicycles on the ground and walked a way up the track. Fabien held a hand out, a gesture of invitation, and, producing a stopwatch, said, "Gentlemen . . ."

Even with muscles stiff and sore, the masons moved quickly. Retrieved plastic explosive and time pencils from Fabien's suitcase, molded the puttylike *plastique* into fist-sized lumps, pressed the explosive into the angle where a rail met a tie and pushed a time-pencil detonator into the center. Having practiced this operation at the broom factory, they moved efficiently, adding two more portions of the *plastique* with time pencils set to go off at five-second intervals after two minutes. Then they ran back toward the bicycles and all four men lay flat and waited. Two minutes later they were rewarded with three flashes, each accompanied by a low, flat sound, *crump.*

They returned to the track to find the rails severed and twisted to one side and the ties splintered. Not spectacular destruction but enough—a train moving down the track would have been derailed. One of the masons, admiring the damage, said, "Were we fast enough?"

Fabien consulted his stopwatch. "Not bad," he said. "You'll get faster as you work on real operations."

"When will that be?"

"A few months, as the guerrilla warfare section in London gets organized. There's nothing wrong with ripping a poster off a wall or helping an airman to escape, but tonight you've seen the future of the Resistance."

For Mathieu, a note left in his mailbox at the Saint-Yves. *Please meet me tonight at eight in the spare room in the student district. Urgent.* That could only be Klara Zimmer, he thought. And this meeting had to have something to do with the French Communist Party changing sides and fighting the Germans. Mathieu walked over to the Fifth Arrondissement, then up the Rue Champollion to the building above a student restaurant. When he reached the spare room, a visibly agitated Klara, waiting for him at the open door, took his hand, said, "Thank God you're here," pulled him into the room and locked the door behind him.

"What's happened?" Mathieu said.

As she waved him toward the sofa she said, "I'll show you," went to her desk and brought him a sheet of mimeograph paper and a photograph. Then she went to the window and looked out over the street. As Mathieu stared at the sketch-artist drawing of his face and the clandestine photograph of Chantal, Klara sat opposite him on the sofa.

"Where do these come from?" he said.

"I have a friend, a detective, who has been secretly a member of the party for years, and he isn't the only one, in fact there are quite a few, both detectives and uniformed police. After the surrender, some of them were ordered to befriend their Vichyite counterparts on the force—they drank with them, they went to brothels with them, took their wives out for dinner with them. In time, they were asked to join their new friends in some sort of special anti-resistance squad directed by a German officer in the Kommandantur."

Mathieu studied the drawing and the photograph, found Chantal's real name and address written on the back of the photograph. On the other side of the drawing, the single word *Mathieu*. He let his hands drop to his lap and swore.

"I think you had better run for it, Mathieu. Before it's too late." Then she said, "Now. Tonight. Don't go back to your hotel."

Mathieu sighed, "I can't do that, Klara, I have to save my people."

"They are looking for you, Mathieu, and I fear there's no hope for Chantal."

"She has some time, they'll watch her, use her as bait in a trap. That gives me a chance to get her away. Then . . . the others . . . I'll have to work something out."

Klara made a sound of exasperation and said, "You just won't leave now, will you."

"I can't."

She nodded, confirming to herself what she'd suspected. "I knew what you would do . . . you don't change. Anyhow, I tried."

"Klara, why are you doing this for me? Is it politics?"

She did not answer him immediately, her eyes were glistening. "My reasons are not political, they are what the party calls 'sentimental,' and that word is said with contempt."

"Do they know that you are showing me these . . . things?"

"They do not. And I would be in bad trouble if they found out and so would my detective friend. But when I realized what the police had, I couldn't stand the idea of your being interrogated, probably by the Gestapo, couldn't stand the thought of your being hurt like that."

Mathieu stood and kissed Klara on the forehead. "I *will* have to go away, when I'm able, but I will never forget what you did for me. You saved *lives,* Klara."

She closed her eyes for a moment, then said, "I'm going to watch the street when you leave, in case you are being followed. Just look up at the window and see if I'm holding a handkerchief. If not, you are safe."

Mathieu left, walked some way down the hill, then turned back. At the window, Klara's hands were empty.

Now grateful for the darkness of the blackout, Mathieu made his way back toward his hotel, keeping an eye out for document controls. He would buy a hat, he thought, as soon as he possibly could, and eyeglasses—not exactly a disguise, but such differences from the drawing would make it harder to identify him. As would motion—thus he picked up his bicycle at the Saint-Yves and rode it over to the Hôtel-Dieu, the large public hospital on the Île de la Cité. Where he searched for, and eventually found, Lisette's mother, Sonya—born in Russia, emigrated to Paris at age nine—who worked there as a nurse. To speak privately, away from the patients in their beds, the two stood in a corner by a window.

Sonya was breathless, her hands clenched. "What's happened? Is it Lisette?"

"No, but she mustn't go near Madame Vigne's mailbox—she

mustn't work at all. They are looking for me, and Chantal is surely under surveillance."

"What will you do?"

"I need your help, Sonya, to rescue Chantal."

"Anything. Just name it."

Mathieu told her what he wanted to do and she said yes, it was possible.

"Tonight, Sonya. I will telephone you here, can I do that?"

"Yes, there's a telephone at the nursing station, it goes through the switchboard and everyone uses it. You need only call the hospital number and ask to be connected to Ward Five-B, and they'll come and get me."

"I won't say much, just a few words."

Sonya's smile was momentary and grim. "I know how these things work, Mathieu."

He leaned toward her for a Parisian kiss goodby, then left the hospital.

Taking the Pont au Change across the Seine, Mathieu was in a crowd of bicyclists but nobody gave him a second look. The night was warm and sticky and the sweat ran down his sides—only in athletic competition had he ever sweated like this, but he'd had a shock and he was scared. Also he was angry, in the way of what was called a sore loser—in his heart he had believed he could never be caught because he was somehow better than his enemies. *So now you see,* he mocked himself, *what nonsense that was.* But he recovered quickly, working his way through what had to be done. Again and again, trying to make sure he hadn't made some fatal error. Such concentration caused him to speed up and, as he turned off the bridge, he swept past a woman cyclist, missing her by a hair. She called him a name, he shouted an apology.

· · ·

16 July. Sometime after midnight, in the Rue d'Assas, a small street that bordered the Jardin du Luxembourg, the sound of an approaching ambulance, its high-low siren hoarse from overuse. When the ambulance stopped at the third apartment house on the block, some of the tenants came to their windows to see what was going on, and two men in suits stepped out of darkened doorways. The ambulance driver and his assistant moved quickly, taking a stretcher from the back and running into the building. A few people went outside, reaching the sidewalk in pajamas and bathrobes, and spoke in hushed tones. Who is it? What has happened?

A few minutes later, the driver and his assistant reappeared, carrying a woman, wearing only a nightgown, on the stretcher. The two detectives came running and, as the ambulance crew carried the stretcher to the back doors, one of the detectives showed his badge and held up a hand. "Stop," he said. "Who is that on the stretcher?"

"This woman has had a heart attack," the driver said. "She's dying, monsieur, if we get to the hospital in time she may live."

The detective, now joined by the other, pointed the beam of his flashlight directly onto Chantal's face, which was waxy and dead white. She raised a hand to keep the light from her eyes, coughed, and put her head over the side of the stretcher as if to be sick. The detective, fearing for his shoes, stepped back. Chantal waited for a few seconds, but she did not get sick, lay back on the stretcher, held her hand over her heart and said, in a whisper, "It hurts, please . . ." One of the tenants, a pompous, pigeon-chested little gentleman wearing a maroon bathrobe with satin lapels, stepped forward from the crowd and said to the detective, "What is the *matter* with you? Have you no heart?" The detective gave him a dark look but the little man was fearless and said, "Let her go, you mean sonofabitch."

The detective asked the driver what hospital they were going to. "The Hôtel-Dieu, Officer, but if we wait much longer, the morgue." The detective turned to face up the street, took a police whistle from his pocket and blew two shrill notes. In response, a car engine came to life, accompanied by the dim glow of blue-painted headlights.

At the Hôtel-Dieu, the two detectives accompanied the ambulance crew in the elevator and followed the stretcher into Ward 5B. Sonya hurried over and said, "You can't stay in here, Officers."

"This woman is wanted for serious crimes, nurse. Our job is to watch her."

"It is against the rules at every hospital in Paris, messieurs, because of contagion. And we've had the police here before, they have always stationed themselves just outside the entry to the ward."

The two detectives held a whispered conversation, then left the ward and stood at either side of the ward's entry, facing the elevator. In the ward, Annemarie wasted no time. She said to Chantal, "How are you feeling?"

"Not so good," Chantal said, her voice barely audible.

Sonya smoothed Chantal's hair back from her forehead, knelt by the side of the bed and tied a thin rope around her waist. "Too tight?" she said.

Chantal nodded that it was.

"Not for long, dear. When the ambulance driver handed you the powder, did he explain what was going to happen?"

"Yes, I had no idea the police . . ."

"Well, now you are going to go for a little ride, and then you'll be hidden. The powder is effective for a few hours—you'll be fine in the morning."

When the elevator door opened, a crowd of people, nurses, doctors, patients, flowed out into the hall and this flurry drew the attention of the detectives. A woman in the bed next to Chantal's, watching the activity outside the ward, said, "Now." Sonya helped Chantal to stand up, then half carried her to a laundry chute set in the wall a few feet from her bed. Chantal crawled into the chute and, with Sonya hanging on to the rope for dear life, slid three stories to the basement laundry room where, amid huge steel machines that rumbled and steamed, she landed in a canvas rolling bin filled with sheets.

The driver and his assistant were waiting for her, put her back on the stretcher and carried her out the hospital service entry to the ambulance. With siren bleating as loud as it could, they took the Pont au Change across the river and then drove north on the Boulevard Sébastopol, turned left on the Rue du Cygne, and parked in the alley by the back door of the Le Cygne nightclub. Mathieu and Max de Lyon helped Chantal onto the landing of the stairway that led to the nightclub's spare room and, with Mathieu's arm around her waist and de Lyon's across her shoulders, walked her slowly up the stairs. "How are you doing?" Mathieu said.

"I'll be better in the morning, the nurse said. Do you have anything I can cover myself with? I'm practically naked."

"The bed's already made up for you," Mathieu said. "Clothes in the morning."

Poor Oberst Pfeffer.

A good boy, once upon a time, from a good family in Stuttgart, where he'd been first a leader in the Boy Scouts, then a captain in the Hitler Youth. He had been a diligent student and earned high grades, attended university in Munich, and, after graduation, had met his devoted wife at a tea dance, then fathered two adorable girls. After working for his father-in-law as an accountant, Pfeffer joined the Wehrmacht and rose in rank and position until he was a colonel, a respected staff officer. Now he served on the general staff of the occupation forces, headquartered in Paris.

For Oberst Pfeffer, the City of Light was exceptionally illuminating. Soon after his arrival in Paris he joined fellow officers at a brothel, his first experience of such a place where, for the first time in his life, a woman took him in her mouth, a curvaceous woman wearing a harem costume. Never had he had such pleasure and he would have it again. And again. Thus the newly enlightened Pfeffer, who gambled up in Deauville and watched sexual exhibitions in Pigalle. Most evenings he wrote his wife: "Dearest, so much do I miss you, and sweet Gretel and Liesl . . ." then went off to the Le Cygne nightclub to drink champagne and dance in the conga line. The club's owner, Max de Lyon, was like nobody he'd ever known and Pfeffer admired him as only a naughty boy can admire a naughty man. Pfeffer believed that Max de Lyon was his friend— after all, in private they called each other Max and Willy.

In private, because he had to visit the office from time to time when he needed a loan. The sinful life had turned out to be sinfully expensive. Oh what a licking he'd taken at the casino in Deauville! And, yes, when he tipped the already high-priced harem girls in their gauzy costumes, they would make him so happy that he tipped them again. In fact he now had a favorite, the luscious Mimi, sorely missed when he was with his wife on leave in Stuttgart. So he had to visit the office with some frequency, to see his generous pal, Max. But then, on the seventeenth of July, disaster.

De Lyon had come down to the nightclub and asked Pfeffer to stop by his office when he had a moment. This had never happened before and it made Pfeffer faintly uncomfortable.

"Willy!" de Lyon said as he let Pfeffer into the office and slapped him on the shoulder. "Come in, come in, I have a brandy waiting for you." When Pfeffer sat across the desk from de Lyon, they toasted Paris. "No place like it," de Lyon said. "Whatever pleasure you desire, it's right here . . ."

Pfeffer clearly liked that idea.

". . . but it has to be paid for."

For a moment, de Lyon looked a little glum, then he explained. Such nonsense, really, but the nightclub owners of the city had received a formal written order from the commanding general of the occupation forces: under no circumstances were they allowed to loan money to military personnel and, if there had been such loans, they must be repaid immediately. "You and I may think this is ridiculous but, as you know, Willy, an order is an order and must be obeyed. So, we'd best put things right between us."

De Lyon opened his desk drawer and brought out a piece of paper that Pfeffer recognized immediately; a ledger sheet. When de Lyon handed it to him, Pfeffer's eyes went to the number at the bottom of the column—a great deal of money. "So much . . . ," he said.

"Well, over time . . ."

"I always meant to repay the loans, Max."

"Of course you did! Now, let's put this behind us—how long will it take you to gather your funds?"

Pfeffer swallowed hard and said, "I don't have any funds, Max."

De Lyon was surprised. "You don't? I always thought that, back in Stuttgart, you had, umm, private means."

Clearly miserable, Pfeffer shook his head.

"Could you borrow the money from your family? From your wife's family?"

"That is impossible . . . how would I explain?"

"But then, what shall I tell the general's office when they inquire?"

From Pfeffer, silence. At last he said, "Do you . . . do you *have* to tell them?"

"No, maybe I don't, but what if they find out? I will be in real trouble, Willy, they will close the nightclub."

Pfeffer said, "Please, my friend, think of some way out of this."

De Lyon tried, drummed his fingers on the desk, working on the problem. But then, suddenly, he brightened. "There is one possibility . . ."

"Yes? What is it?"

"I do need a favor, Willy. In return, I'll keep quiet about the loans."

"Of course, I will do anything."

"An officer of your rank usually has a car and driver."

"I do. A grand Mercedes-Benz."

"I have a friend, you know, a *petite amie,* a girlfriend, and my life goes much better when she's happy. At the moment, she is very worried—her grandfather in Geneva is ill and she must go to see him, before it is too late. Unfortunately, there is no train to Geneva until next week, but what if your driver were to take her there? It's about five hours, faster with a Mercedes-Benz. If you can do me that favor I will cancel your debt, what do you say?"

Pfeffer thought it over. "I don't see why not. It is irregular, of course, so we will have to be quiet about it."

De Lyon agreed, then stood and offered Pfeffer his hand. "Let's shake on it, an agreement between gentlemen."

The following morning, de Lyon visited his friend at the Swiss embassy and a three-month visa was arranged.

Two of the dancers from Le Cygne had shopped for hours and spent lavishly to produce a new version of Chantal who, sitting in the back of the Mercedes, looked just as the doxy of a nightclub owner should: clothing a little too tight and sexy. One of the dancers, Lulu, whose audition Mathieu had observed, had contributed an oversized pair of glittering, fake-diamond earrings, the perfect finishing touch. At the French border, the German guards saluted and waved them through and they paused only briefly at the Swiss control. Then the driver took Chantal to the hotel she'd named and, when the doorman let her out of the car, headed back to France.

Chantal would be staying elsewhere, at a *pension* Mathieu had found for her, so, valise in hand, she crossed the street to a small park at the edge of Lake Geneva and sat on a bench facing the water. She would have to, sooner or later, find someplace to change her clothes before going to the *pension* but, for the present, she wanted to do nothing—a luxury not available to her for the past months. At this distance, she understood too well what had become of her city under Occupation—its spirit had been damaged but would, she thought, heal itself with time. The Germans would go away and then, whenever that might happen, she would see it once more.

Chantal's escape raised all sorts of hell.

The detectives who'd lost her were furious. First they drove around the neighborhood, probing alleys and doorways with their searchlight, then returned and questioned anyone who'd been in the vicinity of Ward 5B: doctors, nurses, and patients, but getting nothing for their trouble. Their style—*You better tell me what you know, or else*—did not work well with sick people who wanted to get well and go home and had no interest in becoming witnesses to—*anything,* much less a woman in a nightgown sliding down a laundry chute. In fact, they'd had a bellyful of being policed—permits, controls, curfews. Enough. The doctors had actually not seen the escape—that left Sonya and one other nurse, who was her friend. The detectives might have arrested Sonya, who they suspected of aiding the escape, but she claimed that Chantal had discovered the laundry chute and used it.

"With a heart attack?"

"Some people, when they are afraid, have great strength of will."

In the end, they let her go, aware that she was the sort of individual who could not be bullied into a confession. So, in the morning, one of them telephoned Madame Passot who, voice icy and rigid, told him that he and his partner would be transferred back to their old jobs. Now that the bird had flown, all the border controls were given Chantal's picture and they arrested two or three women who bore some slight resemblance to her. Wasted time and effort, and one of them wrote a letter.

Then, Broehm. Madame Passot tried to be apologetic, but was so utterly unused to apologizing that she made Broehm even madder and, if possible, even more silent. Finally, he said, "They knew."

"I would say they did, though how they found out is beyond me."

Broehm did not want to have the wound-licking conversation and, polite as always, told Madame Passot she could go back to work. When her hand was on the doorknob, an afterthought. "One more thing," Broehm said. "Have the café owner arrested and brought here. Now."

Jules had been warned. Early in the morning, from a telephone in an unused office at a department store, de Lyon had called Jules, Annemarie, Ghislain, Daniel, Madame Vigne, and several others who worked in the escape line and told them it was time to be elsewhere, saying that the business was bankrupt and had to be shut down, then wished them well on their upcoming vacation. Contact with Kusar had been limited to Chantal and Mathieu, as for the rest, they were likely safe but getting out of town for a while was probably a good idea.

After de Lyon's call, Jules didn't know what to do. He had never been outside of France, and finally decided to go to some other city for a time. His best waiter would run the café but he started his shift at noon, so Jules waited for him. Then, an hour later, the detectives showed up and, in front of a silent crowd of midmorning patrons, manacled Jules and led him away. This saved his life.

In his office at the Kommandantur, Broehm interrogated as was his custom; the removal of the manacles, the coffee, the pipe, the mild tone of voice, but Jules wasn't impressed.

"Your café was used by the Resistance, monsieur, and you had to know about it. So, unless you wish to be forthcoming with me, I can promise you some time in prison."

"Forthcoming?"

"Give me some names, the names of people who associated with Chantal."

"Who's Chantal?"

"Do you know Mathieu?"

"I know a dozen Mathieus. More. This is a common name in France, where we name for saints."

"This Mathieu," Broehm said, showing Jules the drawing.

Jules squinted at the drawing, then took his spectacles from his apron pocket and tried again. "No, monsieur, you have found a Mathieu I've never seen. I used to have a patron who resembled the fellow in your drawing but I haven't seen him for years. Somebody said he'd moved to Lyons, maybe you should look for him there. Or was it Bordeaux?"

I hate these people. "How can something like this resistance contact go on in your café without your knowing about it?"

"Monsieur, do you know what goes on in the cafés of Paris? Everything. Of course, one may have a glass of wine, a coffee, and something to eat, but there is more. Love affairs begin, love affairs end, swindlers meet their victims, victims meet their lawyers. But, mostly, the café is a place for people to go. To keep warm in winter, to write a letter, to read a newspaper, to stare out the window at the people in the street, while in summer they do their staring from tables on the *terrasse*. In the midst of all that, how do I know if someone is making contact with the Resistance?"

Thus was Jules sent from the Kommandantur to Fresnes prison. He was to make the café speech again, in a longer form, in court, where he was defended by the cell's excellent lawyer, who had gone to the Sorbonne with the prosecutor. As for Jules, the judge quite liked him and, in the end, he did a year.

An hour after Jules had left his office, Broehm telephoned the vice-minister from the Foreign Ministry in Berlin who had recruited him to run the operation against the Resistance. The vice-minister, when his secretary told him who was on the line, picked up the phone with a hearty greeting. Then Broehm delivered the bad news: his first agent penetration had gone wrong—they had discovered the identity of one of the escape-line operators and put her under surveillance but she had vanished. They had, however, learned much from this failure and would do better in the future.

"Major Broehm, I regret to say that there will be no future. The Fuehrer has determined that the French will never be our allies, so the time of coddling is over. The Resistance will now become the concern of the Sicherheitsdienst—the security service run by Himmler—and the Gestapo. You know their techniques, Major, unappetizing but they produce results."

"Thank you, Vice-Minister, for the opportunity to serve."

"A Gestapo officer from the Paris headquarters will be there to relieve you this afternoon. Again, my regrets. You will return to Hamburg in your old job of senior inspector. Have you any questions?"

"The penetration agent, Stefan Kusar, what shall I do with him?"

"Where did you find him?"

"In Fresnes prison, on his way to Zagreb to stand trial for murder."

"Well, put him back there, and he'll be off to whatever awaits him in Zagreb."

At three in the morning, they came for Kusar in his room at the Hotel Magenta. When they knocked at his door, he thought they might be bringing news of his next assignment. Previously, he'd been contacted by means of an anonymous slip of paper, and he thought this personal visit was simply a change of procedure. But it wasn't and, as they forced his hands behind his back, he realized that the people who had saved his life had no further use for him.

Earlier that day, the Gestapo officer had been ushered in to see Major Broehm. He was a tall, lean young man wearing a dark suit and crisp white shirt and, in his approach to Broehm, was formal, very courteous and correct. But his manners did nothing to soften what Broehm saw in his eyes: a fixed stare, cold and relentless, that suggested there was nothing he would not do to you. Clearly, he *would* get answers to his questions, though not from Jules, who was safe in Fresnes prison.

. . .

After the warning from de Lyon, Annemarie had sat in her quiet apartment, trying to figure out what to do. It was wiser, she finally decided, to heed the warning and, at least for a time, disappear. But where? How? And, particularly, for how long? She had some money in her apartment but not much, and she would need a lot of money, that much her work in the Resistance had taught her. Money from her family was paid, once a month, into her account at a private bank in Paris, but what if the police knew this? What if they had somebody watching the bank? How to disappear if you must return to the city every month? In time, she realized that there was only one way to acquire a large sum of money and called her mother.

"I am thinking of dropping by this afternoon," she said. This was not usual for Annemarie, she hadn't seen her parents for months.

"Any special reason, dear?"

"No, simply to say hello."

"What's wrong? I am your mother and I can hear it in your voice."

"Nothing, nothing at all."

The connection wasn't the best—there was a low buzz on the line as mother and daughter did not speak. Then, finally, her mother said, "Your father and I are planning to come into Paris today, why don't we stop by your apartment?"

Annemarie's parents lived in Chevreuse, an enclave for the rich on the outskirts of the city, thus Annemarie had time to change clothes, dressing for her parents, and soon enough her doorbell rang.

Her parents settled in the parlor, Annemarie made tea. "Would you like to tell us what's happened?" her father said. He was a tall man with waves of white hair above a hawkish face, one of the wealthy men who fully supported the Vichy regime, their barrier against the ravening Bolsheviks, and Annemarie loathed him.

"I am in some difficulty and I need money," Annemarie said.

"You have money," her father said.

"I need more, just now."

"And so I should hand it over, is that what you think? We've provided for you amply, but now it seems you've gotten yourself into some kind of trouble. Some kind of trouble you don't want to talk about."

Annemarie's mother intervened. "My dear, the car is parked downstairs, why don't you come home with us and spend a few days?" Annemarie's father was allowed to have two cars, one of them the de luxe Citroën. "You can rest and relax, you do look a little tired, and we'll talk things out. Please say yes, dear, I worry about you so, what with the . . . situation here."

She knows, Annemarie thought. Her mother was seated in such a way that her husband could not see her face and, for the barest second, flicked her eyes at Annemarie's father. *Trust me to get around him,* the glance meant.

"Very well," Annemarie said. "Let me put a few things in my valise."

Ghislain fled twice. First to Nîmes, in the Unoccupied Zone, then, three months later, to New York. There, with the help of a few words in the proper ear provided by Margaret Mead, he joined the anthropology department at Columbia University. He found American students very different than their French counterparts. The latter attended lectures, took notes, and volleyed back that information in their examinations, while the Americans sought insight, spoke up in seminars, and were instinctively curious—they were certainly curious about him.

"Yes? Mr. Cohen?"

"Professor Bernard, when you were living in Occupied France, did you join the Resistance?"

"No, I can't say I did. I had a few friends who took part, and now and then I helped them."

"Can you tell us more about it?"

"Yes? Miss Bailey?"

"In your book, you claim that the Kahwa people often . . ."

Madame Vigne wasn't sure what to do. She dearly loved her shop—her beautiful white candles, her crucifixes, Saint Christopher medals, and paintings of saints with halos—and didn't want to leave it. She could, she supposed, sell it and live on the money in some little place somewhere. Where she would be a hunchbacked old lady, eccentric, a little dotty, perhaps. *No.*

Still, the telephone call from de Lyon had been frightening. Would they arrest the woman she had just described to herself? She wasn't sure—would the French police do such a thing? Would the Germans? Well, she supposed, it would depend on the individual commanders—their personal politics, their commitment to the laws, or the quotient of good to evil in their souls.

Her German customers were nice boys, from a country where the Nazis had attacked and suppressed religion, and they liked handling the religious articles, sometimes buying a small crucifix to hide away. She had also some older German customers, spiritualists like herself, who came to the shop for conversation and, rarely but it had happened, a séance—they wanted to contact the spirits of the departed, friends and loved ones, to make sure they were content and in a better place.

These men would not want to arrest her, she thought. And, anyhow, arrest her for what? For receiving and sending messages for the Resistance. *Oh no,* she thought, *the messages!* She went to her office and looked in the drawer where she kept the messages. Yes, there they were, a dozen slips of paper awaiting delivery. *For Chantal: They will be on the 8:30 train from Bourges.* She crumpled them up, found a china-painted plate with the image of a shepherd holding a crook and a lamb, and set the papers alight. She greatly disliked the smell of burning paper so lit a stick of sandalwood incense. Much better, her shop now smelled as it should.

It happened that there was a deck of tarot cards on a bookshelf next to her chair and, almost idly, she began to lay them out. Nothing was clear, of course. In tarot, all was implied, open to interpretation. So, here was the Fool, about to walk off the edge of a cliff, but it could be read as throwing caution to the winds. A few cards later, the Seven of Pentacles, which suggested that she was involved in an undertaking that would flourish and grow. Was that not her shop? She completed the pattern of cards but saw nothing of danger. So, the cards had told her what she needed to know. *I shall stay in Paris,* she thought. And, if she *were* arrested, then fate had spoken and there was nothing she could do about it.

But fate had no arrest in store for Madame Vigne, neither was she questioned nor summoned to a Préfecture, and, as the months passed, her heart eased and she was quietly elated that she hadn't given in to panic, that she had saved her lovely shop.

For Daniel, the warning from de Lyon presented an opportunity, an opportunity to do something he had long wanted to do. On the evening of the seventeenth, he prepared to leave his tiny basement room in the Marais, throwing a few things into a pillowcase, including a Spanish Astra automatic with a wooden grip, given to him by a friend who was headed out of the country. Then he looked around at what was left, knocked on his neighbor's door and asked her if there was anything in the room she could use. Graciously, she wondered if he would like to have a few francs in exchange. He shook his head and said, "Take what you want, you've always been good to me."

Later on, some German investigators found her standing on the corner of the Rue Saint-Denis where she worked, offering herself to the men who roamed that street, and questioned her about Daniel. There was little she could tell them; she had sometimes cooked dinner for him, and, before he left, he had given her a towel and a few dishes. When the investigators were done, they took down her

name and address. As she was the last person known to have seen
Daniel alive, they explained, they might need to question her further.

Otherwise, rumors. It was said that Daniel had joined an assassination squad, all of them members of the Communist Party, all
of them Jewish boys, fifteen and sixteen years old. The leader of
the squad was called Binyamin. His photograph in the newspaper,
when he was finally captured, showed a boy with curly hair, soft
skin, and thick eyeglasses. Binyamin's group was not the only Jewish gang in Paris, the exploits of a group led by Gilbert Brustlein
were highly publicized: the shooting of seven German soldiers,
each followed by massive reprisals, then other actions at Nantes.
The gang was believed to have been organized and armed by a
French Jew who had fought with the International Brigades during
the Spanish Civil War.

Daniel had changed his nom de guerre more than once, and
changed his appearance, which made tracing him almost impossible. Was he in the group that ambushed a French collaborator in
Paris? Or the lone wolf who shot a Wehrmacht officer in Lille? Or
among the teenagers who hurled a hand grenade through the window of a restaurant much patronized by German officers? Nobody
could say for sure. Some people believed that Daniel had been
killed during a gunfight in a garage, others that he had fled to
North Africa, or gone to Palestine. There was no question that he
had sought revenge against the Germans for killing Jews, but whatever might have happened to him in that mission was unknown.

At last, on the twenty-ninth of July, the storm that all Parisians,
wilting in the heat wave, had longed for. It began after nightfall;
lightning flashed above the city, illuminating the blacked-out streets,
while the claps of thunder were sharp and explosive, the air was
suddenly chill, and then, driven by a stiff wind, the rain pelted
down, filling the drains at the edges of the sidewalks and flooding
over the cobblestones.

Joëlle reached the Saint-Yves in the middle of it, walking fast beneath a dying umbrella. She stopped in the doorway of the hotel, closed the umbrella, shook the water off, then entered the lobby. Sitting on a battered chair was a large man, perhaps a dangerous man, wearing a black rubber raincoat, hair pounded flat by the rain, drying his face with a handkerchief. As Joëlle passed the reception desk, he stood up. Apparently he was there to see her and, intuition told her, this visit was somehow connected to the missing Mathieu. The man approached her and said, his voice marked by a Slavic accent, "Pardon, madame, are you Madame Joëlle?"

"Yes, that's me. Have we met before?"

"No, madame, I am called Stavros and I am sent here by a friend of yours, a very good friend, I think, and he want to see you."

Joëlle let out a breath she didn't know she'd been holding. *He's alive.* "Is he well, this friend?"

"You can see for yourself. I will take you where he is."

"Now?"

"Yes, now."

To reach the Mabillon Métro, they took the Rue de Buci and there, on the wall of an apartment house, was a poster that showed the drawing of Mathieu and offered a reward for information leading to his capture. Joëlle stopped dead and stared at it, transfixed, heart pounding. Stavros took her elbow, said, "Just keep walking, Madame Joëlle," and led her up the street.

They got off the Métro in the neighborhood of crumbling tenements near the Les Halles market, passed the giant doorman at the entry to the Le Cygne nightclub, then walked some way down the alley behind the building. Stavros opened the door, then pointed at the stairway and said, "It's the room on the first landing, Mathieu waiting for you there."

Joëlle ran up the stairs, knocked at the door, and, when Mathieu appeared, he wrapped her in his arms and crushed her against him. She'd had only a glimpse of his face, but sufficient to see a pale and exhausted Mathieu with dark shadows beneath his eyes.

It was a small room, the only furniture a straw mattress with a blanket thrown over it, while an open valise stood at the foot of the bed and served as a closet. As they sat side by side on the edge of the mattress, Joëlle ran her hand up and down his upper arm, nursing him as best she could. Although there was no window in the room, the storm outside was present: thunderclaps exploded one after the other, then echoed away, the splash of the rain loud on the pavement in the alley. "I had to see you," Mathieu said.

"I was afraid you were gone." She paused, then said, "You look, so tired."

"I am tired, being hunted will make you tired."

"Are you going away, Mathieu?"

"Yes, perhaps tomorrow, it will depend on the weather, and the moon."

"I shall stay with you until then."

"Two things I must tell you: later I will introduce you to a man named Max de Lyon, who owns this nightclub. If you need anything, money, anything, he will help you. Next, here is the key to my apartment, I would like you to stay there with Mariana."

"I keep her in my room, now. She was waiting for you all night by the door."

"She will do better in her usual place and she will read you, will trust I am coming back if you believe it."

"Are you coming back, Mathieu?"

"Yes, someday, I will come back to you, to our city."

"I want to lie on the bed with you."

He lay next to her and she pressed herself against him. He sighed at the warmth of her and held her closer, then closed his eyes. She worked her hand between the buttons of his shirt so that she could touch the skin of his chest. "I think you must sleep now," she said.

He was fading fast and his voice was faint, but she heard him well enough when he said, "I love you, Joëlle."

·   ·   ·

30 July. The storm had passed, leaving behind a deep blue sky. *Good flying weather,* Mathieu thought, *and a clear sky for the full moon.* It was Edouard who had arranged his escape, telling him he could no longer stay in France, thus he was to meet a contact in the town of Nemours who would take him to a wheatfield where a Lysander could land. In the second-class car of the train to Nemours, all the compartments were full, so Mathieu stood in the corridor, a dense crowd packed around him. A silent crowd: worn faces amid the scents of garlic, sour wine, and tobacco.

Now it happened that Mathieu noticed a short man wearing a very expensive brown hat with a high crown, their eyes met for a moment, then Mathieu turned away, too aware that the wanted poster had been pasted to walls all over Paris. The crowd stirred, the man in the brown hat was trying to move to a position where he could get a better look at Mathieu, who glanced at him once again to see him smiling in a certain way, smug and sly, in control, invulnerable. *Secret police,* Mathieu thought and cursed his bad luck. The train would reach Nemours in fifteen minutes and then he would be safe, hidden away, but the man now moved closer.

If he was trying to flush Mathieu from cover, he was successful. Mathieu decided to move to the following car and, as he began to work his way through the crowd, was the recipient of a few sharp elbows and muttered curses. When he at last reached the entry to the next car, he turned sideways, to see his smiling pursuer patiently following him. Which secret police, he wondered, they were everywhere now, Vichy French, German, from this organization or that, and they were more than capable of recognizing a face despite a hat and eyeglasses.

As he entered the following car, people in the crowd turned toward him with a look that said, *We really don't have room for you, where do you think you're going?* Mathieu pushed his way to the middle of the car, then, as he tried to move away from his pursuer he saw, looking through the windowed door at the rear of the carriage, railway track rolling away behind the train—he was in the last car. He would have to make a stand, he thought. Then the short man encountered a beefy, stubborn fellow who didn't want to get out of his way, but the pursuer leaned toward the fellow and said a few quiet words that caused him to step aside in a hurry.

Now on the run, Mathieu tried to wedge himself between a middle-aged couple who straddled two large suitcases. The man put his hands on Mathieu's shoulders, gave him a hard shove, saying, "Mind your manners!" Mathieu shoved back, with enough force that the man toppled over backward, drawing gasps from the passengers. Mathieu stepped over him as the crowd, aware of the near brawl, made way for him. He was quickly at the end of the carriage, where he opened the door, stepped outside, and found himself on a small platform with a gate across it. He needed only a few steps to reach the gate—the sound of the locomotive now loud in the open air—then he turned to face his pursuer.

The man didn't follow immediately but waited on the other side of the windowed door, his smile now broad and beaming as he enjoyed the plight of his prey—cornered, nowhere to go. Next he paused to adjust his hat, making sure it hadn't been knocked askew during his passage through the crowd, then opened the door.

Mathieu climbed over the gate and hung on to the top, his legs dangling beneath him, then, as the short man took a step toward him and slid his hand inside his jacket, let go. He fell flat on the track, one knee bounced off the iron rail, the other scraped across the gravel bed beneath the ties. Mathieu rolled away from the track and tumbled down an embankment, waiting for the shot, waiting to be killed. But there was no shot and Mathieu, sore and bleeding, watched as the train chugged away into the distance and, at last, disappeared.

1944.

Before the war, the Brasserie Heininger had been one of the merriest restaurants in Paris. Just down the street from the Place Bastille, it was all vast, gold-framed mirrors above dark red banquettes, where waiters with fin de siècle whiskers hurried among the tables, balancing bottles of champagne in ice buckets and platters of *choucroute garnie* on silver trays. At the beginning of the Occupation, the brasserie had remained open for two weeks, then, as Papa Heininger wearied of the crowd of German officers, he shut it down and went off to live with his sister's family.

In August of 1944, Paris was liberated and Papa Heininger rushed to get his brasserie reopened. It wasn't yet as it had been but the food was good and the crates of champagne in the cellar had been hidden away from German eyes. The old customers came back when they heard the news. Two of them, a couple whose apartment was in sight of the Bois de Boulogne, visited the Heininger on the night of the fourteenth of September and were seated at the favored table 14, where the mirror above the banquette still bore a bullet hole from the time a Bulgarian headwaiter, having played émigré politics, was murdered on a spring night in 1937. The couple, called Benoit, ordered the *choucroute garnie* and made small talk as they waited for their dinner to be served.

Then, Monsieur Benoit interrupted some story his wife had been telling, saying, "Aha, look who's here," and nodded his head at a man and a woman, accompanied by a beautiful Tervuren shepherd, who had just arrived.

"Who are they, dear?"

"Jean Leveque and his girlfriend."

"And they are . . . ?"

"Before the war, Leveque owned a weekly newspaper, the *Chronique de Paris,* never all that popular but it was entertaining. It had a good deal of sports news, bicycle races and prizefights, the horse-racing tips were second only to the Communist *L'Humanité,* the astrology column, *Queen of the Stars* it was called, was one of the best. Also, a good crossword puzzle, hard but not *too* hard."

"It is once again published?"

"I believe so, though newsprint is still hard to come by."

For a moment, Madame Benoit stared at the couple, then said,

"You know, dear, dogs are always allowed in cafés but I've never seen one in a brasserie."

"True, but this is a special dog. In 1941, Leveque led a resistance organization, using the alias Mathieu. When he was betrayed he escaped to London, where he worked on de Gaulle's staff and was of such standing that, a month later, his Parisian girlfriend and dog were flown across the Channel so they could join him."

"That de Gaulle!"

"A very independent man, the general."

"Tell me, is this just a story? Or did it actually happen?"

Monsieur Benoit shrugged. "It's generally believed but, these days, people tell all sorts of tales about the Occupation."

"So, he was in the Resistance. And did he do well?"

"Yes, a hero, it's said."

PHOTO: © RAINER HOSCH

ALAN FURST, widely recognized as the master of the historical spy novel, is the author of *Midnight in Europe, Mission to Paris,* and many other bestsellers. Born in New York, he lived for many years in Paris, and now lives on Long Island.

alanfurst.net
Facebook.com/AlanFurstBooks

ABOUT THE TYPE

This book was set in Sabon, a typeface designed by the well-known German typographer Jan Tschichold (1902–74). Sabon's design is based upon the original letter forms of sixteenth-century French type designer Claude Garamond and was created specifically to be used for three sources: foundry type for hand composition, Linotype, and Monotype. Tschichold named his typeface for the famous Frankfurt typefounder Jacques Sabon (c. 1520–80).